Utopian Day

By C. L. Wells

Copyright © Christopher L. Wells (2015)

All rights reserved

This book is a work of fiction.

Any resemblance to actual events or persons, living or dead, is entirely coincidental.

Table of Contents

Chapter One 6

Chapter Two 9

Chapter Three 13

Chapter Four 16

Chapter Five 19

Chapter Six 24

Chapter Seven 28

Chapter Eight 32

Chapter Nine 37

Chapter Ten 41

Chapter Eleven 45

Chapter Twelve 51

Chapter Thirteen 55

Chapter Fourteen 60

Chapter Fifteen 64

Chapter Sixteen 71

Chapter Seventeen 76

Chapter Eighteen 82

Chapter Nineteen 88

Chapter Twenty 93

Chapter Twenty-One 98

Chapter Twenty-Two 106

Chapter Twenty-Three 111

Chapter Twenty-Four 116

Chapter Twenty-Five 121

Chapter Twenty-Six 126

Chapter Twenty-Seven 132

Chapter Twenty-Eight 140

Chapter Twenty-Nine 149

Chapter Thirty 155

Chapter Thirty-One 161

Chapter Thirty-Two 167

Chapter Thirty-Three 172

Chapter Thirty-Four 177

Chapter Thirty-Five 180

Chapter Thirty-Six 185

Chapter Thirty-Seven 189

Chapter Thirty-Eight 194

Chapter Thirty-Nine 200

Chapter Forty 206

Chapter Forty-One 213

Chapter Forty-Two 219

Chapter Forty-Three 224

Chapter Forty-Four 230

Chapter Forty-Five 235

Chapter Forty-Six 239

Chapter Forty-Seven 245

Note from the Author 250

Thank You 252

Acknowledgements 253

About the Author 254

Chapter One

James stood on the dock wondering about the events that had led him to this point. Just months before he had been a prisoner serving time in a U.S. prison. Then, unexpectedly, his sentence had been reduced and he was given a chance to start a new life and go straight – a chance he was eager to make good on. But now he was in a foreign country, on the run from the FBI, and framed for a crime he didn't commit. He watched, feeling helpless, as the man who had set him up sailed away on a yacht. Could things possibly get worse? His mind drifted back to that fateful day that had started the whole bizarre journey....

Six months earlier:

As he looked across the table at his client, Cecil Brody Jr. felt pity and sadness. In his years as a public defender he had seen many such young men follow a similar path. A troubled youth with a difficult or non-existent family life had a brush with the law and ended up in juvenile detention. They made friends with the wrong crowd while inside, and went from bad to worse once they were released from prison. Years and numerous incarcerations later – assuming they lived that long – they ended up right where this young man was.

Today, however, was different. Cecil was here to offer his client something that none of his other clients had ever received. He was, dare his frequently cynical mind admit, excited about the possibility that today might be a turning point for the better. Today might be the beginning of a genuine shot at rehabilitation for this young man.

The guard who had brought his client in finished securing one handcuff to the table to ensure the lawyer's safety, and exited the room. Cecil, who had been lost in his thoughts, had his contemplations cut short as he heard the door shut and the loud mechanical lock engage. He brought his gaze up to meet the eyes of his client.

"James, it's good to see you."

He paused before continuing, but the prisoner did not respond. "I have some good news for you. You have been selected to participate in a special rehabilitation program that could cut ten years off of your sentence."

James sat up a little straighter in his chair and leaned forward, obviously interested. He had so far been incarcerated for two years of a twenty-five year sentence for armed robbery. The idea of cutting his remaining sentence almost in half seemed surreal. He wanted to make certain he had heard correctly.

"Ten years?"

"That's right. Are you interested?"

"Is grass green?" James responded.

"O.k., here's how it works." The lawyer slid some paperwork and a pen across to his client. "It is a highly selective and relatively unknown project the department of corrections has been running for years. I didn't even know it existed myself. If you sign up and keep your nose clean, your sentence will be reduced by ten years. Everything you need to know is right here."

He slid the form across the table and paused while James picked up the paper and began to read. James was sharp. He may have been a criminal, but despite his bad choices he had graduated high school with a 'B' average. He'd even been looking at colleges before his life began to fall apart with break-neck speed. Cecil patiently waited for the questions he knew would begin coming once he finished reading the agreement.

"What is this about 'prisoner waives all rights,' and 'prisoner authorizes implantation of required devices'? Am I agreeing to be experimented on or something?"

"No, nothing like that. This is just the legal paperwork required for you to get into the program. I've been briefed on the program and I think you are going to like it much better than here. You will be living in a facility with only nine other people. There won't be any cells like they have here. You will have a real room all to yourself. The 'devices' they refer to are for electronic surveillance purposes only."

Cecil watched James' eyes as he read back over the paperwork. James didn't appear to be as interested as Cecil had initially hoped he would be.

"Listen James," Cecil began as he stared straight into the younger man's eyes. "Chances like this don't come around that often. In fact, I can almost guarantee this chance won't come around again. If you don't sign this deal today, I walk out of here and you stay here for the next twenty-three years, barring an early release, which we both know won't happen in this state unless hell freezes over."

Cecil paused again to let his words sink in as James stared down at the paperwork in front of him. This was James' third serious conviction with jail time – by far the longest sentence. He thought back to his previous sentence of five years and how he had almost committed suicide in the fourth year because he was so depressed. He was on medication now, but it didn't really help much. He knew in his heart that he would never make it twenty-three more years. But thirteen, and in a better environment… maybe he could make it. He would still be young enough to build a different life when he got out, maybe go straight the way his mom would have wanted him to. Just maybe this could be the first break he had seen in a long time.

James picked up the pen and signed his name.

Chapter Two

Mia was in a sour mood, and it wasn't because of the dining experience at Del Posto. On the contrary, the baked striped bass had been excellent. Followed by the fette biscottate for dessert, it could hardly have been a more delicious meal.

Mia's mood had everything to do with the fact that she was about to end a three month long relationship with Thomas Pendleton. He was a nice enough man, an investment banker, and he was fun to be around. They had met at a party for a mutual acquaintance. She had been working at the time – the only time she ever went to such functions.

Thomas had tried to strike up a conversation with her, and she had politely told him that she was working and could not stop to talk to him. He had given her his number and asked her to call him so they could have lunch sometime. She had thanked him, stuffed the number in her pocket, and continued working. A few weeks later she had called him up and they had been seeing each other ever since.

But now, however, there was a problem. It was the same problem Mia always had with anyone she had dated. Once it started getting too personal, a switch flipped inside of her head and she started feeling like she was being suffocated. After that, the relationship was doomed. She would normally break it off within a few dates after she started getting that feeling. *This* date was *that* date.

Thomas reached his hand across the table and gently caressed Mia's hand. It made Mia tense up, though she tried not to show it.

"I've just bought a new sculpture from an up and coming artist and I'd like to show it to you. Why don't we go by my apartment before I drop you off at your place and you can see it?"

She knew where this was going. Tonight was the most expensive restaurant that he had taken her to so far. He might as well have asked her outright if she wanted to go back to his apartment and have sex. She was glad she had already made plans to take the subway back to her apartment building after she ended the relationship. She felt a twinge of guilt about dumping him after he had just spent over three hundred dollars on dinner, but it couldn't be helped. Now was the time.

"Thomas, I really like you, but I am just not ready to get serious in a relationship right now. My work keeps me very busy, and I don't think it is fair to either one of us to continue to see each other right now. I need a break. I'd like to keep your friendship, but not the dating relationship."

She had given this same speech so many times she should have a patent on it. It rolled off of her tongue like the well-rehearsed script that it was and to the desired effect. Thomas slowly withdrew his hand back across the table, crestfallen. This was the worst part. At least he wasn't getting angry. A fair number of men became belligerent after being dumped. She even had one man follow her to her car and try and force himself on her. He hadn't made it to first base, but he did manage to get to an ER to get treatment for his broken nose afterwards.

"But we've been having such a good time together. If things are going too fast, I can slow down. I don't want you to feel pressured. I think we've got a good thing going here and I'd like to give it a chance. I really like you Mia. So… I'll back off and give you space, then in a few weeks I'll give you a call, and see if you still feel the same way. Fair enough?"

"O.k. Thomas, we'll see. I really need to go now. Thank you very much for dinner."

Thomas held up his finger to a passing waiter.

"Check please," he said with a forced smile.

"No, Thomas, I'm taking the subway back to my apartment."

"But, Mia…"

Before he could finish his sentence, Mia stood up, and walked away from the table and out the door.

When Mia had first started experiencing what she had started to call 'the Mia phenomenon', she had blamed the men for being too pushy. But when it happened over and over again, she started to believe it was just something wrong with her. She read a few books trying to figure out what was wrong, even going to a psychologist for a while. The psychologist had listened for several sessions, and then she had suggested that Mia was having trouble trusting men. She theorized that whenever the relationship started to progress past a point where minimal trust was required, Mia bolted.

Mia found the suggestion believable. She'd had a difficult

relationship with her parents and had ultimately left home at a young age because she felt that they had betrayed her and could no longer be trusted. But at this point in her life, she wasn't sure what to do about it.

Mia caught the subway home, went into her apartment, lay down on the sofa, and cried.

Nick was feeling on top of the world. The big project he had been working on for some time was finally coming together, and the payoff for all of the hard work was now within sight. On top of that, he had just crushed Jerry in a singles tennis match.

After showering and changing clothes, he met Jerry in the club dining room for lunch. He was enjoying the review of the game when he had a sudden pain in his stomach. He winced slightly, and hunched forward a bit.

"Are you o.k., Nick?" Jerry asked.

"Just a bit of a pain in my stomach, that's all. Probably a touch of indigestion or something; nothing to worry about."

He took a sip of seltzer water and continued talking about the match. He had been having indigestion quite frequently lately, and made a mental note to go to the doctor after he closed this next project. There was no reason to take time out of his busy schedule now for a doctor's visit when some over-the-counter medicine would probably suffice for the time being.

As he drove back to his office, his cell phone rang. Tom Freeman's name came up on the screen.

"Hello Tom. What do you have for me?"

"I talked to that cop who owes you ten grand. He's willing to take the job."

"Good. Go ahead and make the arrangements. Make certain it can't be traced back to us."

"Will do."

"Oh, and Tom. When this is all over, see to it that any history of his activity on any of our gaming sites is removed from the host servers and all the backups. I don't want any potential investigation to turn up anything. This has to be clean or we'll all end up in trouble."

"Consider it done."

A file lay open on the workbench beside J.T. Thornbacker as he finished up the last few cuts on the wooden carving, the base of which was held tight in a vise. It was a woman's face. She was staring up into the sky with her eyes open, her hair swept back as if it was being blown by the wind, and a beautiful smile on her face. He stepped back to admire his handiwork. After staring at it for a few moments, he smiled and put down the carving tool beside the file on the workbench.

He opened up the file folder and stared down at the mug shot of the soon-to-be newest member of their dysfunctional little tribe. James Marlowe, twenty-six years old, convicted of armed robbery. The profile went on to state that James had attempted suicide and was on anti-depressants, was above average intelligence for the prison population, and had been in and out of jail since he was a juvenile.

"I hope, my friend, that you can find peace here with us," J.T. said out loud.

He thought back to his own introduction to Utopia and all of the life-changing experiences he'd had here. This place had helped turn a bitter, angry man who thought he was the center of the universe into someone who actually cared about other people and had learned to live in peace with himself and others for the most part. He had seen the same transformation in many of his fellow-prisoners.

As he left the warehouse where his workshop was located and headed to the library, he enjoyed viewing the orange glow of the sunset over the desert horizon. He took a deep breath of the rapidly cooling air and felt happy to be alive. Here in Utopia, each day was a chance to grow, a chance to experience a new level of inner freedom and peace. It was strange to admit it, but he was glad he had come to this prison. It had helped save his life. But the world as J.T. Thornbacker knew it at that moment was about to permanently and irrevocably change forever....

Chapter Three

James woke up in his hospital bed slowly, groggy from the anesthesia. His hands were in restraints and he was beginning to feel the odd sensation of the monitoring device that had been surgically implanted underneath his skin on the back of his neck, near the spine. After about fifteen minutes, a nurse came in to check his vital signs and then left without saying a word. In another half-hour, a doctor came in and asked him a series of questions, then pecked on the screen of his tablet computer for a few minutes, punctuating his flurry of activity with miscellaneous utterances - 'hmmm', 'o.k.', and then finally a 'looks good' before leaving the room.

The next person James saw was a man in a business suit, wearing glasses with small, circular lenses. He had an intense gaze and black hair that was just starting to grey. His demeanor was pleasant, but formal. He took a few moments to look at James' face before he spoke.

"Good afternoon, James. How do you feel?"

"Groggy at the moment."

"That should wear off completely in a few hours. How does the implant feel?"

"Irritating."

The man shook his head up and down slightly, acknowledging the response before continuing.

"You will be in this facility for a week. During that time we will run a series of tests on the monitoring device we implanted, and you will learn about your job at the new facility. Part of the program includes a six-day, eight hour a day work schedule to help rehabilitate you to a normal productive life for when you leave the facility. You will be helping to assemble a mechanical device on an assembly line. At the end of the week, assuming all goes as planned, you will be transported to the new facility. Should you attempt to leave this facility, you will be removed from the program, your sentence reduction will be eliminated, and you will be put back in the prison you just came from for the remainder of your sentence. Is that clear?"

"Yes," James responded. He was encouraged about the possibility of any improvements over his previous incarceration. He liked working with his hands; at least he wouldn't be bored to death.

"Good. One of the reasons we picked you is that you appear to have intelligence above many of your fellow inmates incarcerated for the same crime. We hope this will enable you to better appreciate that you have been given a great opportunity, and that you will therefore endeavor to successfully complete the program. In short, we want you to succeed. If you do, it makes all of us look good and you will be rewarded with an early release per our agreement. If you don't, you will make all of us look bad, in which case we both lose."

The man let the last sentence hang in the air for effect, all the while holding James' gaze without blinking. When the man spoke again, he almost seemed to be a different person. It was as if he had just completed a script that he had given many times before, and now he was slipping out of character and back into a more comfortable, friendlier role. He seemed less official, more excited, and more likeable all at once.

"You know, James, this program has the potential to completely change everything about our current methods of incarceration. For you personally, it has the potential to change your life for the better. We chose you out of hundreds of candidates."

His gaze grew more intense as he spoke the next few words very deliberately.

"I believe in you, James."

Without waiting for a response, the man turned and left the room as quickly and as deliberately as he had arrived.

Out of all the things that had happened to James during this whirlwind of change since Cecil had first told him about the program, up until this very moment, nothing had impacted him more those five words this nameless bureaucrat had just spoken to him - "I believe in you James." James had been told many things in his life by government functionaries. He had been told he was nothing but a convict, that he should be ashamed of his behavior, that he was headed down the wrong road, that he was a career criminal, and many other such things, but no one had ever told him that they believed in him. Those words rang around in his head for hours after the man left and James wondered exactly what they meant to the man who said them. And inside his heart, somewhere deep, where the last bit of hope glowed like a tiny ember in a pile of ashes - the remains of a fire that had long since begun to go out – that hope began to glow a bit brighter.

Chapter Four

Over the last twenty-four hours, James had been shuttled between an SUV, a government plane, an army Humvee, and now he was in a helicopter. Just before take-off in the helicopter, he had been given a special helmet to wear which prevented him from seeing anything. He had no idea where in the United States he was. In fact, he wasn't even certain he was in the United States any longer.

After about an hour and a half, the helicopter landed. His armed escort led him out of the cargo area of the helicopter and into a building that looked like a 1950's era diner. The guard removed the helmet and handcuffs, and promptly went outside to the waiting helicopter and flew away.

James squinted to adjust to the daylight. At the far end of the diner, sitting at a booth facing him, was a man who appeared to be in his late forties. He had a full head of greying hair and a bushy beard. He was drinking a cup of coffee and staring amiably at the newcomer. When he spoke, James thought he detected a slight Southern accent.

"Welcome to Utopia. Coffee pot is behind the counter. Help yourself."

"Thanks," James replied. He poured himself a cup of black coffee before seating himself opposite from the man who had just greeted him. He closed his eyes and inhaled a long breath, savoring the aroma of the coffee before taking a sip.

"How was your trip?" the man asked.

"A bit disorienting."

"Yeah, they like to mix it up when they bring folks out here. It's a bit too James Bond if you ask me."

He took another long sip from his own coffee before setting down the mug and reaching his hand across the table.

"Name's J.T."

James reached out and shook his hand. The first thing he noticed was how big the man's hand was – it engulfed James' own hand. The second thing was how firm the grip was.

"I suppose you already know my name," James responded.

J.T. chuckled. "Yeah, I know quite a bit about you, James. Unless I miss my guess, they didn't tell you Jack-crap about this place. Am I right?"

"I just know I signed my life away to get here in return for a reduction to my sentence."

"Par for the course," J.T. continued. "Well, I'm the longest serving inmate here. Been here for the better part of ten years. I'm not in charge of anything, but I'm the one who gets to show you the ropes. For starters, I'll go ahead and tell you that the implant in your neck is not just to monitor your whereabouts; it serves as a behavior control device. If you try to leave Utopia or do something they don't like, you will be zapped with enough voltage to send your brain into temporary overload. You don't want to go there, trust me. Think of it like a stun gun pointed at your head 24-7."

"Great, the gift that keeps on giving."

"Oh, and another thing: once we leave this diner, don't touch anyone. Outside of this diner and a couple of other places, touch is considered out of bounds and you'll be zapped if you do it. Now, you will start to feel a buzz in the back of your neck if you get too close to someone, and that's your chance to back off before you get zapped."

J.T. tossed a small manual across the table. "Just about everything else you need to know is in that manual. Read it *tonight*. If you have any questions, ask me."

"Will do."

J.T. pointed in the direction of the refrigerator behind the counter.

"There's sandwiches in the refrigerator. Better go grab you one if you want to eat anything tonight. Curfew is at 8:00 p.m. You have to be in your room before then, or you will start feeling a low-grade headache, courtesy of your implant. If you aren't in your room by 8:15 p.m., you get the full shock treatment." He simulated an explosion with his hand motions and said, "Ka-pow!"

James retrieved a sandwich from behind the counter before following J.T. out of the diner and down the street to what looked like a motel.

"Your room is lucky number seven. Here's the key."

J.T. handed him a key with a tacky plastic red number seven key fob attached to it.

"What's with the retro 1950's decorations around here?" James asked.

"Well, that's a bit of a mystery. From the geography around here and the fact that I've never seen any planes fly over us, except military planes, I believe we're somewhere in Nevada – probably some military base. My guess is that this place was built during the cold-war to practice war-games in an invasion scenario. Whatever it once was, it's your new home now."

He turned to go, and said over his shoulder as he left, "I'm room 34 if you need to call me on the phone to ask me anything; just dial the room number. I'll be by to pick you up at 6:15 a.m. Don't leave your room before 6:00 a.m. or...." He pointed his finger back behind him towards James as he continued to walk away.

"...or I'll get the shock of my life," James responded.

J.T. gave him a thumbs up without turning around.

James unlocked the door to his room and went inside. The 1950's era decorations were complete, right down to the vintage bedspread, tacky lamp, two-drawer dresser with a cheap veneer faux wood finish, and the metal trash can with a western motif painting of a stagecoach on it. He smiled as he thought about how much better this was than going to sleep each night in his former jail cell back East.

He sat down on the bed, propped some pillows up as a backrest, and began reading the manual J.T. had given him.

Chapter Five

From the manual:

　　Inmates are expected to follow all the rules set forth in this manual. Failure to comply will result in disciplinary measures which can include revocation of any suspended sentence agreement and removal from the program.
　　A central part of the program are the five practices. All inmates must participate in the following:

1. Participate in the daily exercise regimen.
2. Attend the scheduled group sessions and individual counseling sessions.
3. Practice an approved hobby.
4. Read a book from the approved book list for one hour per day.
5. Contribute to the community by performing approved acts of service.

　　James was awakened from a deep sleep by an alarm clock noise coming from a speaker positioned in the corner of his room. After the alarm sounded for about ten seconds, a pleasant-sounding automated voice came over the speaker: "Please report to the exercise field for your morning exercises in 30 minutes."
　　James barely had time to shower and change into a jumpsuit he found in the closet before he heard a rapping at the door. He opened it up to see J.T. in a similar-looking jumpsuit.
　　"Come on in. I'm just putting on my shoes."
　　"No can-do," replied J.T. "We cannot go into another inmate's room." J.T. pointed up into the sky. "Big brother is watching."
　　James finished tying his shoes and followed J.T. down the street to what looked like a small park. Gathered in the middle of the park were six other people in jumpsuits. J.T. greeted the group

as they approached.

"Good morning, troops! This is our new recruit. His name is James."

James began to move forward to begin shaking hands with the first man, who looked to be in his late forties, about five-foot-six, and slightly built. The man held up both hands and took a step back.

"Whoa! Don't touch me or you'll be shocked."

James immediately backed off. "Sorry about that. Not used to the rules yet."

"That's o.k. We just wave around here," the man replied. "I'm Samuel." He waved his hand at James for effect.

"Hi Samuel." James waved his hand back.

Before the conversation could continue, the same automated voice came over some well-hidden speakers.

"Position yourself to begin morning exercises in 30 seconds."

The group, James noticed, had grown to the full complement of ten inmates. Everyone quickly spaced themselves out to begin the exercises. James had read about the exercise routine the night before in the manual. Stretching, followed by aerobic calisthenics and body-weight exercises, finishing up with some Tai-chi and a 1 mile walk/run. The whole work-out was intended to be about 30 minutes long for most people, but 45 minutes was allotted to account for some people taking longer to finish the walk/run at the end.

James was surprised to notice that there were five women in the group. No one had told him that this was going to be a co-ed facility. He was liking this new facility better by the minute. When the group started the run, he positioned himself beside one of the women who had short, blonde hair.

"How long have you been here?" James asked.

"Not interested," she replied.

"Not interested in what?"

"Look," she responded, "we both know you're just starting this conversation because you're attracted to me. I'm just letting you know up front that I'm not interested. No big deal, just not interested."

Before James could respond, the woman picked up the pace and ran ahead of James. James sped up and came up alongside of her again.

"Hey, I get it, o.k.? But since we're both stuck in here, maybe we could be friends."

She turned her head to the side and rolled her eyes. Next, she sped up the pace again. James tried to keep up, but it was clear he was in no shape to catch her, so he finally started slowing down. J.T. soon came jogging up beside him.

"Don't mind her. She's got a chip on her shoulder."

"Why's that?" James asked.

"You ever wonder why you were picked out for this program? Why anyone was picked out for a program years after it started when only ten people were selected to be in it?"

"I haven't had time to think too much about that yet."

"One of us died, that's why."

James put two and two together.

"So the one who died was her boyfriend, is that it?"

"Yep. And his replacement is the last person you want to be. Every time she looks at you, she'll remember him."

"What happened to him?"

"Freak accident. He was allergic to shellfish. One of the sandwiches they delivered for us had been mis-labeled and had shellfish in it. One bite and he went in to anaphylactic shock. Died before we could give him the epinephrine shot."

"Wow."

"Yeah, I miss the guy. He was a real corker. So anyway, I'd leave her alone for a good six months if you ever want to be on speaking terms with her."

"Thanks for the tip," James replied.

They finished the run and everyone headed back to their rooms to change into their work clothes. James had been trained on his job before arriving, so it was no surprise when he walked into the small warehouse and found his assembly station looking very similar to what he had been trained on. The ubiquitous automated voice came over the speaker system and announced the count-down to the beginning of work. Thus began James' first day of work in the program.

It was easy enough to remember his job. Put the bolts in here, apply the gasket there, place the completed part in the bin for the next person in line to do their job. Overall, it was mind-numbingly boring, but it was better than staring at a cell wall for most of the day, so he wasn't too bothered by it.

Dinner was in the diner and was very different from any of the prison meals James had ever had before. Men and women sat together, and it felt more like a pot luck dinner at your grandmother's house than a prison cafeteria. James sat in a booth with J.T., Julie, and Malcolm. Julie was very up front about the fact that she was incarcerated for insurance fraud. Malcolm was about fifty years old and was telling jokes throughout the meal that made Julie laugh so hard she snorted.

    Afterwards, once it was announced that dinner was over, everyone took their dishes and utensils to the counter where three of the group, who were apparently on kitchen duty, took them and began washing them. Everyone else exited the diner and began walking down the street. James followed along, wondering where they were headed as they continued in the opposite direction from their rooms at the motel. Soon they were in front of a red brick single-story building. Three steps led up to the entrance of the building. There were four concrete columns at the entrance to a small portico which sheltered the doors to the interior of the building. Over the door, etched in stone, were the words, "Utopia Public Library".

    Everyone but J.T. and James split off once they entered the library. James could see that there were several seating areas spaced throughout the long middle corridor that ran the length of the building. The cushioned seats were dated, but comfortable looking. The inmates began sitting down in the different areas, each with one or more books in their hands that they had retrieved from a shelf near the entrance.

    "I assume you've read the manual?" J.T. queried.

    "Yes. But it was a bit short on the particulars," James replied.

    "There are around 100,000 books in this building, with 200,000 more accessible on the intranet from the computer terminals in the back," J.T. explained. "The computers are on a closed network, so you can't get to the web – just in case you were wondering. You pick a book and read it. When you are done, you punch in the book code on one of the computer terminals and you take a short test that basically proves you actually or probably read the book, and that's it. Books range from fifth grade reading level through college level. Classics to modern. No trashy romance novels, no porn, and nothing that encourages violence or criminal behavior, but beyond that, the field is wide open. Oh, and I almost forgot – the books can't leave the building. There are sensors at the door and the cameras are watching." J.T. pointed up to where James could see several black orbs protruding on stems from the ceiling.

"What happens if you don't get the answers right or just refuse to read?"

"Well, I'm thinking you can guess what your options are..." J.T. began.

"Tow the line or get kicked out of the program?" replied James.

"You see?" J.T. responded. "I knew you were a smart one the moment you walked in. Happy reading." With that, J.T. wandered off into the library to find his own reading material for the night.

James had done well enough in school, but he had never been much of a reader. Between helping his mom out by working a job after school and doing his school work, he never took the time to explore non-required books. He wandered up and down the aisles, looking at the shelves full of books he had mostly never heard of. He wound up in the history section and his eyes lighted upon a thin book entitled *The Autobiography of Benjamin Franklin*. Without much interest other than fulfilling his required reading obligation, he found a comfortable-looking chair and sat down to begin to read.

Chapter Six

James woke up to the sound of the automated voice instructing him to dress for work and proceed to the workshop at 451 tenth street. He looked at the clock positioned on the bedside table and noticed he had been awakened a full hour earlier than normal. He stared at the ceiling momentarily, wishing he could sleep in, but knowing that wasn't an option, so he got up anyway. He showered, dressed, and headed out the door just as the sun was rising on Utopia. The street lights were still on and the night chill was still in the air.

Utopia was designed with one main street going down the middle of town, with short side streets jutting off that were themselves perpendicular to the main road at every block. The side streets were numbered sequentially, so it was easy to find 10th street. James found his destination just behind the first row of buildings.

The workshop was a brick building with a metal roof. It had large metal sliding doors facing directly toward the street, and a smaller door off to the side for pedestrian access. James knocked on the door three times and waited. There was no answer, so he went inside.

The ceiling to the workshop was about thirty feet up, where huge gas-powered lights shown down on the contents of the building below. There was an empty area directly in front of the large sliding doors, leading to the alleyway that was big enough to park a couple of large vehicles. Beyond that were several rows of industrial-sized shelving units two-stories tall and about ten feet wide each, which spanned the remaining length of the building.

"Good mornin'," J.T.'s familiar voice echoed out in the

cavernous space. James looked up to see J.T. peering down at him from the second story of one of the large shelving units. "Come on up," he continued as he waved his hand at the metal staircase attached to the end of the shelves.

James climbed up the stairs and followed J.T. through a narrow middle passageway that eventually opened up into what looked like a woodworking shop. Natural light shown in from the opaque skylight directly above the area. Shelves lined the open space with what appeared to be wood carvings of mostly people's faces. James noticed that the faces on one end of the area were filled with pain. Some were crying, some were simply sad, and others looked like the faces of despair and anguish. As he moved down the line, he noticed the faces began to change. They began to display softer emotions, even happiness, some of them bordering on what could be described as joy. J.T. remained silent as he watch James taking it all in. Only when it was apparent that James had surveyed the whole area did J.T. speak.

"As I'm sure you've read in the manual, everyone here has to have a hobby." He spread his arms out wide, indicating the sculptures before them. "This is mine – wood carving."

James walked up to one of the shelves and picked up one of the sculptures of a crying woman, looking at it closely and turning it from side to side so he could see it from different angles.

"Why are so many of them sad?"

J.T. walked up beside James and looked at the same sculpture. His eyes were pointed at the carved sculpture, but he was looking somewhere else. Somewhere in the past. When he spoke next, his voice was subdued and his tone echoed not so much guilt as acknowledgement.

"Because I'm a thief, James."

James looked up from the sculpture into J.T.'s eyes and the man met his gaze, looking intently back at him.

"I stole from people. I took things from them. I stole their money like it was mine to take. Only now, I realize I was taking a lot more from them than that. From some of them, I was taking their hope, or a chance to buy medicine for their sick child, or their college fund. I never thought of that before I came here, to Utopia. I carve these images as a type of amends. It's a way to remind myself that what I did hurt real people so I won't ever do it again."

James looked down at the sculpture he held in his hands. He began to think of his mother and about how much he missed her. Tears began to well up in his eyes as he spoke.

"That's what happened to my mom.... She had cancer. The doctors told her it was incurable and that she might live another year or so, but that was it. She found out about this experimental drug she could get in France that might help stop the cancer. She was going to take the money out of her retirement fund to go get the treatment, but right before she was going to get the money out, they told her the money had been stolen by one of the fund managers. They eventually tracked the guy down and took him to court, but they told Mom the class action suit could take years to settle before she would see any of the money. After that, it was like the life was sucked out of her. She knew she wouldn't live that long. She died on my fourteenth birthday."

J.T. reached up and put one of his big hands on James' shoulder.

"I'm sorry, son."

"Yeah, thanks," James replied as he reached up and brushed away the tears that were threatening to cascade down his face.

J.T. waited another moment before he continued in a more upbeat tone.

"We'll need to get to work soon, so I better cut to the chase. You need to pick a hobby. This workshop contains just about anything you need. If you want to paint, learn to play the guitar, build bird houses, create pottery, take photographs, whatever. Take a look around the place and pick something. Your counselor will want to know what you pick – it has to be approved, as I'm sure you are aware. I'm going to head over to work to get ready. We've still got a few minutes, so look around a little before you come over."

With that, J.T. headed back out of the building.

James began walking up and down the aisles of the warehouse. Just like J.T. had said, there was a little bit of everything in there. He saw some machine shop tools, a ping-pong table, art supplies, even a stack of jigsaw puzzles. He heard the automated voice announce that there was fifteen minutes before the work day began and decided to go back to the front of the warehouse by way of one of the aisles he hadn't yet explored. About half-way down the aisle, he saw twenty or thirty bicycles stacked closely together. The sight suddenly brought back a childhood memory of being with his dad.

On his seventh birthday, his dad had bought him a brand-new bike and taught him how to ride. That summer was probably the best summer of his life. He and his dad would ride down to the playground almost every Saturday. That was also the last summer he'd ever seen his dad. Shortly after that, his mom had gotten cancer for the first time and his dad had left for good. He abruptly turned away from the bicycles and headed to the door.

Chapter Seven

The next day, James went through the daily routine a bit more smoothly as he began to assimilate into the scheduled existence of life in his new prison home. He had reviewed the weekly schedule posted on the wall in the diner and seen that today there was a group session after work. The manual was fairly vague on many of the topics it covered, and mention of the group session was no different. It simply stated that : "The group session is designed to assist the inmate in facing and overcoming the challenges of life in the prison environment and in preparing them for returning to normal life as a fully functioning member of society."

After dinner was over and the cleanup was complete, everyone headed out the door to yet another building James had not been to yet. The building appeared to be a well-cared-for 19th century house. The wooden siding was painted a colorful yellow and the large windows revealed period rugs, furniture, and decorations on the inside of the house. The group ascended the steps onto the spacious wrap-around porch and James noted the ornate carving on the porch railing, spindles, and posts – all painted white.

They filed inside and the women grouped together and went down the hall while the men in the group entered the first door on the right. James followed along. The room was spacious, with twelve-foot ceilings and a large oriental rug laid out on the wooden floor. There was a circle of chairs in the middle of the room and a water-cooler in one corner. Bedsides those items, there was nothing else in the room. Everyone took a seat and began talking among themselves as James looked around silently, taking it all in.

Moments later, from the back of the room, a door opened and a man in his mid-forties entered, wearing a tweed jacket and dark-rimmed glasses. His hair was coiffed to perfection, but didn't totally eradicate the slightly nerdy aura he emanated. He was looking down at a computer tablet he was carrying as he crossed the room and sat down in one of the chairs. When he looked up, he quickly scanned the group and fixed his gaze on James.

"Ah, James," the man said with a smile. "Welcome to your first group session."

The man reached out his hand and noticed James' reluctance to respond.

"It's o.k., this is one of the locations in which the monitoring software is not programmed to zap you."

James reached out and shook the man's hand. The man then settled back in his chair and addressed the group.

"Hello everyone. Let's jump right in. As is protocol, since we have a new member of the group, we're going to start with principle one." Turning to James, he continued. "James, this is a twelve-step group somewhat akin to A.A. I could go into a long explanation, but you'll catch on soon enough. Let's introduce ourselves; then I'll read the rules and the first principle and we can begin sharing."

He looked around at the whole group before he continued.

"My name is Greg, I struggle with commitment issues and insecurity."

When he stopped speaking, everyone but James spoke in unison.

"Hi Greg."

J.T. was seated to Greg's left, and continued the introductions.

"My name is J.T.. I struggle with stealing and pridefulness."

"Hi J.T.," everyone but James replied.

When it came time for James to introduce himself, Greg interjected.

"James, you don't need to tell us what you struggle with today if you don't want to. You can just tell us your name and something else about yourself if you want."

James felt strange telling everyone who he was when they already knew, but he did it anyway.

"My name is James, and as you all know, I'm the new guy."

"Hi James," everyone responded.

Once the introductions were completed, Greg clicked on his tablet and began reading. He read some rules about not interrupting and not trying to tell someone how to fix their problems, as well as a few others. The last sentence, Greg read very slowly and deliberately, as if he were reading to a small child that might not understand the sentence if he read too quickly.

"We admitted we were powerless over our destructive, compulsive behaviors and that our lives had become unmanageable."

He looked up from his tablet and took a look around the room.

"Who would like to begin sharing?" he asked.

Samuel spoke up.

"Hi, my name is Samuel, I struggle with anger and desire for revenge."

"Hi Samuel," the group responded.

This time James joined in the response. Samuel continued.

"I think I'm beginning to forgive my father for never being there, for always working and not spending time with me. I realize now that he grew up in a dysfunctional home too, and part of what drove him to work so much was a feeling that his value in life came from his bank account. I think he neglected me not because he didn't love me, but because he felt so worthless himself that he felt he constantly had to be working harder to make money in order to feel that he had any value as a person."

When Samuel was done, everyone but James said in unison, "Thanks for sharing, Samuel."

The meeting went on with everyone but James eventually sharing something. Some were just as forthcoming as Samuel. James noticed that Greg didn't give any advice, nor did anyone else. They just listened. It was a strange feeling, being listened to. James couldn't recall the last time someone had really listened to him like these men were listening to each other. They weren't making jokes or wise-cracks at what each other were saying. They were just listening.

Later that night, after James was back in his room, he was laying on the bed and thinking over what had transpired at the group session earlier in the day. He had never experienced anything like this in prison before. He felt a glimmer of hope that this might actually help him break out of the destructive lifestyle he had been in for so long. Maybe he could find a different, better way to live. Maybe, just maybe, he wasn't doomed to follow the road he had been on to the bitter end. Maybe he could learn to change.

He closed his eyes and began to think about what a different life might look like as he drifted off to sleep.

Chapter Eight

Laura woke up in a cold sweat as her body involuntarily sat upright in her bed. She had been dreaming of Paul again. She hadn't gone more than a few nights since his death without having the same nightmare over and over. Only, it wasn't just a nightmare... it had really happened.

She got out of bed and went to the bathroom sink to rinse off the cold sweat with some warm water. She looked at herself in the mirror and began to cry. She vowed to herself that she would never allow herself to be in a position to feel this emotional pain again. It was tearing her apart inside and she wasn't sure how much longer she could take it without having a nervous breakdown – or worse.

The scene played out again in her mind. One minute, she and Paul were sitting across from each other in a booth at the diner here in Utopia, laughing and talking. He had reached his hand across the table and gently caressed hers. They'd looked into each other's eyes, each letting the other know how much they cared for one another in a silent conversation. Then, suddenly, Paul's countenance had changed. He began to make gasping sounds and fell out of the booth onto the floor. His lips began turning blue as Laura slid out of her seat onto the floor. She grasped his hand and shouted out, "He's having an allergic reaction! Someone give me the epi pen, now!"

Malcolm had run around behind the counter to the medicine storage unit, a secure refrigerated unit where any emergency inmate medicine was stored. Malcolm punched in the code on the keypad and tried to turn the handle to open the door, but it didn't turn. Malcolm frantically punched in the code again, but still the door wouldn't budge.

"Where is the pen!? He's dying here!" Laura yelled as she watched the life ebb out of Paul's face and his eyes begin to glaze over. She grasped his hand in hers and looked into his eyes. "Hold on, Paul, help is on the way."

"The code isn't working!" Malcolm shouted back. He shouted out into the air as if to an unseen entity, "Security! The code has been changed! What is the current code to open the medicine cabinet!?"

A nervous human voice came across the loudspeaker, "Ahh, I'm checking now. Hold on!"

Malcolm could hear papers rustling in the background as the guard frantically searched for the needed code. Precious seconds later, the voice returned.

"Try 7238!"

Malcolm punched in the code, ripped open the door, and grabbed the epinephrine pen. He tore around the corner, slid onto the floor, tore the top off the pen, and slammed the needle a bit too forcefully down into Paul's leg in order to deliver the life-saving medicine. It was only then that he realized Laura was no longer frantic, but that a steady stream of tears were flowing down her face.

"He's gone," she said, holding his hand against her face as the tears continued to flow.

Just to be sure, Malcolm checked for a pulse, but could find none. He began trying to administer CPR. A minute later, the on-staff EMT threw open the door to the diner and quickly moved in to assess Paul's condition himself. He saw the pen, but asked anyway.

"Did you give him the shot?"

"Yes," Malcolm replied.

The EMT felt for a pulse but couldn't find any. He took out another epinephrine shot from his medical bag and gave it to Paul; then he took over administering CPR. He tried desperately to blow air into Paul's lungs, but couldn't. After trying to resuscitate Paul for fifteen minutes, the exhausted

EMT sat back to catch his breath. He looked over at Laura, who was still clutching Paul's hand.

"I'm sorry."

The next few days were a blur to Laura. A special investigator was flown out to investigate Paul's death. Everyone was questioned. The medicine chest lock was tested and the code was changed. The new code was printed on the outside of the cabinet so everyone could see it. Then, the following day, everything returned to the new normal. The same schedule, the same activities, the same work, the same food. Except, no Paul.

About two weeks later, in one of the group sessions, they were informed that Paul, who was allergic to shellfish, had accidentally ingested shellfish from an improperly labeled pre-packaged sandwich. The code on the medicine cabinet had been changed during routine maintenance, but the form that was filled out so that the inmates could be notified of the new code had fallen behind a desk and was only found after the investigation into Paul's death.

It was about a month later that James showed up in Utopia. Laura hated to even look at him. His very presence was a constant reminder that Paul was dead. In her heart, she knew it wasn't James' fault, but she needed someone to focus her anger on, and for now, James fit the bill.

There was no use trying to go back to sleep now. It would be a few hours before her mind settled down enough to allow that to happen. She wished she could make herself a cup of tea and sit on a nice couch with a blanket wrapped around her, but that wasn't going to happen either. Even though she was in Utopia, she was still in prison, and in a room with one bed and an uncomfortable wooden chair with little padding on the seat. It would be another few hours before she could leave her room to get that cup of tea. Instead, she lay back down in bed and stared up into the darkness, letting her mind wander back over the years and consider how she had ended up here.

Laura had grown up in a troubled home with abusive parents. She could still remember hiding under the kitchen table while her parents fought, throwing whatever happened to be near them at each other and yelling at the top of their lungs. Her dad finally left when she was seven years old, but instead of things getting better, they got worse. Her mom then began a series of relationships with abusive boyfriends. As Laura got older and began to mature, the boyfriends began taking an interest in her physically. More than one of them would sexually abuse her over the years.

When she was fourteen, she had had enough, and ran away from home. She fell in with a drug dealer and began taking and selling drugs. Her taste in men wasn't any better than her mother's, and she and her drug-dealing boyfriend would have violent fights. She was arrested for drugs on a couple of occasions and did time for possession. Then, one night after getting out of jail for the second time, her boyfriend came home in a drug-induced rage. For the first time in their relationship, she was terrified that he might actually kill her. He beat her so badly that she passed out. When she woke up on the floor, bloodied and bruised from the beating, she crawled into the bedroom to find him asleep in the bed, like nothing had happened. She pulled a pistol out of the bedside table drawer and shot him six times in the head as he slept. Next stop – prison.

The chance to come to Utopia had been a chance for a new life. She had begun dealing with her anger and her past, and had made real progress over the past few years. When Paul came into the program, she kept her distance. She didn't want to get involved with another criminal.

Over time, Paul won her over. He was funny, charming, and he actually respected her. He did little things like asking if he could touch her hand for the first time instead of trying to force himself on her. He shared about his own abusive past with a father that beat him, and how he'd left home after he grew bigger because he was afraid he might beat his father to death the next time he laid a hand on him. He said he didn't want to be the same kind of person his father was. He'd begun stealing cars to make a living at sixteen and eventually ended up in prison, then Utopia.

Laura could relate to him. They thought about things the same way and they both wanted their futures to be different from their pasts. They became allies and tried to help each other change, and encourage each other when things were tough. Slowly, they became best friends. Then he died, and she had been in a tailspin ever since.

The automated voice came over the loudspeaker, bringing her back to the present and signaling the beginning of a new day in Utopia. Normally, she hated that voice, but today she was glad to have something else to focus on besides her own inner voice and the memories that tormented her. Laura got out of bed and began to get ready for the morning exercises.

Chapter Nine

James showed up for his counseling appointment early and sat out in the waiting area. He wasn't quite sure what to expect and wondered if he was going to be asked to lay down on a couch and talk about his childhood or something. It wasn't long before the door to the counselor's office opened and Greg walked out to greet him. He held out his hand to shake and James reciprocated.

"Good afternoon, James. Good to see you. Come on in."

As he spoke, Dr. Greg Thompson stepped aside and motioned with his hand towards the open door with a slight deprecating bow. James entered the small office, seating himself in one of the two comfortably cushioned lounge chairs which faced each other. Dr. Thompson followed him, closing the door before positioning himself in the remaining chair.

"So, James," Dr. Thompson began. "It's been almost a week since you arrived here in Utopia. What do you think?"

James was guarded as he considered his reply. He wasn't accustomed to prison employees being so nice. For that matter, he wasn't accustomed to speaking to a counselor either. It felt strange.

"It's much nicer than where I came from," he replied.

"Yeah, I bet it is indeed," Dr. Thompson continued. "What do you think about the five practices – the exercise, the group and individual sessions, the reading, the hobby, the community service...?"

"It's o.k. It beats being stuck in a jail cell all day, that's for sure."

"What are you reading?"

"An autobiography of Benjamin Franklin."

"Is it enjoyable? Do you like it?"

"I'm not much of a reader, so I get distracted when I'm reading, but so far I like it. It's not like anything I read in school. I mean, I've heard about Benjamin Franklin, but mostly about what he did in the American Revolution. I never heard about the rest of his life before."

"Was there anything meaningful that you learned? Anything that you learned about his life that inspired you or caused you to change the way you think about something?"

James looked over at a plant that was sitting on top of a bookshelf in the corner.

"Yeah. He said something that stuck with me. He said, 'The most acceptable service of God is doing good to man.' He seemed to do a lot of things that helped other people. He started a library, started a fire department, and a whole lot of other things that I never knew about. I guess I never thought of getting up in the morning and thinking about how I can help out other people a whole lot, not since my mom died anyway."

"Do you think that would be a better way to live than the way you have been living?"

James looked at Dr. Thompson suspiciously.

"I know what you're trying to do. You're trying to get me to admit that the way I've been living is the wrong way and that I need to change. Well, I know that already. It's just not that easy. I like nice things. I like to live a certain way and I can't exactly get a great job with a background as a bank robber."

"Do you want to change, James?"

Dr. Thompson let the sentence hang in the air and waited for James to reply. He didn't say it judgmentally or in an accusing way. The question disarmed James and found its way in, past the defensiveness he often wore as a shield when other people asked him questions he didn't want to answer. It was something he had thought a lot about since getting sent back to jail.

"Yes... I do."

Again Dr. Thompson left the empty space alone and let James' response linger in the room.

"Good," the doctor replied. "Very good."

Later that afternoon, it was time to work on his official hobby. James went to the workshop with J.T. and a few of the other inmates who also worked on their hobbies there. As he entered the door to the warehouse, there was a box on the floor. A white sheet of paper was taped to the box with his name scrawled across it. He opened it up and found a bicycle manual and a set of tools, along with some other supplies. He smiled as he picked up the box and made his way back to where the bicycles were stored.

Earlier in the week, he had filled out the required form indicating he would like to fix up the bikes he'd seen in the workshop as his hobby. He had received notice that his hobby was approved, but no one had said anything about getting him a set of tools or a manual. This was definitely not like the prisons he had been in before, he mused to himself as he began rolling out the first bicycle on the rack so he could get a better look at it.

It was a bit rusty, the tires were flat, and the chain had been de-railed. It was painted white and green and had silver fenders over the tires. He found a manual bicycle pump at the end of the row of bicycles and pumped up the tires. The tires had the small cracks in the rubber that were telltale signs of dry rot, but they seemed to be holding air for now. He pressed down on the tires, slightly impressed that they didn't pop outright.

He rummaged around in the box of supplies and found a can of lubricant spray, which he sprayed on the chain after he re-mounted it on the gear cogs. He straddled the bicycle and pushed off tentatively, guarding against a sudden tire blowout. After coasting a few feet without a mishap, he managed to pedal down to the end of the aisle. He turned the bike around and rode back down to the other end. He smiled to himself as he dismounted, putting down the kick-stand and standing back to admire his handiwork. He didn't know why they had the crazy rules they had, but he was beginning to actually like this place.

Chapter Ten

In the weeks since his first encounter with Laura, James had continued to be attracted to her. Her fiery personality reminded him of his mother before she got sick. As they began the morning run, James ran a respectful distance behind Laura, making certain not to get too close to what he had begun to consider as her 'no trespassing' zone. He had noticed some days that she would run faster than others, and today was one of the faster-paced days. Though he had never been much of a runner, he was beginning to develop a bit of a taste for it through the daily repetition of morning exercises.

He kept pace with Laura for the whole mile, maintaining about a ten yard distance behind her until she completed the prescribed mile course. He slowed to a walk once the run was complete and he was headed to his room to change for work, when suddenly Laura wheeled around and came to within a few feet of him, glaring at him as she approached.

"Stop following me!" she shouted.

"Whoa, hey, what's the problem?" James replied as he put his hands up shoulder-high in a gesture of surrender.

She shoved a finger in his direction before saying, "You've been shadowing me for weeks and I'm over it!"

"I didn't know it was bugging you, o.k.?"

"No, it's not o.k.!"

Laura stepped closer and James could feel the low-grade electrical buzz of the device in his neck that began whenever two of the inmates passed too close to one another in a restricted zone. He took a step backwards and felt the buzz subside.

"Hey, watch out, you're getting too close," he warned.

"Too close?! That's exactly what you are, too close! I'll show you what happens when you get too close to me!"

Without another word, Laura ran directly at James at full speed. James began running backwards and attempted to turn around and run, but he wasn't fast enough. The last thing he remembered before he blacked out was the searing pain of the most intense shock of his life.

James awoke to find himself lying on a hospital bed, dressed in a hospital gown. He had the most intense headache he had ever felt and immediately closed his eyes, grimacing against the pain he felt. About ten painful minutes later, Tony, the facility EMT, came into the room with a glass of water and two pills that he held out to James.

"Here, take these. They're migraine pills. Bite down on them before you swallow them and they'll make the pain stop quicker."

James took the pills and the water, doing as he was instructed before handing the empty glass back to the EMT. Tony offered his hand to James.

"Name's Tony."

James shook his hand without saying anything. Tony continued.

"The edge of the headache will wear off in about fifteen minutes if you're like most." He nodded towards a chair by the door where a plastic bag was placed. "Your clothes are in there. You'll need to wash them. The body loses bladder control when the shock hits. There are some scrubs underneath the bag you can wear back to your room to change."

"What's going to happen to me?"

"You mean are you going to be shipped out of here? No worries. Everything is caught on video around here. It was clear you didn't start anything and tried to get out of the situation. You're good to go."

"What about Laura?" James whispered, trying not to agitate his throbbing head any more than necessary.

"Well, that's another story. The docs will decide that. She's obviously one ticked off lady. I give her a 50/50 chance either way. They really don't want to send anyone home if they can avoid it. Makes them and the program look bad. I'll come back in ten to escort you back to town."

Laura had woken up in a hospital bed. The first thing she'd noticed besides the intense headache was that her hands and feet were in restraints. A few minutes after she'd woken up, Tony had come in and offered her two migraine pills, putting them in her mouth and giving her a drink through a straw. It had been about thirty minutes since then. She wondered what was going to happen next. A few minutes later, Sheila, the women's staff counselor, came in the room and sat down beside her on the bed. Laura looked out the window, not wanting to look Sheila in the face.

"I know I blew it," Laura said.

"You think?" Sheila responded. She waited for Laura to continue.

"I just couldn't stand him hitting on me like that."

"So that's what it was, was it?"

Sheila waited again for Laura to speak. Laura's eyes started to tear up, and when she spoke next, there was a different kind of pain in her voice.

"I miss him. I miss him so much."

"It's not James' fault, you know."

"I know. But every time I see him, I think of Paul and how Paul should be here instead of him."

"So you turned your anger about Paul's death onto James."

"Yeah. I guess I did."

"Did it help?"

There was a long pause. Tears were slowly making their way down Laura's cheeks. She began moving her head from side to side.

Sheila let out a long sigh before she continued.

"I'm going to try to keep you here, Laura, but you have to promise me you won't do something like this again."

Laura turned and looked at Sheila.

"O.k.," she replied.

Sheila placed a motherly hand on Laura's forehead and smoothed the hair to one side that had fallen down over Laura's eyes before turning to leave. As she was heading out the door, Laura spoke.

"Sheila?"

Sheila stopped and turned towards the bed, "Yes?"

"Thanks for not giving up on me."

Sheila smiled slightly and nodded at Laura before turning and walking out the door.

Chapter Eleven

James worked steadily in doing his part on the assembly line, but his mind was somewhere else. His job was simple enough that he could perform it while thinking on other things without too much chance of making a mistake. During a break at the water cooler as he leaned against a wall, away from the others, J.T. wandered over in his direction.

"What's on your mind?" J.T. inquired.

James' eyes were staring off into space and J.T.'s question brought his focus back into the room. "Just thinking about stuff," he replied.

"Look, if you don't want to talk, fine by me, just tell me and I'll buzz off. But if you want to get something off of your chest, I can listen," J.T. continued.

"This whole thing... being here in Utopia... I've had some time to think about my life. The counseling, the reading, all of it.... I guess I have a different perspective now than I did when I came here."

"How's that?" J.T. responded.

James started shaking his head from side to side as he continued. "I've made a lot of stupid mistakes. I've been doing it all wrong."

"What exactly do you mean by that?"

"I've been living life wrong. When my mom died, I was angry. I took it out on everybody and I didn't listen to the people who tried to help me. I let that anger lead me to a bad place and did some really stupid things. I took what I wanted because I thought I deserved it and I had the power to take it. I never thought about what my actions might be doing to somebody else... and now I'm here... in prison.... I don't want to live that way anymore."

"Well, James," J.T. replied, "you don't have to. You can learn to live a different way. You know, you and I are a lot alike. Before I was convicted, I lived in much the same way you described. I took what didn't belong to me because I thought I deserved it and I had the ability to take it. Then I came here. It took me a few years being here and soaking up the lessons of this place before I began to get it. But when I did, it wasn't long before I came to the same conclusion you just did. Since then, I've been working my program as best I can, and I can tell I'm really changing on the inside, where it counts. You can change, too, James."

The automated voice came over the speakers.

"Now is the time to return to your workstation... Now is the time to return to your workstation."

James went back to work and, for the rest of the day, he kept thinking about what J.T. had said and about that twelve step statement he heard in the first group session he'd attended: *We admitted we were powerless over our destructive, compulsive behaviors and that our lives had become unmanageable.* He wasn't certain how he could change, but he was sure of one thing; his life had certainly become unmanageable and he wanted to do whatever it took to learn to live a better way.

Later that evening at the library, James sat down at the computer terminal and prepared to take his first book exam. He had read up on the process in the manual the night before in his room. After reading whatever book the prisoner chose, he or she had to complete an online assessment to prove they had actually read the book. The test was to be comprised of four multiple choice questions and a short answer question at the end, asking what they had learned from reading the book. He punched in his user ID and password as they had been printed in the manual, then punched in the code on the back of the book he had been reading. The questions popped up on the screen:

When Benjamin Franklin was twelve years old, what

profession did he begin:

    __ *Candle-maker*
    __ *Printer*
    __ *Painter*
    __ *Farmer*

James selected 'Printer' and moved on to the next question.

About the year 1730, Benjamin Franklin started the first one of these in the American colonies:

    __ *Newspaper*
    __ *Insurance company*
    __ *Public library*
    __ *Firearms manufacturer*

James was fairly certain it was either 'newspaper' or 'public library'. He was glad this was an open book test. After spending a few minutes thumbing through the book, he located the answer. He selected 'public library', and continued to the next question.

Which of the following are descriptions that Franklin gave among his list of thirteen virtues:

    __ *"Speak not but what may benefit others or yourself; avoid trifling conversation."*
    __ *"Lose no time; be always employ'd in something useful; cut off all unnecessary actions."*
    __ *"Wrong none by doing injuries, or omitting the benefits that are your duty."*
    __ *All of the above.*

He thumbed through the book for a few minutes and

eventually found the section where the thirteen virtues were listed. He found all of the quotations on the same page and selected 'all of the above' from the list of answers.

Benjamin Franklin started the first one of these in Philadelphia:

    __ *A fire station named "Union Fire Company"*
    __ *A restaurant named "The Golden Eagle Tavern"*
    __ *A hunting club named "Foxglove Hunting Club"*
    __ *A gambling club named "The Gaming Diversions Association"*

He selected the fire station and continued to the last question.

What have you learned by reading this book:

James looked at the last question and sat back in his chair. After some consideration, he leaned in towards the monitor and began pecking out his response on the keyboard:

Benjamin Franklin started life out without much education. He read a lot, tried to learn as much as he could that would help him move ahead in life, and didn't spend much time getting angry over things other people did to him that were wrong. He also did a lot of things that helped other people. I would like to be more like him in the future.

When he was done typing his answer, James clicked on the "submit answers" icon on the screen. Immediately, his score flashed in front of him:

Congratulations! You scored 100%

He smiled to himself. "That wasn't so bad," he thought. He looked up at the clock on the wall. He still had forty-five minutes left before they were sent back to their rooms for the night. He picked up the journal that Dr. Thompson had given to him during their first session together. He flipped to the page where he had written down the title of the book that Dr. Thompson had recommended he read next, <u>Some Fruits of Solitude</u> by William Penn.

He selected the library catalog program on the computer and typed in the book title, locating the book location code and writing it down in his journal. Then he went and found the book on the shelf. It was another thin book, which made him wonder what Dr. Thompson was thinking about his reading abilities.

He pulled the book off of the shelf and found a good spot to begin reading. It was a bit difficult at first because some of the words the author used had been spelled differently back when the book was written. It caused him to read more slowly than usual. However, it wasn't long until he read something that hit him like a ton of bricks. He read it again and again, letting it soak in to his mind. Then he opened up his journal and began copying the words down so he could read them again later:

> We understand little of the works of God, either in nature or grace. We pursue false knowledge, and mistake education extreamly. We are violent in our affections, confused and immethodical in our whole life; making that a burthen, which was given for a blessing; and so of little comfort to ourselves or others; misapprehending the true notion of happiness, and so missing of the right use of life, and way of happy living.
>
> And till we are perswaded to stop, and step a little aside, out of the noisy crowd and incumbering hurry of the world, and calmly take a prospect of

things, it will be impossible we should be able to make a right judgement of our selves, or know our own misery. But after we have made the just reckonings which retirement will help us to, we shall begin to think the world in great measure mad, and that we have been in a sort of bedlam all this while.

Reader, whether young or old, think it not too soon or too late to turn over the leaves of thy past life. And be sure to fold down where an passage of it may affect thee; and bestow thy remainder of time, to correct those faults in thy future conduct; be it in relation to this or the next life.

- quote from the preface of <u>Some Fruits of Solitude, In Reflections and Maxims</u> - by William Penn, published in 1682

James must have read the passage about ten times in all. He began thinking about the conversation with J.T., the group sessions, the one-on-one session with Dr. Thompson, and about where his own thoughts had been leading him recently. He was beginning to realize that it was all a pattern. It was all guiding him to a destination.

He thought back in his life and recounted the direction he had been taking – the wrong direction. He remembered how even then there had been those in his life who had tried to direct him along the right path. But he was too busy, too angry, or too distracted to really understand that he was in desperate need of the direction that was being offered to him. Now, here in this place, he was being given a second chance. He wasn't sure why they had selected him for this program, but he wasn't going to let this opportunity slip by. He decided that whatever it took, he was going to leave this place a changed man... a man changed for the better.

Chapter Twelve

As he ascended the New York brownstone's steps, Silas McGruder had disturbing thoughts. He thought of what he was about to do and who he was about to do it for. He thought of his wife of twenty years and his teenage son. He thought of their quiet suburban life in New Jersey and their plans to eventually retire in Florida. He thought of how his gambling had put a strain on their marriage and put all of those plans in jeopardy.

He paused at the top of the steps as he was about to press the doorbell. Once he did this, there was no going back. Once he did this, he would officially be a dirty cop. He could still turn around and walk away. He could come clean to his wife and tell her they were about to lose the house because of his gambling debts, and then get counseling – maybe the marriage would survive. He couldn't bear the thought of being without Maggie and their son. Losing the house and having to start all over again with a rental while they slowly built up credit to buy, then trying to fund their retirement plans....

No, not today. He shook his head from side to side. Not when he could possibly stop the avalanche from beginning just by finishing what he'd come to do. He was in the home stretch. After all, it was just information, nothing more. Just words on a piece of paper and a few pictures. He reached down and pressed the doorbell quickly before he could think anymore about it or lost his nerve.

It seemed like an eternity as he waited. Silas had to fight the urge to turn, jog down the steps, and walk down the street to escape. Then the intercom speaker came to life and a husky man's voice spoke.

"Who is it?"

One thing Silas could do was focus when required. It's what made him such a good detective. He was like a bulldog that way: once he got hold of something he never let go until he was good and ready. When he heard the voice come over the intercom, he pushed all the previous thoughts out of his mind. In that moment, he committed 100% to finishing what he had come here to do. No more debate. The decision had been made.

"I'm Johnny D. I'm here to see Mr. Bartonovich," Silas said with conviction as he introduced himself with the prearranged code name he had been given.

"One moment please," the voice responded flatly. In a few moments, Silas could hear the door being unlocked and then a stout-looking wall of muscle opened the door. "This way," he croaked as he motioned to the staircase, pausing only long enough to shut and lock the door before lumbering over to the staircase and leading Silas up the stairs.

The room to which Silas was led was at the top of the brownstone's four stories. His guide opened the door to the study and stood aside for Silas to enter, then closed the door behind him as he went back down the stairs. The room was large and had little furniture in it. There was a bar at one end of the room. At the end of the bar stood a strikingly beautiful woman of Asian descent with shoulder length black hair. She was tall for an Asian, Silas thought to himself, probably about five-foot-seven. She was dressed in closely fitted all-black clothing that a woman who wanted to show off her figure might wear, only she looked classy rather than catty. Judging from her eyes and something about her demeanor, he put her age somewhere between forty and forty-five, although many people who didn't pay attention to details the way a cop did would have guessed about fifteen years younger than that. She watched him like a snake with a gaze that made a slight chill run down his spine as he walked across the oriental rug to the man he had come to see.

The massive oak desk had four huge carved wooden legs supporting it. The two front-facing legs had large lions' heads carved into them at the top, with their fangs bared. The lack of side panels on the desk gave it a cleanly efficient look. On top of the desk was a laptop computer off to one side and a bottle of water on a coaster. Directly in front of the desk and facing it were two burgundy leather wing-back chairs.

Silas didn't bother sitting down in either of the chairs. He wanted to get in and get out. From the temperature in the room, he guessed Mr. Bartonovich was not going to ask him to have a long chat either. His host was turned to the side in a leather swivel chair and talking on a wireless headset. Silas caught the tail-end of the conversation as he waited for his presence to be acknowledged. He was somewhat surprised by the crisp, upper-crust slightly British sounding accent he was hearing, which belied Mr. Bartonovich's East European ancestry. His previous dealings with Mr. Bartonovich had been brokered by someone else and this was the first time he had seen or heard from his employer directly.

"...and I don't really care what your excuse is Myron. You defaulted on the loan and now it's time to pay the piper. I'm sending my man over to pick it up. And don't try to hide it because I know where you live."

Nick Bartonovich hit the disconnect button on the cell phone he had been holding in his hand and turned to face Silas without breaking stride.

"What do you have for me?"

Silas pushed the USB drive across the desk towards his employer. Nick picked it up, plugged it in to his laptop, and began opening files and scanning through the contents.

"Sit," Nick said without any preamble. Silas cringed inside as he sat down in one of the chairs, his hopes of a hasty exit evaporating in the process. Nick spent about ten minutes reviewing the documents and photos on the USB drive before turning to address Silas again. "You are sure the information about accessing the funds in the Cayman Islands is accurate?"

"That copy of the contract came directly from one of the bank's vice-presidents. I flew down there myself and picked it up straight from him in his office at the bank. If it's a fake, it came straight from the top."

Nick smiled slightly, with his mouth but not his eyes, while he continued to look directly at Silas. He seemed to be considering something, and it was several seconds before he spoke again.

"You've done well. Consider your debt canceled. I presume the money I gave you for the expenses covered everything else?"

"Yes, it did," replied Silas.

"Good. Have a nice day, Detective."

Silas nodded his head without saying anything, stood up, and walked out of the room. The Asian woman followed him to the staircase and watched him exit through the front door before returning to the office and closing the door. She crossed the room quietly and sat down in one of the wing-back chairs without saying anything, waiting for Nick to speak.

"Mia, is everything in place for the extraction?"

"Yes, all we need is the green-light from you and it is a go," she replied.

"Do it. Meet me at the airport in two hours. We're taking the jet to the Cayman Islands so we can prepare for our guests."

Mia rose silently from her chair and exited the room without another word. Nick leaned back in his own chair and contemplated the events that were about to unfold. He had waited ten years for this day to come, and now that it was here he was going to savor it like a fine wine. He smiled and relished the thought that his old friend and business partner J.T. Thornbacker had no idea what was about to happen to him.

Chapter Thirteen

Laura walked into the diner for breakfast and she could feel the tension in the room. It was her first foray back into the general population since the incident two days before. She knew everyone must be thinking about what she had done to James and wondering whether or not she was going to freak out again and attack one of them. She walked to the breakfast bar and began serving herself breakfast, trying to act as if nothing had changed.

James was already seated at the far end of the diner and saw Laura come in. He decided to try and act as normal as possible, considering what had happened the last time they had spoken. His plan was to eat and get out the door without speaking to her at all. Better to not do anything that might trigger another outburst, he thought to himself. Even though the implant devices wouldn't shock anyone while they were in the diner, there were still forks and table knives available, and he didn't want to take any chances.

He tried to keep his focus on his own plate, but out of the corner of his eye, he noticed that Laura was walking towards him with her plate and a glass of orange juice. "Great," he thought to himself, "now I'm going to have orange juice and breakfast food all over me." Laura stopped about three feet from his table, too close for comfort.

"James, I have something to say to you," she said.

James looked up from his plate timidly.

"O.k.," he replied.

"Look, I know I was out of line the other day. I wanted to say I'm sorry and to let you know that it won't happen again."

"O.k., thanks," James replied, not certain how to

respond.

Laura turned away from him and went to a booth farther towards the door, where she sat down and began eating. James realized he had been holding his breath and exhaled. The tension in the room dropped several notches and everyone continued eating their breakfasts.

The next day, right before the group began their one-mile run, Laura walked by James and said matter-of-factly, "You can run with me if you want." Then she started jogging down the running course. James wasn't sure whether it was a good idea to follow her or not, but curiosity got the better of him and he started off after her. He came up on her right side, a respectful distance away just to be on the safe side, and kept pace with her for about a minute, not saying anything.

"I was angry, you know," she said. "Paul dying the way he did…. It felt like… well, I was really angry about it and I took it out on you, but it wasn't your fault."

James remained silent, giving her space, not sure what to say.

"I just wanted you to know that we could be friends. After all, we're going to be stuck in here for a long time," she said, saying the last sentence somewhat sarcastically.

"Laura, I'm sorry about Paul. I want you to know that."

"Thanks."

They ran for another minute in silence. James saw the end of the course coming up and they both began slowing down as they neared it.

"I would like very much for us to be friends, Laura," James said.

Laura smiled slightly as she turned towards her room and went to get ready for the workday.

As nighttime fell and darkness descended on the town of Utopia, three all-black ATVs silently approached the town's perimeter. They each sported a state-of-the-art electric motor that made them virtually silent except for the sound the wheels made as they rolled over the terrain – sounds not audible over the song of the desert Cicada, which sounded like a symphony after dark. Each ATV was manned by two commandos, dressed in all-black and armed for the occasion.

The trio of ATVs stopped just outside of the town and two of the commandos dismounted. One moved silently to the back of the building where the night watchman kept tabs on all of the town's extensive video monitoring feeds. Selecting one of the electrical wires, he took out a pair of wire cutters and cut it in half. The other commando had positioned himself near the front door. As soon as the power went out, he unlocked the door with a skeleton key and entered the building.

Inside the control room, the monitors and lights went dark and the emergency lights kicked on in the hallway. The night watchman cursed, got up, turned on his flashlight, and began making his way down the hall to the circuit-breaker box. As he rounded the corner, he felt a stinging in his chest. He grabbed at the area where the tranquilizer had penetrated his uniform reflexively, moments before the dart's payload took effect. The commando at the other end of the hallway lowered the blowgun from his lips. The watchman slumped into the wall and slid down to the floor, his flashlight rolling down the hall noisily. The commando silently crossed the hall, turned off the flashlight, and headed out of the building to re-group with his team.

James was dreaming of his mother. In the dream, he was a young boy, and he and his mother were rowing out into the ocean in a small rowboat. She had brought the fishing poles and they had begun fishing. Suddenly, James had a bite. He jerked the line to set the hook and began trying to reel the catch in. As he reeled, he saw a fin break the top of the water. He had hooked a shark, and it looked like a big one.

"Mom, cut the line and let's get out of here," he said.

His mother looked at him and smiled, seemingly oblivious to the shark that was fast approaching.

"Good boy, James, you've got something. Reel it on in, honey," she said, smiling.

"Mom, I've hooked a big shark and he's headed right for us! I'm scared! Let's cut the line and get out of here!"

Just as he finished his sentence, the big shark rammed the boat and his mother fell out, into the water. She surfaced quickly and began to laugh as if nothing was wrong.

"Mom! Give me your hand!"

James stretched his hand over the side of the boat towards his mother, but he couldn't quite reach her. She was close enough to reach him, but she just smiled and looked at him as she continued to tread water. Suddenly, his mother jerked to the side and a cloud of blood began to rise around her, but still she continued smiling.

"Mom!" James cried as he grabbed the oars, trying to re-position the boat closer to his mother so he could pull her to safety.

"It's o.k., son," she said. "I'm o.k."

The door to James' room burst open and two darkly clad figures with headlamps shining blindingly into his face came rushing through the door. James sat bolt upright in bed, awoken from his nightmare by their theatrical entrance. He raised an arm to shield his eyes from the light. He heard the crisp report of two tranquilizer darts leaving the chamber of the dart gun, feeling the sting as they embedded themselves in his upper torso. The last thing he felt was someone sliding something around his neck before he was swallowed by the darkness.

Chapter Fourteen

When James finally began to wake up, he could feel the floor moving under him. At first he thought it was the after-effects of whatever he had been drugged with, but the smell of the salt air and rhythmic movement of the floor made him realize he was probably on some sort of boat. His mouth had been taped shut with duct tape, his hands were bound behind him with plastic restraints, and his feet were likewise bound.

He re-positioned himself, pushing himself up on one elbow and then into a seated position. It was then that he saw the armed guard dressed in black, staring at him from across the room, and the two other bodies lying on the floor near where he was positioned. At first he could only see their backs, but as they too began to wake up, and move around a bit, he realized with astonishment that J.T. and Laura were his fellow captives.

Laura's eyes grew wide with fear as she began to look around, but as she saw James and J.T., her panicked look gave way to confused bewilderment. J.T. came around a few minutes later. His look betrayed neither fear nor confusion, and James wondered what thoughts might be running through his mind at this very moment.

After all three were fully awake, the guard spoke into a two-way radio.

"Leader 1, they are awake."

He said nothing else, but continued to look back and forth between the three of them as if trying to determine exactly how coherent each of them was. A few minutes later, another man dressed in black came through the door. He was big and burly, with a shaved head that was beginning to show signs of hair growth stubble where his sparsely spaced hair was beginning to grow. His three-day beard growth offset the unlit cigar now protruding from his mouth.

He knelt down beside Laura first, and with a huge thumb, he attempted to push her eyelid upwards to get a better view of her eye. Laura shook and pulled away, glaring at him with daggers. The big man abruptly grabbed a fist-full of her hair and held her still, repeating the maneuver with this thumb as he spoke.

"Be still, you little tramp. I'm just trying to see how dilated your eyes are."

James could tell Laura was seething, but she didn't try to pull away again, not that it would have done much good if she had. He then removed what appeared to be a neck-brace from Laura's neck similar to the one he was wearing. The big man repeated the procedure on J.T. and James. Once this was done, he appeared to be satisfied and stood up again, addressing them all.

"I can see you are all awake and none the worse for wear. I'm sure you have a lot of questions, which I will likely not be willing to answer, so I'll keep it simple and tell you what you need to know. You will not be harmed as long as you cooperate. There's no use trying to escape since we are in the middle of the ocean and there is nowhere to go. I'm going to have my man here remove the duct tape from your mouths, and as long as you don't start screaming, I'll leave it off. We'll be at our destination in about four hours."

He looked at the guard and gave him a quick nod before exiting the room as abruptly as he had arrived. The guard came by each of them and removed the duct tape without much tenderness or apparent concern that gentleness in that procedure was desirable. As soon as Laura's tape was off, she began peppering the guard with questions.

"Where are we?" No answer. "Where are we being taken?" No answer. "What are you going to do with us?!" No answer.

Before she could ask question number four, the guard paused, picked up some earbuds that had been draped around his neck, and plugged them into his ears, smiling as he did so. He could not hear the obvious curses Laura was hurling in his direction, but he could tell by her reddened face that they were not very polite, and he chuckled out loud. Laura, seeing her attempts to gain information were futile, let out an audible sigh and slumped back against the hull of the ship.

Meanwhile, the guard produced three water bottles with straws and proceeded to go between each of them, letting them drink as much as they wanted before moving on to the next person. Having accomplished this task, he resumed his original position in the corner, continuing to listen to whatever music was playing through his earbuds. Seeing they were now apparently free to talk, James spoke up.

"Is everyone o.k.?"

"I'm just peachy," Laura replied with obvious sarcasm.

"What about you, J.T.?" James continued.

"I feel like I've been rode hard and put up wet, but besides that, I think I'll be o.k."

J.T. repositioned himself, stretching a bit and grimacing slightly at the soreness he felt from his poorly positioned night's repose on the floor of the ship.

"Does anyone have any idea what is going on?" Laura asked.

"Well," J.T. replied, "I'd be willing to bet that when we arrive at our destination, we're going to find one of my former business associates on the other end."

James and Laura both looked at J.T. in surprise.

"Why do you say that?" James asked.

"Back in my robber-baron days, I stole a great deal of money. Not all of it was recovered. My guess is, one of my former business partners thinks I still have some of it squirreled away somewhere."

"Do you?" Laura queried.

J.T. turned and looked at her straight in the eyes. "No, I do not. But he doesn't know that."

"Oh, crap," James responded.

"'Oh crap,' is right!" Laura chimed in. "You know exactly what's going to happen to us if this guy doesn't get what he wants. We'll all be fish food! What are we going to do?!"

"Now just calm down a minute," said J.T. "We don't know for sure it's who I think it is or that he (or they) want what I think they want. But if I'm right, you two better leave the talkin' to me when we get where we're going."

Chapter Fifteen

Silas came into the police precinct carrying the coffee that he had made at home just like he did every morning since he'd become a detective. He plodded up to his office and sat down at his computer to begin reading his email and reading over the news before the business of the day had him going in a hundred different directions.

When he saw one of the news headlines, he felt a knot form in his stomach. The tag line read, *'Notorious corporate embezzler J.T. Thornbacker and two others escape from Nevada prison'*. He clicked on the link to read the whole story, but it was just a short blurb from one of the newswire services. He focused intently on the few lines and read them over and over again, trying to absorb any hint of additional details that might give him some relief from the weight of dread he felt pressing down upon him, but found none.

> *Three inmates escaped yesterday from the Nevada prison system. Two men and one woman believed to be traveling together have been identified as J.T. Thornbacker, James Marlowe, and Laura Bristo. Prison officials offered few additional details on the breakout, stating only that the three should be considered armed and dangerous. Officials have requested that individuals having information on the whereabouts of these convicts contact the FBI.*

Silas slumped back in his chair, his mind racing. The day before, he had turned over information to Nick Bartonovich on the banking operations of a non-profit corporation based in the Cayman Islands named the Porfiry Group. The group was very secretive and only the law firm of Handle and McQueen was mentioned in most of the documents. He wasn't hired to read the legal documentation, just to track down where the money was coming from that Handle and McQueen had been funneling out to various individuals for the past two years. But he didn't feel good about the job, and so he had read through the bank documents to see if anything set off a red flag. Nothing did. It all seemed like legalese to him. But he had managed to find one person's name buried towards the end of the document: J.T. Thornbacker.

He clicked on the links at the end of the article to the FBI website where images of the three escaped convicts were posted. He studied them closely for a few minutes, then printed them out. He grabbed the printouts off of the color laser printer and headed back out the door he had just come in through a few minutes before.

Thirty minutes later, Silas was marching up the steps of Nick Bartonovich's brownstone. He knocked on the door and waited, but the speaker remained silent. He leaned over the side rail and looked into the windows. Fortunately for him, the drapes were not drawn. He saw no one milling about or lounging at the dining room table that was viewable from his perch. He went down and behind the stairs to the ground level entrance, peering through the windows to make certain no one was there, and then he put on a pair of rubber gloves before picking the lock.

He opened the door and quickly confirmed that it was wired to an alarm system by locating the tell-tale contact strip attached to the top of the door. After locking the door behind him, he took out his cell phone and dialed the precinct dispatch officer.

"Yeah, this is Silas. I just witnessed a break in on

3rd street, house number 1900. No, it's just some kid, probably looking to watch porn on the television while the owner's at work. Anyway, no need to send a patrol by. I'll take it and run him in. Yeah, you too. Bye."

Silas cautiously made his way up to the office on the top floor, just in case his earlier assessment proved wrong and there was anyone in the house. Once he entered the office, he crossed to the desk and sat down in the leather chair that Nick had been sitting in hours before. It was just as comfortable as it looked, he thought to himself as he opened the desk's one drawer and began going through its contents.

He lamented to himself that more and more people were keeping the information he needed as a detective on their electronic devices. It made it more difficult for an old-school detective like him to quickly find what he needed, particularly with someone as careful as Nick Bartonovich. He had apparently taken his laptop with him, so even if Silas had possessed the technical skills required to access the computer's data, they wouldn't have done him much good at the moment.

There were few items in the desk drawer. A herringbone letter opener, some writing pens, a pad of post-it notes, a few paperclips, and some other odds and ends. A small, black leather business card holder caught his eye. He opened it up and found several business cards for Nick Bartonovich, President of CES Enterprises. Nick's picture appeared in the corner. "Thank you, Mr. Bartonovich," Silas thought to himself.

Silas took out one of the cards and replaced the holder in the desk drawer. He put the card on the desk and took out his phone, taking a picture of the card and then a close-up of the photograph in the corner. He put the card in his pocket and then dialed a number. After three rings, a man picked up on the other end. He was greeted with a hearty, "Hello?" in a thick island accent typical of the Cayman's.

"Marty, it's Silas," he began.

"Oh! Silaaaas! It is good to hear from you, my friend. What can I help you wit today?"

Silas could picture the tall islander with his colorful shirt and sandals. He had been very helpful tracking down the information Silas needed to get for Mr. Bartonovich before. He hoped he would be as helpful this time.

"I'm going to send you some pictures. I want you to go to the same bank as before and call me as soon as you see any of these people anywhere near the bank. Can you do that?"

"Ya mon, I can do it," came the reply. "You got sometin' for me now?"

"Yeah, same rate as before."

"O.k. mon, I am on it."

With that, Silas hung up the phone. He took out the three pictures he had printed off before and took pictures of each of them with his phone, sending them to Marty along with the photo of Nick Bartonovich. He couldn't risk sending them from his work computer, so this would have to do for now. He completed his search of the office without finding anything else of value, and left the brownstone the same way he had come in, making certain to lock the door on the way out.

Next, he called Darby Jones of the white-collar crimes division.

"Detective Jones," he answered.

"Hey Darby, I need to locate a plane."

"Hello to you, too, Silas. Who does it belong

to?"

"Belongs to a guy named Nick Bartonovich. It may be registered under a company by the name of CES Enterprises."

"Hmmm… let me check."

Silas could hear Darby typing feverishly on a keyboard in the background. About a minute or so passed before Darby spoke next.

"Yeah, looks like he has a plane out at Newark International."

"Any chance you could tell me where that plane might be at the moment? He may have left town yesterday afternoon and I need to know where he's going."

More typing could be heard in the background.

"Well, I checked the public flight plan database and it's not there. Looks like he had his plane put on the BARR list, which means his flight plans won't be publicly accessible in this database. But I have a buddy who's been working on a program to pull the audio between the planes and the air traffic control towers. They run it through this program which translates the audio file data into text, saves it to a database, and posts it to this website he set up. You wouldn't believe it - there's this whole sub-culture that records this stuff for all the major airports and they share it online. He just downloads it and…"

"Darby," Silas interrupted. "I just need to know where the plane was headed."

"Yeah, o.k., just a minute," Darby replied, slightly disappointed that he hadn't been able to finish his monologue on the technical aspects of the process.

"O.k., yeah, it looks like he was headed for the Cayman Islands, Grand Cayman to be exact."

"Thanks a million, Darby, I owe you."

"No problem, that's why we're here, to serve and protect," Darby replied.

"Seriously, next time I see you at the bar, drinks are on me."

Silas disconnected the call. Everything was falling into place. Whatever the end-game was, it was going to happen soon and in the Cayman Islands. He was willing to bet his pension that it would be at the bank he had been researching and that J.T. Thornbacker was involved. He reviewed in his mind what he knew so far:

1. There was a bank account in the Cayman Islands with a large sum of money in it.
2. According to the documents he had obtained for Nick Bartonovich, only J.T. Thornbacker could withdraw or otherwise transfer funds from that account if the amount was more than twenty thousand dollars in a month.
3. J.T. Thornbacker had escaped from prison.
4. Nick Bartonovich's private jet had left from Newark International Airport bound for the Cayman Islands the night before.

Silas had a decision to make. He had used his position and resources as a police officer to perform work for Bartonovich, which was illegal. By doing that illegal work, he had likely (albeit unwittingly) contributed to the escape from prison of one J.T. Thornbacker. If he didn't do something to stop this train wreck, then he was likely helping a convicted felon withdraw enough money from a foreign bank to disappear forever. That was aiding and abetting a known criminal, which could get him jail time in addition to getting him fired.

The knot in his stomach, which had disappeared

with all the activity of the past few hours, was returning with a vengeance. He couldn't tip off the FBI, even anonymously, without risking his own role being discovered. Should he do nothing and hope J.T. Thornbacker and Nick Bartonovich got away with it, and his role was never revealed? Should he intervene and try to bring J.T. Thornbacker back to prison, developing a cover story that would obscure his own involvement in the affair? He cursed under his breath as he considered his options – none of which were appealing. He had the distinct feeling that this was not going to end well for one Silas McGruder.

Chapter Sixteen

The leader of the commandos came in through the cabin door. The guard, who had been listening to his music, got up out of the chair he had been sitting in and pulled one earplug out so that he could hear any instructions that might be given.

"Listen up," said the man as he looked at his three captives. James, Laura, and J.T. all stared in his direction, each wondering what was going to happen next.

"We're going to move you to the top deck, where you will be transferred to a smaller boat and moved to another location. We're going to cut your foot restraints off so you can move about. Don't get any ideas about jumping ship and swimming anywhere. We're in the middle of the ocean and there's nowhere for you to go. If you do decide to try anything, you'll get a nasty shock from one of these." He pulled a Taser from a side holster that was strapped to his leg, adding emphasis to his threat. "This little beauty will light you up with 50,000 volts of electricity, after which you will still be going where I want you to go. So don't try anything."

After the leader's speech was concluded, both he and the guard came around and cut the foot restraints of all three unwilling passengers. They were led out of the cabin and up on deck, where they were greeted with a bright, sunny day, crystal blue water, and not a speck of land for as far as the eye could see in any direction.

James squinted at a small dot off in the distance and thought he could just make out another boat. The two commandos who had brought them up to the top deck helped them down into two awaiting inflatable boats. James and Laura were offloaded into one, where there were two other commandos waiting. J.T. was placed in the remaining boat, which the lead commando entered, along with their guard.

As the two boats sped away from the larger craft, they headed in the direction of the boat that James had thought he spotted when they had first come on deck. In a few minutes, they were approaching a one hundred foot long yacht. The first inflatable boat pulled up alongside of the boarding ladder and one of the commandos climbed up, then turned around to help bring J.T. aboard. Once the first inflatable was secured, the boat that James and Laura were in similarly unloaded their occupants.

After everyone was on deck, James, Laura, and J.T. were led to a seating area at the back of the boat where a table had been set with a lavish lunch. James' stomach rumbled as he was reminded that they hadn't eaten anything since being abducted the day before. The lead commando headed off into the interior of the boat, while the remaining three commandos positioned themselves around the deck and watched the three prisoners.

Moments later, Nick Bartonovich came through the sliding glass door leading on to the back of the boat, followed by Mia and the lead commando. Nick smiled devilishly as he saw J.T.

"Well, hello, J.T., it's been quite a long time."

"Hello Nick," J.T. responded flatly. Turning to Mia, he added, "Hello Mia."

Mia nodded, with a slight smile. Nick turned to address the lead commando.

"Let's not leave our guests tied up; they won't be able to eat."

He crossed the deck and sat down at the head of the table along with Mia. The guards cut the hand restraints and they all began massaging their hands where the restraints had been hampering their circulation. Nick motioned to the table.

"Please, come sit down and enjoy some lunch. We

have much to discuss."

Each of them took a seat. As Mia and their host began to eat, both Laura and James began serving their own plates, while J.T. looked warily at Nick.

"What do you want with us, Nick?" J.T. asked.

"In due time, my friend. Why don't you try some of this shark? It's delicious and fresh. I just caught it this morning." He motioned towards a plate in the middle of the table with his fork as he took another bite.

J.T. could tell Nick was enjoying himself and thought that there was no reason to deprive himself, considering the situation, so he began serving his own plate.

"I've thought about you often these past several years, J.T. Languishing in that prison all by your lonesome. I have to say, I appreciate that you didn't give me up to the prosecutor during the trial in exchange for a deal."

James and Laura eyed each other.

"But what I didn't exactly appreciate," Nick continued, "was that you took eighty percent of our hard-earned profits and stashed them away somewhere."

Nick watched J.T. closely for a reaction. He leaned forward, keeping his gaze fixed on J.T. as he spoke the next sentence. "I want it back, J.T." He broke his gaze and focused back on his plate, cutting another bite of shark and eating it.

"I don't have it," J.T. replied. "I had to give the feds something or they would never let me out of prison. I turned it over to them in exchange for a deal."

"J.T.," Nick feigned an offended expression as he spoke, "I'm hurt. After we spent so many years building up that little nest egg and leading others astray in the process, do you really think you can lie to me and I won't know it?" He took a sip of wine and sat back in his chair.

"Look around, J.T. Can you hazard a guess as to where we are?"

J.T. continued to look at Nick.

"I know you can't see land from here, but the climate and the color of the ocean should give you a clue," Nick said mockingly. "We're anchored just off the Cayman Islands, my friend."

J.T. sighed heavily and sat back in his chair. Nick looked over at James and Laura before continuing.

"You see, James and Laura," Nick continued, "Ole J.T. here thought I wouldn't find the eighty million dollars he hid in a bank in the Cayman Islands. He hid it very well. It has taken me years to track it down. In fact, he may have gotten away with it altogether if he hadn't gotten all soft-hearted. Apparently, J.T. here started feeling guilty about how we accumulated all of that money, and decided to give some of it back. About two years ago, he had his lawyer visit him in prison and start up a sort of social security for all of the people who lost their jobs or their pensions because of what we had done."

"Now, I had been watching very closely and had just about given up on getting any of that money back until the money started flowing out of the lawyer's office to all of those poor creatures. Once that started, all I had to do was follow the money trail back here, and *voilà!*"

Nick paused and turned to stare at J.T., watching delightedly as the reality of the situation sank in for him.

"By the way," Nick continued. "If you are counting on being rescued, don't. Those neck braces effectively blocked the transmission from the tracking devices they implanted in you. Now they are so far out of range that they are virtually untrackable."

"O.k., so what's the plan, Nick?" J.T. finally responded. "You want me to waltz right in to the bank and take out the money, or else you are going to hurt these two people who had nothing to do with it? Is that it? You really think I'm stupid enough to believe you aren't going to kill all three of us once you get what you want?"

"I'm not planning on killing anyone, J.T. That's really not my style," Nick replied.

"Really?" replied J.T. "Tell that to Jacob Styles' widow."

"Now, that was an unfortunate accident, J.T. As I recall, he died from a massive heart attack – not my doing."

"Yeah, while he was in the hospital from injuries he sustained at your direction!" J.T. said accusingly.

"Come now, J.T. You remember the situation. He was the last vote we needed on the board to sell us the Jenkins auto-supply factory. We nearly lost the deal when he died. If I hadn't been able to bribe his replacement, the whole thing would have collapsed. Besides, if we had known he had a weak heart, I would have asked Mia to go easy on him."

Laura looked at Mia with surprise. Mia returned a cold stare that sent shivers down her spine.

"Look, I don't want us to get off on the wrong foot. You should be thanking me. I rescued you from that desert prison you were in and I'm offering you a chance to be free when this is all over. If everyone does what they are supposed to do, I'll let you keep ten million and let these two have a million each for their trouble. Then we can all go our separate ways. Think about it."

Nick stood up from the table. "Mia will show you to your accommodations."

With that, he turned and went back inside the yacht.

Chapter Seventeen

Mia led the way back inside the yacht and below the first deck. Two of the commandos followed behind James, Laura, and J.T. to ensure they went where they were told to go. They were deposited in a cabin at the bow of the yacht. It was a small room with two bunk beds on either side of the entrance, a small table in the middle, a closet off to one side of the door, and a bathroom/shower on the opposite side. Once they were inside, Mia closed the door and Laura heard the clicking sound of the lock as it slid into place. She sat down on one of the seats at the far side of the room and leaned her head back on the cushion.

"What just happened?" she wondered aloud.

"I think you and I were just offered a million dollars apiece to help take some money out of a bank," James responded, somewhat bewildered.

Laura lifted up her head and looked at J.T.

"What is going on, J.T.? You said you didn't have any of the money this guy was after."

J.T. sat down at the table and looked over at James and Laura.

"I know. I had hoped to keep that hidden from these guys in case they were listening in on our conversation back on the other boat, but Nick already figured that out."

"So just who is this guy?" James asked.

"His name is Nick Bartonovich. He and I met in college when he was running bets for the college sports games. We hit it off and started working together once we were out of college. We raised money to take over vulnerable companies, then sell off assets and unprofitable business units. We would create shell companies – companies that only existed on paper

– to hide the losses from some of the legitimate businesses, which we would then sell for far more than they were worth. The new owners would think they were buying a solvent business, only to find out that what they'd actually bought was a bankrupt company. The people working for these companies would then lose their jobs when the new owners had to liquidate the company assets to pay off their creditors. Often, the retirement plans the company had invested in relied heavily on the same company's stock, so most of the people who lost their jobs also lost their retirement money."

"One of the lawyers we used to help set up the shell companies was arrested for having sex with a minor and decided to spill the beans on our operation in return for leniency from the judge. The lawyer didn't know Nick, but I'd had a meeting with him once and he knew I was in on the scheme, so he gave the prosecutor my name. The prosecutor had a field day, and I was convicted and sentenced to twenty-five years in prison, but before I left, I created my own insurance policy. Nick and I had this offshore account where we had kept the operating funds that we used to conduct all of our under-the-table deals. We had a hundred million in it. Right before I went to prison, I had eighty million dollars of that moved to a bank here in the Cayman Islands, and left twenty million for Nick. I hoped he would be satisfied with that and leave the rest alone, considering I'm the one who went to prison."

"O.k.," Laura finally responded, "but that doesn't explain why James and I are here. He only needs you for this deal to work. Why bring us, too?"

"Leverage," J.T. responded. "If I don't go along with it, you two get squeezed."

"You mean tortured… or worse," James replied.

"But why us?" Laura persisted.

"He needed someone close to me – that's why you're here Laura. I don't have any family left alive, so people close to me in the program are the closest thing I've got to family. As to why James was picked, I don't know. He's new in the program, so it doesn't make sense to me from that perspective. But one thing I've learned over the years is that Nick has a reason for everything he does. I'm sure he will use James as leverage, I'm just not sure how he plans to do it yet."

That night, the three companions went to sleep in paradise, wondering what their fate would be at the hands of their new jailer.

The next morning, one of the guards came to unlock the door and led everyone up to the dining room, where a sumptuous breakfast was served. Nick was reading the news on a tablet computer while he finished his breakfast, which consisted of a bagel, a poached egg, and a glass of freshly squeezed orange juice.

"Have a seat and enjoy some breakfast," he said as they entered the room. After everyone was seated, he continued. "It seems you have made front-page news in the *Nevada Free Press*, and even received a mention on the nightly news, J.T. You are a wanted man."

"Did you think breaking me out of prison was going to go un-noticed?" replied J.T.

"No, not at all, but you should consider the situation you are in. No one knows that I kidnapped you against your will. For all they know, you three planned the whole thing together. Do you really think that anyone will believe the truth?"

"What's your point?" James chimed in.

"The point is that, should you choose not to cooperate with me, all I have to do is drop you off anywhere in United States jurisdiction and make a call to the FBI for you three to be sent back to prison with a long extension to your current prison sentences. Sentences not likely to be served in the same cushy circumstances that I found you in, I might add."

James' appetite was suddenly much smaller. The thought of spending even longer than his current sentence in a regular prison was something he didn't think he could face. He would rather die. He stared at his plate, unwilling to take the next bite of food, temporarily frozen in contemplation of the possibility of going back to a regular prison.

"What exactly do you want each of us to do?" asked Laura.

"Well, that's the easy part," Nick proceeded. "All you and James need to do is behave yourselves and enjoy a two-week vacation here on the yacht. You can eat great food, entertain yourselves in the library – fishing, swimming, sunbathing, whatever you like, so long as you follow a few simple rules."

"J.T. will have the slightly more demanding task of accompanying me to the bank every day to withdraw the money. You see, he had a provision put in when he set up the bank account that he could not withdraw more than one tenth of the cash balance from the account on a given day unless the account was going to be closed out. In that case, the balance could only be withdrawn in ten equal amounts over a ten day period. Evidently, he anticipated that such a day as this might eventually come." Nick looked directly at J.T. as he spoke the last sentence.

"And it's a good thing I did, too," J.T. replied.

"Mia," Nick said without taking his gaze off of J.T. "Please give J.T. a change of clothes. He will be accompanying me to the bank shortly." Addressing J.T., he continued. "We leave in an hour; don't be late." With that, he returned to reading the news on his tablet computer and finishing his breakfast.

A few minutes later, Mia arrived with a tailored suit on a hanger. "I have your suit, J.T.," she said. "Time to get dressed." J.T. stood up from the table and began walking back to the cabin they were assigned to stay in. When he reached the door, he turned to take the suit from Mia, but she held on to it when he tried to take it from her grasp. "Nick wants you to shave your beard off, so you'll look more business-like."

"Do I have a choice?" J.T. retorted.

Mia raised one eyebrow to let him know that he did not.

"Do you really think this is going to work, Mia?" J.T. asked.

"Yes," Mia replied with a determined look that J.T. knew well. "I intend to see that it does."

J.T. looked at himself in the mirror as he shaved off the last remnants of his beard. He was racking his brain, trying to decide how to get out of this situation without getting himself, or James and Laura, hurt. The one thing he had on his side was time. If he kept calm and looked for an opportunity to get a message out, he might be able to pull it off. He might be able to get Nick's tablet for a few minutes and send an email to alert his lawyers and have them contact the FBI.

He bolstered himself with that thought as he dressed in the suit Mia had brought for him. It felt nice. He hadn't been in a suit since his last appearance at trial seven years before. This was a nice Italian suit with Gucci leather shoes. He wondered where they had picked it up and how they had gotten his size right.

When he opened the door of the cabin, he encountered one of the guards, who motioned for him to go in front of him. Up on deck, Nick was waiting, similarly dressed.

"Shall we?" he said as he motioned to the awaiting fifty foot cigarette boat docked at the back of the yacht.

J.T. got into the boat along with Nick and two of the commandos, who were suitably attired for the occasion. One of the commandos took the controls and began to pull the boat away from the yacht. J.T. thought to himself that it was a beautiful day in a beautiful place, and in other circumstances, he would have been able to enjoy it, but his mind quickly returned to what they were about to do. He and Nick had made a lot of money, and needlessly hurt a lot of people in the process. Many of those people had lost everything they had. He had begun the process of making amends to those he had wronged, starting to restore what he had taken, but now all of that was being put in jeopardy. He prayed a silent prayer as they sped towards the island. "God, somehow, someway, please get us out of this."

Chapter Eighteen

Mia explained the rules to James and Laura, and posted a copy of them on the inside door of their cabin:

1. Stay away from any navigational or communications equipment, including computers, tablets, phones, or the yacht's radio.
2. Stay away from the other watercraft, such as lifeboats.
3. You must be accompanied by a guard if you go anywhere except your own cabin.
4. If you go swimming, you must stay within sight of the yacht.
5. All other cabins but your own are off-limits.
6. After dinner each night, you will be escorted to your cabin where you will stay locked in until someone comes to get you for breakfast.

"Beyond these rules," Mia said, "you can do pretty much anything you want."

Later in the morning, Laura decided to make the best of their captivity in paradise and do some sunbathing. She found a suitably sized swimsuit in their cabin and, after changing, she went to lay down in one of the lounge chairs on the deck of the yacht. James came and sat down in the chair beside her a few minutes later, and pretended to be focusing on the ocean view. He spoke quietly, hoping that the nearby guards wouldn't hear too much of their conversation.

"Laura, what are you going to do when this is all over?"

Laura didn't open her eyes as she responded.

"I'm still just trying to process everything that has happened. To tell you the truth, I've never been too much of a planner. That's kind of why I ended up in prison; I just flew by the seat of my pants. Right now, I'm just trying to enjoy the sun. We've got almost two weeks to figure out what we're going to do, right?"

"That depends on whether or not this Nick character is telling us the truth or not."

"Well, he has treated us pretty good since we arrived here. Why wouldn't he keep his word?"

"A better question is why would he? We know what he is doing, what he looks like, what his name is. We know everything the FBI would like to know about this guy, and with J.T.'s testimony, this guy could go to prison for a very long time. Dumping our bodies somewhere in the ocean seems like a simple solution to that problem."

"Yeah, but like he said, who's going to believe us if we talk? We're just a bunch of convicts. Anyway, if he keeps his word, I've got about a million reasons to keep my mouth shut. J.T.'s the one who should be worried. He's the one with the real details that could sink this guy."

James sat quietly for several minutes, thinking about the whole situation.

"What if he does keep his word and pay us, and let us go like he said he would? We couldn't go back to the states without going back to jail, and serving out the rest of our sentences. That's 13 years for me, longer if I get convicted for breaking out. And like Nick said, that could be back in a high security federal penitentiary."

Laura pushed herself up on her elbows and turned to look at James.

"You're really worried about this, aren't you?"

"And you're not?" James replied.

"It's on my list, but right now, I'm just going to enjoy the moment," Laura responded as she smiled and faced towards the sun. "The sun feels too good to worry. Cheer up, we'll think of something."

With that, she lay back down and closed her eyes. James couldn't stop thinking about their situation, but with Laura obviously not in the mood to talk about it more at the moment, he sat there in silence.

J.T. Thornbacker and Nick Bartonovich entered the lobby of the Grand Cayman Central Bank along with their escorts and made their way up to the circular desk in the middle of the atrium where a young dark-skinned woman was seated, staring at a computer terminal. As they arrived in front of her, she stopped what she was doing and looked up to address them.

"Welcome to the Grand Cayman Central Bank. How may I assist you today?"

"I'm Mr. Bartonovich. I have an appointment with Mr. Takata."

"One moment please," the young lady responded. She picked up the phone and dialed a number. "Mr. Bartonovich is here to see you." After hanging up the phone, she turned back to Nick. "He will be down momentarily, please have a seat." She motioned to her right where there were a number of leather couches and chairs. The group moved over and everyone took a seat.

"You cleaned up well, J.T.," Nick said. "You no longer look like the hippie guru you appeared to be when you came aboard yesterday. I'm glad to see Mia's recollection of your suit size was correct."

"It'll do the job," J.T. responded. "Let's just get this over with and get out of here."

A short Asian-looking man in a three-piece suit came briskly across the floor towards where they were seated. As he came near, he walked directly to where Nick was seated and extended his hand.

"Welcome back, Mr. Bartonovich," he said.

Nick shook his hand and turned towards J.T.

"This is my colleague, of whom I spoke to you earlier."

Mr. Takata extended his hand towards J.T. and they shook hands. "Hello, so glad to meet you." Mr. Takata motioned towards an elevator at the far end of the atrium that was flanked by two armed guards. "Please, follow me."

As they walked, J.T. spied a pen on the circular desk counter. When he passed by, he pretended to trip on the back of his shoe, putting his hand out to catch himself on the counter and palming the pen. One of the guards reached out to help steady him. "Thank you," J.T. said. The whole incident took no longer than a few seconds, and no one seemed to notice he had pocketed the pen.

They entered the elevator and Mr. Takata took the key card from around his neck and slid it into a card reader in the elevator control panel, then punched in a code. The elevator began moving down, below the first floor. Less than a minute later, the doors opened to reveal a red carpet leading up to a wall of bars, behind which was a layer of bullet-proof glass. Two guards with machine guns hanging down by their sides were stationed beyond. As Mr. Takata approached, one of the guards on the inside punched a number in an electronic keypad and opened the door for them to enter.

Once the door was closed, Mr. Takata proceeded around the corner, where the room opened up to reveal yet two more armed guards flanking a vault. Mr. Takata turned to face the group. "Mr. Thornbacker," he said, addressing J.T. by name for the first time. "Please place your hand on the scanner to verify your identity."

He motioned to the hand scanner mounted to the side of the vault door. A bar of light passed up and down the scanner screen, scanning J.T.'s hand, and then the whole screen turned green. Mr. Takata then scanned his own hand with a similar result. Finally, he placed his key card in the card reader and typed in a code on the keypad. The electronic locks could be heard disengaging from the large vault door. Mr. Takata turned the manual locking wheel counter-clockwise and slowly pulled open the eighteen-inch thick door.

He was only inside for a few moments before he returned, pushing a cart before him which was stacked high with large bundles of one hundred dollar bills. He motioned to one of the guards, who shut the door and locked it. The large locking pins could be heard sliding back into place once again as Mr. Takata pushed the cart over to a table that was off to the side.

"Seven million, nine hundred and ninety-five thousand dollars in one hundred dollar bills, as you requested," Mr. Takata announced. He handed J.T. a clipboard with a withdrawal slip attached to it, then handed him a pen. "Please sign here Mr. Thornbacker."

J.T. signed the slip and handed it back to Mr. Takata. Nick opened the briefcase he had brought along and produced two duffle-bags that, when expanded, were large enough to hold the huge pile of cash sitting on the cart. The two commandos helped divide the money between the two bags, each taking one. The group then proceeded back the way they had come and up to the bank lobby. Mr. Takata shook hands with Nick and J.T., then made his departure.

On the way back to the marina, Nick, who was seated in the front of the car, turned around to face J.T. "I'm afraid I'm going to have to ask you to put on a blindfold, old friend." Nick nodded to the commando in the back seat. The commando produced a blindfold and secured it in place, covering J.T.'s eyes.

About thirty minutes went by while he was blindfolded. The car stopped for about ten minutes. It sounded like two people exited the vehicle, but when J.T.

started to reach up and loosen the blindfold, a strong hand reached over and prevented him from doing so. "No. Leave the blindfold on," came a stern warning.

A few minutes later, the car started moving again. When the car finally came to a stop, J.T.'s blindfold was removed and he saw that they were back at the marina where they had left the cigarette boat earlier in the day. They got into the boat and headed back in the direction of the yacht.

Chapter Nineteen

Later that evening, dinner was served on the yacht. Angel-hair pasta topped with a local variety of fish that James didn't quite recognize, with grated Parmesan cheese and diced jalapeños to top it off. It was better food than he had eaten in his whole life. Laura seemed to be enjoying herself, and even J.T. seemed more relaxed than he had been at breakfast. James allowed himself to relax a bit and even enjoyed the banter back and forth. The guards standing around with guns at their sides seemed the only reminder that they were still prisoners.

Shortly after dinner, they were dismissed to their cabin for the remainder of the evening with a complimentary bottle of wine. The door was shut and locked in place. Laura sat down on the couch and reached out her hands towards the corners of the room in a long stretch before interlacing her fingers behind her head and leaning back on the comfortable cushions. She seemed like she didn't have a care in the world.

J.T. walked over to the table where the bottle of wine had been placed and proceeded to open it up, letting it breathe for a few minutes before pouring himself an inch of the dark red liquid in one of the glasses they had been provided. He closed his eyes and lifted it up to his nose, inhaling slowly and deeply. At last, he sat the glass down on the table, finished filling it along with the two others, and then walked over to Laura, stretching his arm out to hand her the glass.

"Here, take this," he said.

Laura opened her eyes and reached out her hand to take the glass.

"Thanks, although I'm not certain I could put anymore

in my stomach right now."

"We have some decisions to make," J.T. responded cryptically. He walked over to the table and handed James the other glass before sitting down on a chair that he had placed between them so that he could see them both equally well. He motioned for them to draw in close to him and he began to speak in a whisper.

"They may be listening to us, so speak quietly. We have to decide what we are going to do."

J.T. took a sip of wine before he continued.

"I know that Nick has offered you each a lot of money to go along with his plan. I think that we need to look at all of our options and decide together what our next move is going to be. Whatever we do, we need to do it together. First off, I'm not entirely certain that Nick won't decide to kill us all. However, if he doesn't and he keeps his word, then we need to think it through. If any one of us decides to go back to the states and turn ourselves in, then we should all go. Otherwise, those who don't go back will be hunted down all the more quickly."

"Wait just a minute," Laura interrupted. "What do you mean, turn ourselves back in? Like Nick said, if we turn ourselves in, there is no guarantee that we won't get even more jail time tacked on to our sentences. And even if we don't, we all have long sentences to finish, regardless. If I have a million dollars to live on, why do I want to go back and turn myself in?"

"Well," J.T. responded. "There are a few things you need to consider. First off, if we don't go back, there is the fact that the FBI takes a very dim view of escapees. We are all likely on the most wanted list by this point, which means that a team of FBI and other law enforcement officers are looking for us this very minute. If they catch us, and they often do catch those on the most wanted list, then we are all likely to end up with more jail time than we can shake a stick at, and in a maximum security prison."

"If they don't catch us, then we are going to be looking over our shoulders for the rest of our lives, waiting for the moment when someone might. I don't know about you, but that is not the way I plan to spend the remainder of my life on this planet."

"So what do you suggest we do?" asked James.

"I'm not suggesting anything just yet. Let's just put all the cards on the table first and see what kind of a hand we've got. Let's consider what happens if we go back. Turning ourselves in is easy enough. We show up at the United States Consulate in George Town and tell them who we are and that we want to surrender. What happens after that is debatable. We will likely each get interrogated separately for as long as it takes to convince them that we are telling the truth. If we tell them the truth, then any money we have been given by Nick will be forfeited. Next, we get shipped back to prison – and likely NOT Utopia, to serve out the remainder of our sentences. Unless, of course, they don't believe us and decide to revoke the contracts we signed, and put us in for the remainder of our original sentences and then some. If we try to lie and pretend we didn't get any money, then we're depending on them not finding out that information. If they catch Nick, then he will tell them outright we have the money and we're on the hook for lying to the FBI – not a good idea."

"So you're saying we're screwed either way," Laura lamented. "There's no way they are going to believe us. We're three convicted felons! It's not like we're all paragons of truthfulness or anything."

"Listen to me," J.T. continued, "I'm not saying I have this all figured out either and I'm certainly not suggesting we decide tonight. We have almost two more weeks before we're going to be cut loose, whatever that means. All I'm saying is that we should begin to consider our options and come up with a plan together. Can we agree on that?"

After a few moments of silence, Laura responded, "I'm willing to talk about it, but that's all I'm going to commit to at this point." She took a long drink from the wine glass, wanting to rewind to the good feeling she'd had after dinner, before she was so abruptly confronted with the reality of their situation.

J.T. looked over at James, who had been silently considering everything that had been said. James slowly nodded his head up and down. "O.k., let's make a plan. But like she said, we're just talking. I'm not ready to commit to anything either."

Satisfied that they had at least agreed to talk about making a plan together, J.T. stood up from his chair and walked over to the starboard portal, where he could just see the sun setting in the distance. He stared at it for several minutes, finishing his glass of wine and watching the darkness descend.

Silas McGruder immediately spotted the slightly beat-up silver van and the lanky driver who was sticking his long arm out of the window and waving at him as he exited the terminal at Owen Roberts International Airport. He ambled over to the passenger side of the vehicle and deposited his tired body in the seat, uttering a tired greeting to his driver as he did.

"Hi, Marty."

"Helloo, Mr. Silas," came the cheery response. "Welcome back, my friend."

Marty pulled the van away from the curb and guided the van back towards George Town.

"Tell me everything you saw," Silas prompted him wearily.

"I see dah man in dah nice suit from dah picture you sent me. He came in with tree otha people." He held up three fingers to emphasize the point.

"You mean three other people?" Silas asked.

"Dat is what I said, mon, tree otha people," Marty continued. "One of dem look like dah man in dah orange shirt wit dah beard, but he had shaved it off."

"Yeah, I could tell from the pictures you sent me. What I want to know is, where did they go after they left the bank?"

"I try to follow dem, but dey take da narrow streets, mon. I could not follow dem o dey see me. So I did what you tell me to do. I stop an' call you."

"Good job, Marty. Good job. Now get me to my hotel before I pass out."

The rhythmic noise and vibrations from the road lulled Silas to sleep as he leaned his head against the window. When he awoke, the van was pulling in to the hotel that he had booked the night before on the internet. He turned to Marty as he got out of the van.

"Pick me up tomorrow morning at 6:00 a.m. I want to make sure we get everything ready before they come back to the bank tomorrow."

"O.k., Mr. Silas, I see you den."

Silas checked in to his room and sat down in one of the chairs. He took out his cell phone and began scrolling through the pictures that Marty had sent to him. From the pictures, he could tell that the two unidentified men were probably the hired security. It wasn't going to be a walk in the park, but he had about ten days or so to plan things, so time was on his side. He set the alarm on his phone for 5 a.m., took off his shoes, and laid down on the bed. As he fell asleep, he thought to himself, "J.T. Thornbacker may have pulled off the great escape, but the game is definitely not over, not by a long shot."

Chapter Twenty

The alarm on his phone was blaring and Silas wearily opened his eyes, willing the alarm to silence and allow him another hour of sleep. After a few seconds of fumbling, he retrieved the phone and turned off the alarm. He located an energy drink he had purchased at the airport the day before, opened it up, and drained the bottle. He was going to need all of his wits about him, and quickly, if he wanted to get the jump on these guys.

He grabbed a cream-cheese bagel at the continental breakfast bar provided by the hotel and was finishing off the last bite as Marty drove up under the awning to pick him up. It was one of the things he liked about Marty – he was punctual.

He had Marty drive him to the bank and go over everything, step by step. Next, he had him drive the route that Thornbacker's car had taken once they had left the bank. Marty stopped at the narrow alleyway where he had lost the car the day before. "And dat is where I stopped following dem," Marty said, pointing at the entrance to the alleyway.

"Drive down the alleyway," Silas instructed.

The alleyway led to a small open park where five other streets dispersed.

"This is perfect," Silas said out loud.

"What do you mean?" Marty replied.

"This is the perfect place to lose a tail," Silas replied. "Anyone following them would need to wait to come down the alleyway or else they would be recognized. Once they make it here, though, they have five choices to take them where they really want to go. By the time anyone following them makes it to the park, they are long gone." Silas excitedly turned to Marty. "O.k., here is what I want you to do. They will probably use this same route every day. You stay here in the park on that bench over there, facing the alleyway. Once they come out, make sure you see which street they take next, but don't make it obvious. If this is going to work, they can't know someone is onto them. I'm going back to the bank and follow them from there as far as the alley. I'll call you when they leave the bank."

Back at the bank a short while later, Silas saw J.T. Thornbacker and Nick Bartonovich get out of the car with their escorts at 9:30 a.m. sharp. Nick was carrying a briefcase. The way the two guards looked around, surveying the area, he would have bet money they were former military. Silas drove slowly past the front of the bank and was just able to see J.T. Thornbacker sit down on one of the couches beside the central desk before he drove out of range. He turned the van around and positioned it so he could see their car clearly and follow them when they left.

They were inside the bank for about fifteen minutes before they came back out, got in the car, and drove away. Silas thought it was odd that Mr. Thornbacker got in the back, while Nick sat in the front. "They must not like each other very much," Silas thought to himself.

He called Marty to let him know they were on their way and followed them to the alleyway where Marty had lost them. He kept his foot off of the accelerator after breaking as the car carrying J.T. Thornbacker slowed to make the turn down the alleyway. He wanted to coast past the alleyway slowly, without needing to break and possibly draw attention to the van. As the alleyway was almost out of his peripheral vision, he thought he saw their tail lights go on. He quickly pulled over to the curb and got out of the van, walking back in the direction of the alley. He stopped and pretended to be window shopping in front of an old antique store directly across from the alleyway. He tried to be nonchalant as he studied the alleyway's reflection in the store's large plate glass window.

The car had indeed stopped. They were close enough that he could tell that one of the passengers in the back was putting something on the head of the man next to him. Then they proceeded down the alleyway. A minute later, his phone rang.

"I see where dey go, Mr. Silas."

"Yeah, o.k., I'm coming to pick you up."

As he drove down the alleyway, he stopped right where the other car had stopped, got out of the van, and looked around. There was nothing there. He processed what he had just seen, trying to make sense out of it. In a few moments, it came to him. "J.T. Thornbacker was kidnapped," he said out loud. He smiled as he jumped back in the van and drove down the alley to pick up Marty.

"Did you see anything unusual about one of the men in the back of the car?" he asked Marty, once he was back inside the van.

"Yes, I did. One of dem had a black cloth over his eyes."

"Yes!" Silas exclaimed. "This is good."

"Why is dis good?" asked Marty.

"J.T. was kidnapped!" Silas exclaimed, proclaiming his earlier revelation as if he had just won the pot at a poker game. "Why else would they blindfold him? Ole' Nick Bartonovich kidnapped J.T. Thornbacker and is using him to get the money out of the bank. That explains why he sent me down here to get the bank documents, the blindfold, the fact that a guard rides in the back with J.T., the whole business. They aren't in business together; J.T. is simply the key to the piggy bank." He slammed his hand down on the dashboard of the van for emphasis.

"I am glad you are happy, Mr. Silas," Marty proclaimed. "Dis is good, yes?"

"This is very good, Marty, this is very good!" Silas responded. "Now I need you to find me the best pick-pocket in all of George Town."

"What do you need wit a pick-pocket, Mr. Silas? A pick-pocket can never get what is in dat briefcase."

"Just trust me, Marty. Just trust me."

James had decided to swim around the yacht to see if he could shake the sense of cabin fever that had been building since they'd arrived. He had become accustomed to the daily exercise regime in Utopia and needed to burn off some energy to calm his nerves. As he swam, he thought about both the future and the past.

He thought about how he was potentially about to get the big score he had dreamed of before, when he was planning a bank robbery. He had thought that would make everything better. He had thought that his problems would be solved by a big wad of cash. Yet now that the big score was potentially in his sight, he only wanted to rewind to a few days earlier when he was serving out the remainder of his sentence in Utopia, headed for a changed life, a life free from being chased by law enforcement officers. He'd just been beginning to believe he could find a better, more peaceful, and fulfilling way to live. Now all of that seemed so far away. *How do I get back there?* he thought to himself as he swam.

Even if he got the money, he would never be able to go back to the States without looking over his shoulder constantly. And even if he stayed here or somewhere like this, a million dollars wouldn't last him forever. He would need to find some other way to make money eventually, and being a criminal was all he really knew how to do. He couldn't think of a way out of it. He knew in his heart that he couldn't live the rest of his life on the run, but he also knew that he couldn't survive twenty-three more years in prison – or longer if they threw the book at him once he got back.

As he swam lap after lap, he came to a decision. Whatever the consequences, when this was all over, he was going to turn himself in. If he ever wanted to be free, then he would need to do the time he had been sentenced to serve. Maybe they would be lenient on him, maybe they would even reduce his time for having come back – who knew? And if he ended up getting more time added on, well, he would cross that bridge when he came to it.

He felt a weight lift off of his shoulders as he swam a final lap around the yacht and climbed back up the ladder, where the ubiquitous armed guardian watched his every move. He grabbed his towel and dried himself off.

Chapter Twenty-One

Laura was curled up on a couch in a spacious room on the main deck of the yacht, reading a book when James came in from his swim. He sat down on a chair next to the couch and finished drying his hair.

"Are you getting your hour a day of reading in?" James joked.

Laura smiled as she looked up from her book.

"Yeah, the habit kind of grew on me when I was in Utopia. They don't have much of a selection here, though."

"What did you think about the program at Utopia?" James inquired.

"I think it was good for me," Laura responded. "My life was definitely a mess when I went there. I think the structure was good for me. It helped me level out and clear my head. The twelve step stuff helped me, too. I was a bit weirded out by the whole 'Higher Power' thing to begin with, but after a while, that sort of began to make sense to me, too."

"So you believe in God?" James asked.

"Yeah, I do. I mean, I look around at all this," Laura waved her hand at the seascape that could be seen through the windows, "and I think there definitely must have been a creative being that made it all. I don't think it happened by accident. What about you?"

"My mom believed in God. She prayed to Him to heal her when she had cancer and to help me stay out of trouble – neither one of those prayers were answered. God certainly doesn't do things the way I would like Him to."

For the first time since they'd known each other, Laura looked at James and felt empathy with him. She could identify with feeling like things hadn't worked out the way she wanted them to.

"I guess that's the reason for steps two and three," Laura responded.

James looked at her with a puzzled look.

"Steps two and three of the twelve steps," Laura continued. "Step two is basically believing that there is a Higher Power Who wants to help straighten our lives out, and step three is where we make a decision to turn our lives over to that Higher Power. Thinking back on all of the crappy things that have happened to me in my life, being sent to Utopia was the best thing that ever happened to me. I mean, if I hadn't been sent there, I'd probably be dead by now."

"Yeah," James concurred, "me, too. I mean, I believe there is a God, and I want to be a better person than I was before I went to prison. Like you said, being sent to Utopia was one of the best things that has happened to me in a long time. I liked the reading thing, too. I never really read much, but now that I'm away from Utopia, I miss the books I was reading."

"What were you reading?" Laura asked.

"It was a book by William Penn – the founder of Pennsylvania. It was called *Some Fruits of Solitude*. I still remember a quote from the introduction of the book. I wrote it down in my journal and read it over and over. 'We understand little of the works of God, either in nature or grace. We pursue false knowledge, and mistake education extremely. We are violent in our affections, confused and immethodical in our whole life; making that a burden, which was given for a blessing; and so of little comfort to ourselves or others; misapprehending the true notion of happiness, and so missing of the right use of life, and way of happy living.'"

There was a long pause after James finished the quote. Laura felt a hint of something inside that hadn't been there for a while. She felt that James might not be that different from her after all.

"That's beautiful, James. That quote describes what my life was like before Utopia."

James turned and looked at her, directly in the eyes.

"What about now?"

"What do you mean?" Laura asked.

"I mean, what about after this is all over and we get a load of cash? Then what? How do we get back on track to learning how to live a better way than we did before? How do we do that, while we're fugitives? Money can change a lot of things, Laura, but I know enough now to understand that money isn't going to make me a better person." James looked down at his feet and shook his head. "I just don't know what to do."

There was another long pause, but the silence was broken by the sound of the cigarette boat engine approaching the yacht.

On the boat ride back from the island, J.T. thought to himself about how the run to the bank had followed the same routine as the day before. After they entered the car with the day's allotment of cash, they had driven to a narrow alleyway where he was blindfolded. Next, they drove for another fifteen minutes before stopping, where he was fairly certain that Nick and one of the commandos got out of the car. After a few minutes, they returned and drove back to the marina, where the blindfold was taken off and they boarded the boat for the return trip to the yacht.

He had been paying close attention to the surroundings today to see where the best opportunity might be for delivering a note to someone at the bank to let them know he was being held prisoner against his will. He thought that the best candidate was likely the receptionist in the atrium. His main concern was what she would do with the information. If she took it to her boss, Mr. Takata, would he tell Nick or go to the authorities? If Nick had paid him off as part of this whole scheme, then Nick would be notified. It was risky either way, but then again, desperate times called for desperate measures. The next hurdle would be to find some paper on the yacht to write a note on. The place had been cleaned out of anything to write on – a move no doubt initiated by Nick in order to prevent just what J.T. was planning to do.

Once they were back on the yacht, the afternoon and evening followed a predictable pattern, even down to the bottle of wine that was delivered to their cabin once they were locked in for the night. He surveyed the room and found a small shelf of books. He immediately went over and began to casually thumb through each book, finally selecting one that had a blank page at the back of it. He could remove this page and use it for writing an S.O.S. note. He turned it back to the front cover and noticed that it was a copy of *Twenty Thousand Leagues Under the Sea* by Jules Verne. He smiled to himself as he sat down and began to read. It was a book he had read once in high school and enjoyed immensely. No time like the present to reacquaint himself with it, he thought.

He read for about an hour as both James and Laura each showered and appeared to be getting ready to turn in, each of them dressed in the designer pajamas that Nick had so graciously provided for the occasion. Nick was certainly going out of his way to make everything seem as hospitable as possible. It was an attempt, no doubt, to lure James and Laura over to his way of viewing the situation, and illicit their support. Now it was time to see just how far that effort had gone.

J.T. went over to his bunk and put the book on top of his pillow. As he turned around, he noticed that both James and Laura were reading books of their own. Utopia, it seemed, had had some positive effects on them all. He hoped it would be enough of a common bond to help see them through the difficulties that remained to be faced. "Can we talk about our plans?" he said out loud.

He spoke quietly, but loudly enough to be heard by both James and Laura. He sat down beside Laura, who reluctantly put down her book. James came over and sat down on the other side of Laura so they could communicate with a minimum of volume.

"I have a plan," J.T. began. "There is some danger involved, but I think it just might work."

"Let's hear it," James responded.

"I was able to get a pen at the bank yesterday, and I found some paper that I can use to write an S.O.S. note on. I think I can deliver it to the receptionist at the bank without being noticed. If so, and if she helps us, she could contact the authorities and let them know we are being held captive."

"And then what?" Laura replied. "We wait for the police to storm the boat and rescue us? Have you forgotten we have four armed guards and that lady guarding us while you are gone? They may be able to rescue you on land well enough, but out here, anyone getting within a mile of this boat will be seen. James and I are likely to be killed in the process."

"Like I said," J.T. continued, "There are risks."

"Why don't we just go along with Nick's plan?" James mentioned. "I mean, he seems like he has no intention of harming us. Once he's done with us and lets us go, we can do whatever it is we want, right? Why go ahead and risk getting killed on an escape?"

"Yeah," Laura agreed, glad to have James thinking along the same lines as she was. "What's the rush?"

"The rush is," J.T. proceeded, "that Nick may not intend to let us live once this is all over. Why would he give us eleven million dollars just for our cooperation when he can just as easily put a bullet in our heads and dump our bodies in the ocean? This man is a thief, remember that. Secondly, I'm concerned about recovering the money. He's taking it somewhere; he's not storing it on the boat. If I lose track of it now, I may never get it back."

"So that's what this is about?" Laura said angrily, raising her voice to a level which risked their being heard by the guards.

"Keep your voice down. Laura!" James whispered cautiously.

Laura lowered her voice, but not her intensity as she continued. "This is all about you getting that stolen money back, isn't it?! And you are willing to put us at risk to do it!"

"Look," J.T. lobbied, "you have to remember that is money that I'm using to pay back the people who got fired or lost their pensions when Nick and I destroyed the companies they worked for. That money is being used to pay mortgages, provide college tuition, pay medical bills. If I lose it now, I may never get it back. I'm trying to do the right thing here."

The fire ebbed in Laura's eyes and her voice toned down as she responded. "O.k., I get that. But I'm not willing to risk my life so you can make amends for the things you did. Remember that program you talk so highly about? I seem to recall that amends are only to be made when you won't be hurting someone else, or have you forgotten that?"

J.T. was silent for a moment as he recalled the ninth step of the program, the steps he had tried to live by the past few years.

"You're right," J.T. said in a subdued tone, "I guess I forgot about that in the process of trying to think about how to save the money. But the first part of what I said is still a good reason to think about it. What if Nick's plan is to kill us when he has all the money? I still think it is worth the risk, but I won't try it unless we all agree."

He paused and waited for James and Laura to consider what he had said. Finally, James spoke.

"There's another possibility."

"What's that?" J.T. queried.

"You could get caught trying to deliver the note. Then

Nick might not be as accommodating as he has been. Who knows what he might do? We already know he is willing to kidnap the three of us and risk being caught doing it by the FBI. If we try to blow the whole deal for him now, he may decide to go back on what he promised us and kill us after all."

"James is right," Laura added, "I don't like our chances. I say we wait it out and take our chances on Nick keeping his word."

J.T. sat back and let out a long sigh, running a hand through his hair as he did. He was obviously disappointed.

"O.k.," he said, resigned, "I guess I'm out-voted. I'll continue to go along with Nick's plan and hope for the best."

As J.T. lay awake in bed that night, he considered the possible outcomes that might befall them. Losing the money was regrettable, but the possibility of being killed within the next ten days was front and center. As he lay in the darkness, he uttered a silent prayer.

"God, grant me the serenity to accept the things I cannot change, the courage to change the things I can, and the wisdom to know the difference." And with that, J.T. Thornbacker drifted off to sleep.

Nick opened up his laptop and quickly reviewed the transcripts just delivered to him on the USB thumb drive by the man in the radio room. With so much riding on this operation, he was leaving nothing to chance. The video and audio devices he'd had installed in the cabin where his new guests were staying ensured that any movements and any conversation, no matter how hushed, would be captured for his review. A note at the end of the transcript indicated that nothing unusual had appeared on the video feed for the evening. As he re-read the transcript of the conversation that had just taken place, he smiled and congratulated himself.

The psychological dossiers he'd had prepared on each prisoner at Utopia had helped him choose just the right accomplices to his plans.

Chapter Twenty-Two

The next day, the routine of the previous two days continued. J.T. and company arrived at the bank and went through the withdrawal process. They got in the car and went on their way as they had done previously. The car exited the narrow alleyway per the usual route and circled around to the third road before exiting the round-about.

No one in the vehicle thought anything about the man at the end of the road who was walking slowly along the sidewalk. Silas had positioned himself so that he would have a perfect view down the street and be able to tell if the car turned anywhere.

Silas bent down and pretended to be tying his shoe when they got close to where he was standing so that Nick wouldn't get a good look at his face and possibly recognize him. With a hat and sunglasses, it wasn't likely, but Silas had known stakeouts to be blown for simpler reasons.

The car continued down the street, almost to the end, before abruptly turning into an alleyway. Moments later, two men, each carrying a duffel bag, came out of the alley and walked down the sidewalk to one of the shops, and then went inside. A few minutes later, they came back out, got back in the car, and continued down the street going in the opposite direction from Silas.

Silas took out his phone and dialed Marty, who was positioned in an alleyway at the end of the street with a rented moped.

"Marty, he's coming your way. Follow him, but not too close," he instructed.

"O.k., I see him," Marty replied before disconnecting the call and putting the phone back in his pocket.

The car drove past where Marty was waiting. He waited a few seconds for good measure and then pulled out behind them, following from about half a block away. This time, they drove along busy roads where he could blend in with the local traffic and not be noticed. Marty stopped when they pulled in to the Barcadere Marina parking lot. He got off the moped and began to walk in their direction, being careful to act as if he was in no hurry. He was close enough to see that they boarded a cigarette boat and quickly began moving away from the dock, out to the open ocean.

After putting his phone away, Silas began walking down the street to see where the car had been parked and to examine the shop that the two men had entered. He was fairly certain that one of the two men had been Nick Bartonovich. The alleyway offered no surprises. It was too narrow for more than one car, and dead-ended into another building. He came out of the alleyway and made his way to the shop door where the two men had entered. It was a bakery on the first floor, with a wooden staircase leading up to the second floor. An acrylic sign hung down from the ceiling over the staircase that read "CES Enterprises".

"Bingo," Silas thought to himself. He wandered over to the bakery counter and picked out some delicious looking croissants. After paying for them, he left and headed back down the street to where he had parked the van. He took out his phone and called Marty.

"Did you find out where they went?" he asked when Marty answered the phone.

"Yes, I did. Dey went to da marina and left in a boat."

"Good work, Marty. Meet me back at my hotel; we've got some planning to do."

Once they were back on the boat, J.T. went to his cabin to change out of his suit. As he hung the pants up in the closet, something slid out of the pocket and onto the floor. He bent down to pick it up. It was a small pen with a piece of paper taped to it. He unfolded the paper and began reading what was written on it:

> J.T. – I know you are being held hostage and that Nick Bartonovich is using you to withdraw money from the bank. I am here to help you escape. I need to know as many details about your daily routine as you can give me: where you go each day, and where you are being held would be very helpful. Write them out on the back of this paper and slide it between the cushions of the couch where you sit each day when you go to the bank. I will place further instructions in the same place for you to retrieve the following day. – A friend who can help.

How did this get into my pocket? J.T. thought to himself. He carefully reviewed the errand to the bank from earlier in the day, trying to focus on who had the opportunity to pass him the note. He finally remembered a man who had brushed against him as he left the bank. That must have been it. He quickly walked over to his bunk and stashed the note and pen under his mattress before heading back up to the dining room for lunch.

The afternoon consisted of various leisure activities. Reading, fishing, swimming – everything you might expect from a vacation except for the armed guards. At one point, Nick even tempted Laura and James into going water-skiing. James had done a bit of water-skiing with a local boys club as a young man, and after a few bungled attempts, he was able to hold his own. Laura, on the other hand, had never skied before. Before the end of the afternoon, though, she was able to stay up on the skis and even jump a few small waves created by the wake of the boat. Mia and Nick took their turns on the skis, as well. They were both quite accomplished skiers, and Nick showed off his skill as he slalomed on one ski.

While everyone but the three remaining guards were off skiing on the cigarette boat, J.T. went down to his cabin and prepared the note for his new friend:

> *We are being held on a yacht about an hour out from Barcadere Marina. There are two other people being held captive with me. Each day I am taken to the bank to withdraw money. Nick, two armed guards, and myself go into the bank. We arrive at 9:00 a.m. and are there for approximately 15 to 20 minutes before we leave. We drive to an alleyway about a block away where I am blindfolded. We then drive for a few minutes and stop. I think two of them get out at that point. A few minutes later, they get back in the car and we drive off. They remove my blindfold just before we get to the marina, where we board a cigarette boat and go back to the yacht. There are five other armed guards who remain on the boat while we are gone to the bank.*
>
> *Do NOT attempt to rescue us without the assistance of the FBI, as it will put us all in danger. Please go to the U.S. Consular office here in George Town and have them contact the FBI to let them know where we are and what our situation is.*

Thank you for your help,

J.T. Thornbacker

When he was done, J.T. put the completed note back under his mattress. He felt a twinge of guilt about what he was planning to do, but he believed it was the right thing.

Now that he had help from the outside and could possibly get the FBI involved in rescuing them, he had to take that chance. If he consulted with James and Laura beforehand, they might actually alert Nick to his plan in order to try and secure the money that Nick had promised them. A million dollars was a big temptation. He just couldn't take that risk. That night, as he fell asleep, he felt that they finally had a fighting chance.

Chapter Twenty-Three

J.T. finished putting on his tie as he faced the mirror in his cabin. James and Laura were still up at breakfast per what had quickly become the daily routine, while J.T. and Nick had excused themselves to dress for their bank excursion. J.T. walked over to his bunk and retrieved the note he had written, placing it in his pocket before he exited the room. When he arrived on deck, he was surprised to find Mia joining them as they prepared to board the cigarette boat for the island.

Mia, who looked like a runway model, was Nick's enforcer. J.T. had once seen her take down three college football players in a bar fight in college when Nick had gotten drunk and insulted one of the player's girlfriends. The three had come to rough up Nick, but Mia intervened before they could get within two yards of him. Mia came out without a scratch, while the other three went to the infirmary. One of the players had to sit out the entire season because of his injuries. Needless to say, she was not an errand girl, and her presence on the boat back to the island was not a good sign.

"Why are you joining us today, Mia?" J.T. tried to ask in as unassuming a way as possible, so as not to betray his concern.

"Oh, just a bit of business I need her to take care of while we go to the bank," Nick replied. He smiled amiably at J.T., who didn't feel any better after getting the answer to his question.

Once on the mainland, Mia did not ride with them to the bank, but instead headed off on foot in the opposite direction. J.T. tried to retrieve the note with as little movement as possible, attempting to disguise the maneuver in the process of exiting the vehicle. He was relieved as they headed into the bank without anyone appearing to have noticed.

Once they were in the bank, the two guards took up their normal standing positions, flanking the leather couch. Nick nodded at the receptionist – who by now knew that was her cue to call Mr. Takata. J.T. tried to sit down on the couch in as casual a manner as possible, and slipped the note between the cushion and the arm rest as instructed. Mr. Takata arrived shortly, and they completed their practiced transaction with a minimum of delay, leaving the bank with their daily trove of cash and heading back to the yacht – or so J.T. thought.

Once his blindfold was removed for the return trip, he immediately noticed that Nick was not in the vehicle.

"Where's Nick?" he asked the guards.

"That does not concern you," the lead guard replied.

The guards were not big on conversation, J.T. had discovered, and he was not likely to get anymore information from either of them, so he contented himself with not knowing the answer to his question as they boarded the boat. He had expected Mia to join them, but the guards did not wait for her, and began the journey back to the yacht without her.

Silas had watched J.T. and Nick enter the bank, then exit again and drive away with their guards. Once they were safely out of sight, he entered the bank, walked across the atrium which served as the lobby, and sat down on the leather couch where J.T. had placed the note. He slid his hand between the cushion and the armrest, retrieving the expected note and putting it in his pocket. He looked around to see if anyone was observing him, waited a few more moments, and then stood up and walked back out of the bank. He headed down the block and around the corner, where he had parked the van out of sight of the bank entrance. The last thing he remembered before blacking out was reaching for the driver's side door handle and feeling a hard blow to the back of his head.

When he woke up, the first thing he noticed besides the sharp pain in the back of his head was that he was duct-taped to a chair. Arms, legs, torso, and mouth were all duct-taped. After struggling in vain for a few moments on the off chance that he might be able to break free, he stopped and looked around. From his surroundings, he surmised that he was in a basement. The chair, it seemed, was bolted to the floor. About ten feet away, to Silas dismay, lay an electric stun baton on a table. Silas began to struggle against his bonds with renewed vigor, attempting to find a weakness in his bonds.

He heard footsteps coming down the wooden staircase located in the far corner of the room. When Nick Bartonovich came into view, followed by the Asian woman he had seen in Nick's home just days before, Silas felt the blood drain from his face and he began to sweat. This was definitely a worst-case scenario.

Nick had removed his coat and tie, and was carrying what looked like a bottle of scotch and a glass with ice in it. He crossed the room and pulled out a chair at the table, setting down his glass and slowly pouring himself a drink. Mia stood in front of Silas and stared at him with those same cold, steely eyes that he remembered from the office visit – emotionless, penetrating, deadly looking eyes.

Nick took a long, slow sip of scotch and put the glass down on the table. He stared at Silas for some moments as if considering what he was going to do next. At last, he spoke.

"You know, Silas, I don't like disgruntled employees who try to take advantage of my generosity. I cancelled a ten-thousand dollar debt of yours in exchange for a bit of detective work on your part, and now here you are putting your nose where it doesn't belong, and attempting to spoil my plans."

"I liked your little note, by the way, very concise. A bit limited in the vocabulary, but that's understandable coming from someone with your educational disadvantages. Now, I'm going to keep this simple for you. I want you to go over every detail, starting from when you picked up the banking contract from Mr. Takata to the point when you arrived here today. If I don't like your answers, then Mia here is going to help persuade you to provide a better answer."

He turned and nodded to Mia, who stepped forward and unceremoniously tore the duct tape off of Silas' mouth. Silas quickly considered what his options were. If he told the complete truth, Nick would know that he had acted on his own and likely had no backup. He also needed to protect Marty if he could, and provide some incentive for Nick to keep him alive. He decided to lie.

"I saw J.T. Thornbacker's name in the bank contract you had me track down. When I heard he had escaped from prison, it didn't take a genius to figure out he would be coming here to get the money. I contacted the police here in George Town. After I told them what I thought was going on, I arranged for them to let me work the case with them. I watched the bank until I saw J.T. come in and I followed you afterwards. That's where I saw the blindfold and figured you were using him to get the money.

"Look," he continued, "they're onto you. Tomorrow, they are going to pick you up and send you and your little sweetheart here back to the States in nice little orange jumpsuits. If you let me go and come in with me now, I'll speak to the judge to see if we can get you a reduced sentence for the kidnapping charge."

Nick sat back, slowly poured himself another drink, and drank it down to the bottom.

"What is the name of the detective you are working with on the local police force?"

Silas felt sick to his stomach. He had no clue what any of the local police officers' names were, so he made one up.

"Detective Jameson."

"First name, please," Nick prompted.

"Detective Andrew Jameson," Silas replied.

Nick took out his cell phone and dialed a number. He nodded to Mia as he did. She deftly replaced the duct tape over Silas' mouth.

"Hello, I need to know some information. Do you have a Detective Andrew Jameson on the force here in George Town? Hmmm. Thank you very much." He smiled as he disconnected the call.

"Silas, I don't think I like your answer very much. You see, there is no Detective Jameson on the local police force."

Mia walked over to the table and picked up the electric stun baton.

"I'm afraid this is going to be a very long afternoon for you," Nick said, right before the electric stun baton touched Silas and he felt a searing pain shoot through his body.

Chapter Twenty-Four

The boat arrived at the yacht as usual, and one of the commandos, along with J.T., disembarked. The remaining commando immediately set off again in the cigarette boat, presumably toward the island to pick up Nick and Mia. J.T. had an increasingly uneasy feeling about the change in schedule, but as there was nothing he could do about it at the moment, he went below to change out of his suit and into something more comfortable for lunch.

At lunch, Laura and James asked about Mia and Nick. J.T. told them what he knew, which wasn't much, and they all continued to wonder what errand they might be on. Laura went to work on her tan after the meal, while James asked J.T. if he wanted to do some fishing. J.T. and James made their way to the far end of the yacht where the fishing equipment was kept.

The guards typically stood farther away whenever they were fishing, so as not to get impaled with a fishhook during casting. James was counting on them keeping a respectful distance so he could talk to J.T. privately.

"O.k., I heard what you said during lunch, but now that we have a bit more privacy, is there anything else out of the ordinary that happened on your trip today?" James asked in a whisper.

J.T. hated to lie to James. He was trying to live more honestly since embracing the program at Utopia, but he had decided he wouldn't reveal anything about the offer of help from the anonymous do-gooder until he had to. He couldn't risk either James or Laura saying something that might compromise their only shot at rescue.

"Everything went as smooth as possible at the bank –

same as the other days," J.T. replied half-heartedly. He put some bait on one of the hooks and cast a line into the water.

James baited his own hook and proceeded to cast his line. They continued to fish for another half an hour before the sound of another boat could be heard approaching the yacht. Both James and J.T. looked off in the direction of the oncoming boat to see if their hosts were returning. The familiar cigarette boat came into view and docked at the side of the yacht.

When Nick got off the boat, he addressed the lead commando.

"Victor, bring everyone to the upper deck."

Victor spoke into his radio headset and the guards began herding J.T., James, and Laura to the upper deck. Once everyone was assembled on the upper deck, Nick turned to face the three captives.

"I have some rather unfortunate news. It seems that J.T. here has decided to try and organize a little rescue."

Laura turned to J.T., her eyes glaring.

"You said you wouldn't do that, you bastard!"

"What have you done, J.T.?" James added, his face reflecting the fear he was feeling as the possible repercussions raced through his mind.

Nick addressed Victor, "Tie their hands to the railing."

"Nick, they didn't know anything about what I did. It's not their fault! I'm the one you should be taking it out on, not them!" J.T. petitioned.

James thought about his chances as he saw the commandos approaching and noted that one of them had his Taser drawn. Laura saw the Taser as well.

"We can do this the easy way or the hard way," the commando stated.

J.T. didn't fight as they used the plastic restraints to lash his hands to the upper rail that ran around the side of the ship. James and Laura submitted as well, deciding that resistance was futile against the six well-armed commandos.

"What are you going to do to us?" J.T. asked.

"You see, old boy, I think it will be much more effective if I punish... her, instead," Nick replied.

"No!" James shouted, "You stay away from her!"

"Mia?" Nick said. Mia came from the back of the group, carrying a telescoping electric stun baton at the ready.

"No!" Laura shouted. "Please, God, no!"

"Leave her alone! Punish me, not her! She had nothing to do with it!" J.T. protested.

Mia touched the end of the baton to Laura's bare thigh and she let out a scream, then started crying. James struggled against his restraints, willing to take his chances with the guards if he could get one good swing at Mia first, but they wouldn't budge.

Nick looked at J.T. and a wild look was in his eyes as he spoke. "You never asked how I made it happen in the old days, J.T. How the votes of all the board members seemed to line up magically, how the regulators always approved the sales. You never asked because you didn't have the stomach for it!" Nick's look was one of contempt as he continued. "Now you're getting a taste of it, my friend."

He walked up to J.T. and grabbed him by the hair, forcing his head to turn and face Laura.

"Do you see that?! That, is what will happen to all of you if you try anything else before I'm done with you!" He nodded at Mia as he finished his sentence.

Mia moved the stun baton to shock Laura again, but James shot out his leg and kicked the prod away as he shouted, "No!" Mia's eyes flashed for only a second, and then she spun around and kicked James in the solar plexus, landing back in the same place she'd started from. With James gasping for air, she easily advanced the baton to its intended target and Laura let out another shriek.

"AHHHH! AHHH! PLEASE STOP! Pleeeease

staaahhhppp!" Laura continued crying and sobbing, tears streaming down her face.

Nick backed up and surveyed his handiwork. Apparently satisfied that he had made his point, he addressed the commandos.

"Cut those two loose and take them to their cabin. They won't be joining us for dinner tonight."

The commandos dutifully cut James and Laura loose, and escorted them down the stairs and to their cabin. Once they were gone, Nick turned his attention back to J.T.

"J.T., I really had hoped to avoid such unpleasantries. I hope, as you spend the day up here on the top deck, out in the sun, that you will reconsider your actions and avoid disrupting my plans further. Oh, by the way, that gentleman who wrote you the note won't be helping you anymore. I've taken care of him."

Nick stepped closer to J.T. so that they were mere inches away from each other, face to face. His countenance was showing malevolent anger as he spoke his next words.

"Just to be absolutely clear, if you try anything like this again, I'll break Laura's legs so badly that she won't be able to walk again. Is that clear?"

J.T. stared straight back as he responded, "Crystal clear."

Nick's countenance changed, a slight smile coming across his face as he backed away. "Good," he responded. He turned and began walking towards the staircase leading down to the deck below.

"I pity you, Nick," J.T. said as Nick was leaving.

Nick turned around, curious. "Why, pray tell, is that?" he asked.

"You are using your considerable talent to gain a pile of money that won't make you any happier. If twenty million won't make you happy, eighty-eight million won't either. You're going about it all wrong. You can change, though... I still believe you can change."

"If that is supposed to make me let you all go, give up the money, and join a twelve-step program to find inner peace, I'm afraid you're going to be disappointed," Nick retorted. "However, since you appear to be so concerned with my happiness, I'll let you in on some information. Money is a means to an end, and happiness is a state of mind. I enjoy what I do. To use your word, it makes me happy. I like the game. It's exciting. You might say I'm an adrenaline junkie. Being a saint is…boring." With that, Nick turned and walked away, leaving J.T. to bake in the scorching afternoon sun.

Chapter Twenty-Five

The sun beat down on J.T. Thornbacker as he sat on the top deck of the yacht. He found that he could just barely sit down on the decking, even with both of his hands secured with plastic restraints to the railing running around the edge of the deck. He had been able to move his shirt over the top of his head so that it provided some shade for his face, but there was no coverage for his arms. He was sure to get some nasty burns if he was left up here until the sun set. Thankfully, he had put on some long cotton pants before being herded onto the deck and lashed to the side railing. He had been on deck for about two hours now. He was sweating and thirsty.

Over the past two hours, he had re-traced his actions since finding the note in his pocket on to when he'd been confronted by Nick about trying to set up an escape attempt. He was wracking his brain, trying to determine how and when he had gotten caught. Did they have a video camera in the cabin where they were staying and see him read the note or stash it under his mattress? Did they see him hide the note at the bank? Or was there something else in play? Did his would-be rescuer even exist? Was it all some elaborate ploy by Nick to see what J.T. would do? After all, the person who had slipped the note in his pocket probably could have been hired by Nick himself.

J.T. finally decided that there was no way to know for certain if the mystery man was a legitimate ally or if it was all set up by Nick as a ruse. He decided that another attempt would be reckless. He believed what Nick said about hurting Laura if he tried anything else. Seeing both Laura and James get hurt because of his failed attempt to get them help this time had been bad enough. Seeing Laura's legs get broken was something he was not prepared to risk. He resigned himself to going along with Nick's plan to the end, wherever that might lead them. He still wasn't convinced that Nick was telling them the truth about planning to let them go with a nice send-off and millions to burn – that part just didn't make sense to him. Time would tell.

Around four p.m. Nick came back up on the top deck. He was wearing sunglasses and a broad-rimmed hat which shielded him from the sun. He was carrying a glass of ice water. J.T. licked his lips almost involuntarily at the sight of the water. He was thirsty, very thirsty. The sun had come around in front of him during the past few hours and he couldn't shield himself adequately from its rays no matter what he did. If he covered his face as best he could with his shirt, his stomach would be exposed. With his upper-torso covered, his face bore the brunt of the sun's rays along with his arms. At this point, he was burned on his arms, and his face and stomach were rosy as well.

Nick pulled up a chair about ten feet from where J.T. was tied to the railing and sat down. He crossed his legs and took a nice, long drink from the glass of ice water that he had obviously brought to torment J.T. with.

"How's it going, old boy?" he said with a vindictive smile.

"How do you think?" J.T. responded.

"You seem to be holding up well enough. Don't worry, I won't leave you out here too long. I still need you to be functional enough to go to the bank tomorrow morning."

"Good thing," J.T. replied.

"You intrigued me earlier with all of your talk about happiness and how I should change my ways and join you on your new-age spiritual enlightenment journey," Nick said mockingly.

"It's not new-age," replied J.T.

"Semantics," continued Nick. "I want to know more

about what makes you tick, J.T., today, not the you from before. I knew you had gone down the repentant sinner path and it was useful to know about your bleeding heart to repay our past victims. I also discerned correctly that you would be motivated by the threat or use of violence against your two compatriots down in the hold. But I would like to know more about why you changed. What was it that made you go soft? It might be useful to me in the future, and if you are willing to regale me on the finer points of your conversion," Nick waved his hand and performed a mock bow, "I am your willing listener." When he was done speaking, Nick sat back in his chair and took another long drink of ice water.

J.T. considered the request. He knew Nick's angle – he wanted to know how he might use whatever J.T. shared in order to manipulate or control him for his own purposes in the future. He had just admitted as much. But was there more? Was it possible that somewhere, deep down, he might be genuinely interested? He decided it didn't matter at the moment. The more he complied with Nick's wishes now, the more likely Nick mightay be to spare their lives and be lenient with them once their usefulness to him was outlived.

"I'm a bit parched to be telling stories at the moment," J.T. responded, looking longingly at what remained of Nick's drink.

Nick sipped at the ice water until it was a mere inch from the bottom before offering the straw to J.T., who eagerly sipped the last bit of liquid from the bottom of the glass.

"Let's hear it then," Nick probed as he returned to his seat.

"The first few years in prison, I was just upset about getting caught," J.T. began. "I had the lawyers exploring every legal option to get me out with a mistrial or get my sentence reduced. As the years progressed, I began to realize I might actually be serving the whole stretch. I was getting depressed. I started taking anti-depressants prescribed by one of the prison docs, but it made my thinking go fuzzy. I couldn't even read the business journal and focus on an article long enough to finish it, so I stopped taking the stuff."

"There was this AA program being offered in the prison I was in, and the prison doc suggested I attend. I figured, 'Why not?', so I went. I started hearing stories from some of the other prisoners about their lives. The messed-up childhoods, the drug abuse, sexual abuse, you name it. Of course, compared to most of them, I grew up with a silver spoon in my mouth. I started thinking about my life, what I had before. I began wondering if I had ever really been happy or if I had simply chased after what I thought I needed to be happy, chased it so fast and hard that I had never really slowed down enough to feel the void that was there all along. I gave that some serious thought. I didn't have much else to do, staring at the walls all day. The more I thought, the more convinced I became that I really didn't have any idea what would make me happy, much less content or fulfilled.

"That's when I hit what we call in the program 'rock bottom'. Faced with the prospect of being in that prison until I was an old man and seeing what a mess I had made of my life, I decided I was ready for a change. I decided that J.T. Thornbacker didn't know squat about how to run his life in a way that would lead to contentment, fulfillment, or peace."

"So that's when you found God and started your bleeding heart campaign to try and save the world with our ill-gotten gain?" Nick asked half-heartedly.

"No. That's when God found me.... And that's when I asked this God Whom I knew nothing about to straighten out the mess I had made of my life. It was a couple of years later when I got to the point where I decided to use the money to try and right some of the wrongs I had helped to perpetrate," J.T. concluded.

"And that," interrupted Nick, "is when I found the money. I suppose I should thank this god of yours for that."

"God had nothing to do with that," J.T. replied.

"Don't be so sure, my friend," Nick said with a smile. He stood up and moved the chair back a few feet before walking to the stairs. "Thank you for the conversation. It has been enlightening," he concluded before descending the stairs and leaving J.T. to suffer some more under the discomfort of the afternoon sun.

Chapter Twenty-Six

At sundown, one of the commandos came up to the upper deck of the yacht and cut the wrist restraints off, then he led a thirsty, sunburned, and tired J.T. Thornbacker back down to the cabin that was his temporary holding cell. The commando unlocked the door and motioned for J.T. to enter, locking it after he was inside.

J.T. stumbled in the door and stood for a moment, stretching his back. James, seated on the couch at the far side of the room, stood up and crossed the room towards J.T., hitting him in the face with his fist when he came within range. J.T. staggered back across the room and hit the bunk beds installed in the wall of the yacht, stopping his backwards progress. James stood there scowling at him, waiting for J.T. to fight back. J.T. reached his hand up and wiped away the trickle of blood trickling down from his lip with the back of his hand.

"I deserved that," J.T. said.

"What were you thinking?" James reprimanded, still staring at him angrily. Laura just stared reproachfully at J.T. from where she was seated, saying nothing.

"Look," J.T. began, "I apologize for the trouble I got you two into today. This guy came to me. He slipped a note in my pocket at the bank, saying he could help get us out, and I saw a chance to end this. I thought it would be better if you didn't know because I thought you might try to stop me."

"At least he's being honest about why he didn't tell us," Laura quipped sarcastically. "Maybe after today, you'll listen to us when we tell you it would be better to just do what Nick is asking you to do."

"I will. I will," J.T. promised.

"How do we know we can actually trust you this time?" asked James.

"I know I let you guys down. I'm sorry about that. I can understand you don't trust me right now. I can't say that I would trust me either if the shoe was on the other foot. But there's nothing you can do about it but take my word for it and wait and see."

"That's what we did the last time; it didn't work out so well for me then," Laura pointed to the burn marks on her leg where she had been zapped with the electrical shock baton.

"I get it," J.T. lamented. "I really do." He edged over to the couch and slumped down into the seat. "Do we have any bottled water? I'm parched."

"You look like hell," James replied, going over to a small shelf where there were some bottled waters and throwing one over towards J.T. It landed on the couch within his reach.

J.T. picked up the bottle, opened it, and began taking small sips. The door lock turned, and one of the commandos came in with a plate of sandwiches and unceremoniously deposited them on the table, along with three cold bottles of water, before exiting again.

"Hallelujah!" James exclaimed as he and Laura both advanced on the food. After eating in silence for a few minutes, Laura noticed that J.T. hadn't moved.

"Don't you want something to eat?" Laura said between bites.

"No. Think I've got sun poisoning. Better off just drinking water for now," J.T. replied.

"I'm still mad at you," Laura said to J.T., "but I'm glad you're o.k."

"Me, too; sorry they used that shock stick on you." J.T. replied weakly. "I won't try anything else, I promise."

"Yeah, I hope you're telling the truth this time, for all of our sakes," James replied.

Over the next several days, the bank routine continued without interruption. Some changes were made in the process to ensure J.T. didn't try to contact anyone else. He was patted down and his pockets were searched before he left the yacht and upon his return.

On the final day of the withdrawal process, after everyone had finished the gourmet lunch that was provided on the yacht, Nick opened up a bottle of champagne. He poured a glass for everyone at the table and handed them out, and then he proposed a toast.

"Here's to the completion of our little journey together, the end of your captivity, and the beginning of this next phase of our lives," he said as he raised his glass.

Mia and Nick smiled as they drank the champagne. James and Laura politely sipped the champagne, not wanting to offend their host, but not quite certain what was going to happen next. J.T. didn't drink at all, but quietly put his glass back down on the table.

"I'm sure you are all wondering if I am going to keep my promise. Toward that end, I've prepared a little briefing for you in the conference room. You can bring your champagne if you like. Mia will escort you there," Nick continued, motioning to Mia with his glass and slightly nodding his head in her direction.

"Please follow me," Mia said, standing up from the table.

James, Laura, and J.T. dutifully followed Mia to the deck below, and into a conference room that they had not seen before. A long table surrounded by leather chairs was in the center of the room, with a video screen hanging prominently on the wall at one end. Three of the commandos followed them, positioning themselves around the edges of the room.

A few moments later, Nick entered the room carrying a briefcase. He opened the briefcase, took out three manila envelopes, and placed them on the table in front of him. "I have information in these folders that you are going to find very interesting. I have a very specific reason for giving you each a very large sum of money. The simple truth is that I need you to remain lost to the FBI and never return to the United States. I need the U.S. government to believe that the three of you planned and executed your own escape from prison, and that you have fled the United States for parts unknown. This way, I am removed from any involvement in the escape and can continue my business activities in the United States without any problems with the authorities." He smiled as he made the last statement.

"Now, I considered the possibility that one or more of you would consider returning to the U.S. and attempting to convince the authorities that you were not complicit in the escape, and give them information about my involvement. Toward that end, I have taken the liberty of providing myself with some insurance."

He tapped the file folders in front of him on the table with two fingers for emphasis.

"A few minutes ago, an anonymous tip was placed by one of my associates from within the United States to the FBI, claiming to have information related to your escape. When the authorities follow up on this tip, they will find a warehouse full of evidence to implicate each of you in the planning and execution of your escape from prison."

"During this past week, I have taken the liberty of collecting numerous items that each of you have touched and left your fingerprints and DNA on around this yacht. I have sent these items to my colleagues in the States to place strategically around this warehouse, providing proof that you all spent time there after your escape. Additional evidence that will be uncovered there will indicate that you all planned to immigrate to Europe under assumed identities, aided by plastic surgery to disguise your appearances."

Nick passed each of them one of the folders.

"I have provided enough information in each of these folders to convince you that what I have just told you is true. Should you ever return to the United States of America, you can rest assured that you three will be convicted of planning and executing your escape from prison and your flight out of the U.S. You will each spend the rest of your lives in prison if you are caught."

He paused to let the gravity of what he had just said sink in. James, J.T., and Laura began looking through the contents of the folders that lay before them. Laura recognized one of the blouses she had worn the week before, hanging in a warehouse locker that she had never seen before. There were photos of a table in the warehouse with glasses she recognized from the yacht. A hairbrush she had used, a towel from the yacht, even the prison clothing that they had worn while at Utopia, all present and accounted for in the warehouse photos.

"We're screwed," she said, staring down at the contents of the folder.

Confident the others would have reached the same conclusion, Nick continued.

"The good news is that I don't want you to be caught. That's why I'm giving you each enough money to live on, why I'm pointing the FBI in the wrong direction, and why I'm leaving you here in the Cayman Islands. I don't want to get arrested for breaking you out of prison, and you don't want to end up going back to jail for the rest of your lives. Furthermore, while murder isn't against my morals, it's too messy for my tastes. This way, you get to live and we can both help each other out."

Nick nodded to Mia, who walked around the table and gave each one of them a backpack. J.T. received a blue backpack, Laura a red one, and James a black backpack.

"You'll find new identification documents along with your promised cut of the money in these backpacks. Victor will escort you back to the island and drop you off at the marina. Have a nice life…and try not to get caught." Nick smiled as he said the last statement. He nodded to Victor, who took his cue and stepped forward to open the conference room door.

"This way, please," he said, motioning with his hand for J.T., James, and Laura to leave the conference room.

J.T. was the last one to leave, and before he exited the room, he turned to Nick and said, "Do you really think you are going to get away with this, Nick?"

Nick smiled as he looked J.T. in the eyes and said, "My dear fellow, I already have…."

Chapter Twenty-Seven

     J.T. looked out over the ocean from the balcony of his home on Rum Point, Grand Cayman Island as he waited for his dinner guests to arrive. He contemplated the many changes that had taken place during the past year since they'd been dropped on the dock at the marina by Nick Bartonovich's hired guns. Nick had indeed kept his word. They each had the promised disbursement of funds and everyone had new identities, complete with background biographies, U.S. driver's licenses, Social Security cards – the whole nine yards.

     After Nick had set them free on the island, it took them a few days to realize they had actually escaped the ordeal relatively unharmed. They had slowly begun to build new lives for themselves. They had all found new places to live. J.T. had bought this place out on Rum Point, and James and Laura had found places to rent in town.

     While none of them had the need to work, they had all developed occupations over the past year. James was bored out of his mind just laying around, so he had begun hanging out at one of the local bike rental and repair shops. An elderly man owned the place, and James had convinced him to teach him the business and sell him the shop once he was ready to retire. He liked doing something productive with his hands, and enjoyed taking the tourists on bike excursions around the island.

     Laura had continued the hobby she had learned while in Utopia – making stained glass. She had set up a room in her small apartment where she made beautiful island-themed stained glass pieces which she sold on the internet. She enjoyed the work and it was therapeutic for her. She had also begun volunteering at the women's crisis center in town that helped abused women by providing them a place to stay, trauma counseling, childcare, and legal services.

J.T. had begun investing in the stock market online. He had helped Laura and James invest, as well, so that they could live off of their investments instead of spending all of the money they had. He had done well enough with his own investments that he was able to keep giving money away to those he had harmed before he went to prison, and still had enough left over to provide for his own living without dipping into the remaining principle investment.

Laura and James had forgiven J.T. for going behind their backs in an attempt to get them rescued, and over time, they had all developed strong relationships with one another. One of the habits they had developed was meeting together once a month at his house for a nice dinner. They would use the opportunity to catch up and talk about what was going on with their new lives.

As J.T. thought about all of this, he closed his eyes and inhaled deeply, relishing the salty ocean air mixed with the delicious smelling food that was waiting on the table in the dining room. He'd had a local restaurant deliver a meal of ackee and codfish, which was one of his favorite local dishes. He was looking forward to tasting it and catching up with James and Laura.

As he opened his eyes, he saw James' car pulling up in the driveway with Laura in the passenger's seat. He turned and went back inside the house, crossing the spacious great room as he made his way towards the front door – which was actually positioned on the side of the house. He made it there just in time to hear James rapping his knuckles on the door.

J.T. opened the door and James crossed the threshold to give J.T. a big bear hug.

"Hey J.T., it's good to see you.

Although J.T. was officially known as Sam Walters –

the new identity that Nick had provided for him, the trio often slipped back into using their real names when they were alone on occasions such as this.

"Hey James, good to see you."

He saw Laura standing behind James, holding something in a plastic container. He gave her a hug too, being careful not to dislodge what was likely a wonderfully tasty dessert from her grasp.

"Hey Laura."

"Hi J.T.," she said as she returned his embrace.

They all made their way over to the dining area and sat down at the table. James started serving his plate immediately, failing to notice that J.T. was patiently waiting for him to stop.

"James, J.T. usually prays, remember?" Laura said.

"Oh yeah, right," James said, feeling slightly embarrassed, putting down the serving spoon and sitting back in his chair. J.T. had started saying a prayer at the monthly meals about six months ago. He had modeled it on the original serenity prayer written by Reinhold Niebuhr. Praying wasn't something James was used to doing before meals, and he still frequently forgot about it whenever they ate together. J.T. laughed at James as he sat back, looking ashamed.

"There's nothing to be embarrassed about. It's not like God is going to strike you down or anything."

"That's a good thing," James replied jokingly.

Laura rolled her eyes at James.

"Can we pray now? I'm starving," Laura pleaded.

"Sure, here we go," J.T. said as he began. "God, give us grace to accept with serenity the things that cannot be changed, courage to change the things which should be changed, and the wisdom to distinguish the one from the other. Living one day at a time, enjoying one moment at a time, accepting hardship as a pathway to peace. Taking, as

Jesus did, this sinful world as it is, not as I would have it. Trusting that You will make all things right if I surrender to Your will, so that I may be reasonably happy in this life, and supremely happy with You forever in the next. And thank You for this food. Amen."

The meal progressed from there with vigor. J.T. opened a bottle of wine and poured everyone a generous portion. The conversation was lively as the three caught each other up on the previous month's activities.

"I just broke one thousand dollars in sales for the first time this month!" Laura exclaimed.

"Hey, good for you!" J.T. replied, raising his glass. "A toast to Laura's stained glass business."

"Here, here," James enjoined, raising his own glass and taking a generous swig of wine along with the other two.

"What about you, James, anything new and exciting to report?" J.T. asked.

"Well... actually there is..." James replied, looking across the table at Laura. She turned beet red and started looking down at her plate.

"Oh, do tell," J.T. encouraged, seeing Laura blush.

"Laura and I are dating," James continued.

"Oh, so you each found someone to date within the last month? Who are these two other people?" J.T. asked jokingly, looking at Laura and enjoying her embarrassment. She took a carrot off of her salad and threw it at him.

"Stop it! You know what he means; we're dating each other."

"Oh, o.k. I get it now," he said, pretending not to have understood what James was getting at. "Well, that's good news," he continued with genuine affection. "How long has this been going on?"

"About three months," Laura replied. "We agreed not to tell you in case it didn't work out. We didn't want it to be awkward between us all."

"Well, shoot fire," replied J.T. "I'm happy for you two."

"What about you, J.T.? Do you have anything new going on?" James queried.

"Well, as a matter of fact, I do. You both know that as part of making amends for my past, that I track down former employees of the companies I helped shut down and help them out. Well, there were a few that were hit particularly hard. Some of them had heart attacks, some of them committed suicide…." J.T. stopped speaking, having begun to choke up. Laura could see tears welling up in his eyes. He paused for a moment to collect himself before continuing. "Over the years I've been doing this, I have made a list of those people and vowed that if I ever got the chance, that I would visit them personally and apologize."

"Wait a minute, J.T.," James interrupted, "you can't be serious about returning to the States. What if you get caught?"

"Now, just hold your horses," J.T. replied, putting both hands up in a gesture of surrender. "I'm not going back to the U.S."

Laura and James both sat back in their chairs, visibly relieved.

"I've arranged for each of these people to be invited on a cruise, supposedly at the expense of their former employer. One of the stops is in Nassau. I'm planning to fly out there and meet with each of them individually at a pre-arranged time in a rental office in one of the hotels there. It's already all been arranged. I'll even be in a disguise so they won't be able to recognize me."

He stared between Laura and James, looking for any indication of alarm.

"If you can think of anything that might set off the alarm bells, let me know within the next week. I can still have one of my lawyers do the meet in my place, but I would rather do it myself if I can. I feel this is something I really need to do."

Laura and James both looked somber, considering what J.T. had just said, wracking their brains in an attempt to see any possible flaws.

"If you get caught, it will lead them right back to us," Laura stated. "Then we're all going back to jail."

"It's only for one day, right?" James asked. "Are you using your real name or your alias for anything?"

"I only used my alias to book the flight to Nassau. Everything tied with the cruise and renting the office will be in the name of my law firm – protected information that they can't legally be forced to disclose under U.S. law. I'm planning on introducing myself as Jack Smith, one of the people responsible for shutting down the business – no more detail than that."

"You can't seriously be in agreement with this?" Laura said to James, obviously upset. "If he gets caught, we all get caught. Our lives would be over, James."

James looked directly at Laura.

"My mom died because somebody ran her company into the ground and she lost her insurance and couldn't get the right treatment for her cancer. It would have meant a lot to me if someone responsible for that would have looked me in the eye and said they were sorry for what they did." He turned to look at J.T. "I think you should go, but only if Laura is o.k. with it. Like she said, we're all in this together."

J.T. looked at Laura, who was shaking her head from side to side.

"Look, Laura," J.T. continued, "you don't have to decide tonight. Think about it. I'm not scheduled to fly out until next Saturday."

Laura stood up and began walking out the door. "I'm going down to the beach. I need to be alone," she said.

James turned to look at J.T. "Let's just give her some space... and eat some of that cake she brought," he said with a smile.

"Darn straight." J.T. replied as they both got up from the table and went to the kitchen counter to open the dessert.

When she arrived at the beach, Laura sat down on the sand and looked out over the beautiful tropical ocean view before her. She was full of conflicting emotions. She was mad that J.T. was planning to do something that could destroy the life they had all worked to build for themselves over the past year. She was also scared that he might actually get caught and get them all thrown back into prison. As she looked out at the waves, she thought about the prayer that J.T. had said before dinner and about her own journey of recovery in the program at Utopia.

"Give me the courage to change the things which should be changed," she said out loud.

She thought about what James had said, about how it would have made a difference for someone to apologize for their role in his mom's loss of insurance and the resulting damage that had been caused. She thought about how it would have helped her heal if any of her former abusers had had the guts to accept responsibility for what they had done and say so to her face. After staring at the ocean for a few more minutes, she stood up and walked back to the house.

Back in the house, Laura found J.T. and James playing pool. James was losing badly, as usual, but he was having fun. She smiled as she walked up to the two. They stopped the game and looked at her, waiting for her to say something.

"I think you should do it. I have one condition, though," she said.

"Name it," J.T. replied.

"You call us once you are in the air on your way back to let us know you didn't get busted."

J.T. nodded soberly, "Will do… and thanks for understanding."

"I think it's great what you're doing, J.T.," Laura said.

"I just hope it can help them move on somehow," he replied.

J.T. went to bed that night looking forward to the upcoming trip, wondering what it would be like. He was both scared and excited at the same time.

Chapter Twenty-Eight

Nick Bartonovich sat in the chair across from the doctor as he was given the results of the battery of tests that had been run over the past few weeks. It was never a good sign when you were called back in to the doctor's office to get the results – they never liked to give bad news over the phone, it seemed. All the same, he hadn't been prepared to hear the 'C' word. Appendicitis, an ulcer, anything but cancer.

There had never been anything that Nick couldn't handle, even since he was a kid. When his parents had died within weeks of each other, he had cried, sure, but he never let anyone else see. He was only ten, but he determined then that he would never let anyone hurt him that badly again. He decided that *he* would be the one calling the shots, making the plans, bending events to his own will and desire. When his uncle tried to get him to take off more time from school to grieve, Nick snuck out of the house and went to school anyway, hitting the books harder than ever. His hard work paid off and he eventually earned a scholarship into college. Once he was there, he started dabbling in running numbers for the college games, found he was good at it, and started the path he was still on today.

But this was different. This wasn't some external enemy he could defeat with the force of his will. He couldn't write a check and make it go away or send Mia out to persuade cancer to change its mind and leave. And for the first time since he'd been that little boy who had just lost his parents, Nick Bartonovich was afraid.

He sat in a daze as the doctor talked about possible therapies for stage two stomach cancer. Surgery would be mandatory, possibly followed by chemotherapy and radiation therapy. All of it coming at him so fast that he felt like a mosquito caught in a rainstorm, having to dodge every word like it was a drop of water, threatening to envelope him if he came too close to it. He came out of his daze at the end of the conversation to hear that he had an appointment the following week with an oncologist.

The doctor slid a card across the desk towards him with the particulars of the appointment before asking if Nick had any questions. Nick could barely breathe. It was as if all of the oxygen had been sucked out of the room and he didn't have enough air in his lungs to speak. So he simply stared at the card and nodded his head from side to side.

He almost had a head-on collision while driving home because he wasn't paying attention to driving – still attempting to process the news he had just been given. He parked the car in the garage and made his way to the den, where he poured himself a scotch and sat down in his favorite chair, looking out the front window. That was where Mia found him when she came in the front door.

Nick had told her to come in around 2:00 p.m. because he had a doctor's appointment and wouldn't be back before then. He had planned on following their usual routine at that time. He would review his various business activities for the day and assign to her any tasks he needed taken care of.

Mia wasn't anything like a secretary. He had a half-dozen of those that worked at his corporate office downtown. He could video conference, call, or email the corporate office administrator from his office here at home should he need something done. Mia was more of a specialized personal assistant. She would handle the coordination of delivery and pickup of funds that were made or lost from the gambling enterprises. If some of the high rollers were having a bad spell and refusing to pay up, she would persuade them to change their minds and come back with the cash. If a business associate needed help deciding to do what Nick was suggesting, Mia was the one he sent to work it out. She was very good at what she did and he had complete faith in her abilities. But today, there would be no such assignments.

Mia could tell that Nick was not in a good mood, so she did what she normally did when she found him in a foul mood – she waited. Ten, fifteen, twenty minutes passed and Nick didn't move. He was just staring out the window, holding the half-consumed glass of scotch in his hand as his arm lay on the armrest of the chair.

Mia could only recall one other time that she had seen him like this. It had been in college when the girl he had been dating had dumped him. He had tried to win her back with gifts and flowers, but she had finally told him that there was nothing he could do to win her back, that she just didn't love him and never would. He had sat in a chair and stared out of the window for the rest of the afternoon just like he was doing now. It wasn't something he could fix. He couldn't force her to love him like he could force someone to pay a debt. He knew that and he was undone by the fact.

At the end of the day, he'd snapped out of his stupor, told Mia to get dressed to party, and they had gone out together. It was the first time Nick had ever asked her to go anywhere with him socially. Before, it had always been business. They had gone to a few bars and Nick was beginning to get drunk. When they entered the next bar, Nick caught sight of his former girlfriend sitting at a table with her new football player boyfriend and a couple of his teammates. Nick began hurling insults at his former flame and her new beau. After the second or third comment, the big football player had stood up, red-faced, and begun coming towards Nick, intent on a fight. He was followed closely by his two teammates.

Mia did what she did best. She protected Nick and looked out for his interests. Before the first would-be assailant had come within striking distance of Nick, Mia had already covered the distance between them, delivering a side-kick to his knee that sent him crashing down to the floor in agony – an injury that would leave him out of commission for the rest of the season. Without skipping a beat, she took another step and leapt into the air to deliver a well-placed knee to the second man's diaphragm. At the same time, she used the palms of her hands to strike his ears violently, leaving him breathless and in considerable pain in the process. The third man was at her side by this time. Seeing what he was up against, he decided not to take any chances. Lady or not, he was going to punch Mia – or so he thought. Mia easily deflected his clumsily delivered haymaker and delivered an open-hand strike to his trachea. He instantly put both hands to his throat and began gagging and gasping for air.

    Nick had been watching the whole time with great amusement. Mia quietly walked over and said to him, "Let's leave before the cops get here." They left the bar and Mia took Nick home, making sure he made it inside to his bed before he passed out. That was what had happened the last time she had seen him look this way.

    She went to the kitchen to make some tea and brought it back in on a tray with two cups and some sugar, setting it down on the coffee table in front of the couch. She poured herself a cup and began drinking it as she waited. After another fifteen minutes or so, Nick spoke.

    "Mia...."

    She waited for a few seconds, expecting him to finish his sentence. When he didn't, she replied.

    "Yes?"

    "Mia...I...I have cancer...."

    The next six months were very difficult. The treatment plan the oncologist suggested for Nick involved a surgery to remove a mass of cancer, followed by chemotherapy. Mia's role began to change. She was still protecting Nick's interests, but now that included driving him to and from doctor's appointments. Helping walk him to the car when he was dizzy, and helping him make some of the common business decisions that he had trouble making because he couldn't think clearly due to the drugs he was taking.

Nick had asked Mia to arrange for a nurse to be around during the day to help him through the recovery process. The nurse was to help bring him pain medication, help him up and down the stairs when he was dizzy, or help clean up when he vomited. One day, Nick called her on the phone.

"Mia...."

Nick's voice was strained.

"Yes, what is it?" Mia asked.

"I've fallen down the stairs and I need your help."

"I'll be right there," she replied.

She depressed the accelerator and sped towards the house. When she came inside, she found Nick sitting in a chair, with his leg propped up on a foot stool with a pillow under it. Marcus, the security man whom Nick usually kept at the house, was bringing a glass of water over to Nick when Mia arrived.

"Are you o.k.?" she asked Nick.

"I'm not sure," Nick replied.

"What happened?"

"The nurse didn't show up today. I thought I could make it downstairs to get myself some breakfast before starting to work, but I began feeling dizzy towards the bottom, and fell down the last four steps. Marcus helped me up and over here to the chair."

He took the offered glass of water from Marcus. But before Marcus could turn and leave, Mia's gaze fell upon him, her eyes burning a hole right through him. He had seen that stare fall upon others and he immediately felt a knot in the pit of his stomach, unsure of what would happen next.

"Why didn't you help him down the stairs?" she asked him, her eyes staying focused on him like lasers.

"I...I didn't know he wanted my help," Marcus replied weakly.

"You should not wait for him to ask. If the nurse is not here, you help him. Understand?"

"Ye.. yes... ma'am. Understood," he replied, unsure whether he was dismissed and should leave the room, or if he should be still.

"Go!" Mia commanded as she pointed out of the room. Marcus retreated hastily into the foyer.

"Don't be too hard on him, Mia," Nick encouraged her. "After all, if it wasn't for him, I'd still be on the floor."

"Not good enough," Mia replied. In Mia's line of work, it was handy to have a doctor on the payroll to patch up any employees who had been recently injured. This frequently happened while rendering some of the more dangerous services required in their business. She scrolled through the contacts in her phone, selecting one and hitting the call icon. In two rings, a doctor answered personally on the other end. Mia did not bother with introductions. "Come to the house; Nick has fallen down. His leg is injured. Hurry." She disconnected the call.

The doctor arrived and, after a thorough examination, concluded that Nick had only sprained his ankle in the fall. He suggested that Nick use crutches until the leg healed up a bit, and that he have someone assist him when he went up or down the stairs. He told Nick that he would come back by in a few days to check up on him and see how the healing process was going. Mia fired the nurse that afternoon and selected a different company. She began a routine of calling Marcus each morning to confirm that the nurse had arrived before she headed to the house herself.

Nick lost all of his hair and so much weight during the chemotherapy that he had Mia buy him a new wardrobe of clothes that fit him more snugly. He said that he refused to look like a scarecrow wearing his old clothes that were now far too big. Eventually, the chemotherapy ended and his hair began to grow back. The side effects of the drugs began to disappear and his sprained ankle healed up so that he no longer needed crutches. Finally, the day came when the doctors declared Nick to be cancer-free.

One day afterward, Mia was heading home after the last business errand of the day when Nick called her on her cell phone.

"Yes," she said.

"Mia, can you come by the house, I have one more thing I need you to take care of before you go home."

"O.k., I'll be right there," she replied.

She pulled up to the house and went up the steps, entering the security code to let herself into the house. She'd started to head upstairs to Nick's office when she saw Nick come out of the den.

"Thanks for coming back," he said.

Mia was still not used to Nick saying 'thank you'. Before his illness, he would ask people to do things and expect it to be done, but rarely did he ever say thank you. While he'd been sick and had needed people to do so many things for him, he had begun to say 'thank you' far more frequently. The illness had definitely changed him.

"Would you come into the dining room, please?" Nick said.

Mia dutifully followed him into the dining room, where she saw the table set for two. Nick walked over to one of the chairs and pulled it out for her.

"I have some business to discuss with you and I haven't eaten yet; would you mind if we had dinner while we talk?"

"O.k.," Mia responded as she sat down at the table. It was a bit awkward as Nick pushed in the chair for her –

something he had never done before.

Nick opened the door to the kitchen and told the chef that they were ready to eat – another oddity, as Nick usually only had a chef when company was coming over. The chef brought out the food and set it on the table. They began eating in silence. After a few minutes, Nick stopped eating and took a sizable drink from his wine glass. Mia could tell that he was nervous – and Nick was never nervous. She was immediately on edge. She wondered if the cancer had returned.

"Mia," Nick began, "this recent illness brought about many changes in my life. I had to rely on many other people to help me in ways I've never had to have help before. You were chief among those helpers, and I wanted to think of an appropriate way to say thank you." He slid a black box across the table before continuing. "Thank you."

Mia looked down at the box, stunned. Nick had never given her so much as a birthday card before. Their relationship had always been solely professional. He paid her well and treated her with respect, but the business line had never been crossed. She slowly reached forth her hand and took the box.

"Thank you," she said, almost as a question.

"Well, go ahead and open it," Nick prodded.

Mia timidly opened the box to reveal a ruby and diamond choker necklace. She stared at it, speechless for several seconds before looking up at Nick with a confused expression on her face.

"Put it on," Nick encouraged her.

Mia picked up the necklace and held it up. It was beautiful. She just stared at it.

"Here, let me help you," Nick said. Nick stood up and came around behind her chair, and took the necklace from her hands. He put it around her neck and secured the clasp for her.

"Why don't you stand up and take a look at it in the mirror?"

Mia stood up and turned around to the large mirror hanging on the wall behind them. The necklace looked even more beautiful around her neck, she thought to herself.

"Do you like it?" Nick asked as he stood beside her and watched her in the mirror.

"Yes," Mia said as she reached her hand up and ran it along the stones, "I like it very much."

"Good," Nick replied, satisfied. "Shall we finish our dinner?" he said as he pulled out her chair for her once more.

They finished eating dinner and Nick did most of the talking. Mia had never been one for chatting, but she liked listening to Nick as he talked about his recovery and how he planned to start keeping a better eye on his health. He paused here and there to ask her questions, to which her replies were predictably short and to the point, but he didn't seem to mind. In fact, he seemed positively giddy – like a schoolboy just let out on summer break. She wondered what was happening. It was confusing to her, but she liked this new side of Nick.

Nick saw Mia to the door and out to the car after they had finished their dessert. He said goodnight to her – something he also had never done before, and went back into the house. Mia drove home thinking about the evening. At one point, she glanced into the rearview mirror to check the traffic behind her and caught a glimpse of her own face. She was smiling. It was something she had not expected to see. Mia did not smile very often. In fact, she couldn't remember the last time she had smiled at all.

Chapter Twenty-Nine

Mia Chen had come to the United States with her immigrant parents. She was an only child whose parents had desperately wanted a boy. Her father opened up a martial arts school in New York City. He pushed Mia to learn the trade just as hard as if she were the son he'd always wanted but never had. He was cruel to her and would hit her if she failed to meet his expectations. Her mother would do nothing to stop him. So Mia determined at an early age that she would not fail to meet those high expectations.

By the time Mia was fifteen, she was able to beat anyone in their studio in the school fighting competitions. She won regional competition trophies and even went to a state-wide championship competition when she was eighteen. She caught the flu the day before the state competition, but her father forced her to compete anyway. She lost. He was irate, berating her and shouting at her all the way home. Once they were home, he hit her in the stomach and she threw up. He was good at hitting her just hard enough so as not to break any bones or cause any lasting physical damage, but the bruises and psychological damage were bad enough. That night, Mia made up her mind to run away.

After she ran away, she began picking up odd jobs where she could. She got a job teaching martial arts at another studio, but her father found out about it and came to take her home. He almost caught her, but she saw his car pull up and ran away through Central Park before he could catch her. After that, she stopped teaching martial arts, afraid he would track her down again.

She saw an advertisement on a local college bulletin board. The ad stated that one of the sororities was looking for a security guard for an upcoming party. When she showed up in front of the sorority house and met the head of the sorority for her interview, the girl almost laughed when she saw this thin Chinese girl was applying for the position.

"I'm sorry, miss," her interviewer began, "but I'm not sure you're...big enough for this job."

Mia looked around and saw a male college student about to enter the sorority house to visit his girlfriend. He was six-foot three and built like a tank. Mia ran up to him.

"Excuse me," she said, "can you help me one moment?"

He looked a bit surprised.

"I need you to come over here," Mia motioned to where her interviewer was seated behind a table with a smirk on her face. The man reluctantly came over to where Mia was motioning, not sure what he was getting into.

"Is this man big enough?" Mia asked the lady.

"Well, yes, he is, but he isn't applying for the job; you are," the lady contended.

Mia ignored her and turned to the man. "Stand here," she said as she positioned him several feet in front of the table at which her interviewer was seated. She held up a twenty dollar bill so that he could see it and placed it on the table, positioning herself between him and the money. It was the last twenty dollars she had to her name.

"If you can pick up the money, you can have it," she said.

The student chuckled, walking forward and reaching his hand out as if he was going to move her aside and pick up the money. Mia grabbed his wrist and twisted it while applying upward pressure with her other hand to the underside of his elbow, putting him in a submission hold that easily deflected him away from the table.

"Try again," she said to him as she released him.

The big student flexed his shoulders up and down, this

time stepping forward and attempting to put Mia in a bear hug to move her away from the table. Before he could step close enough, Mia stuck two fingers towards the base of his neck between the clavicle bones, pressing downward into the epiglottis. The move stopped him dead in his tracks and he reflexively moved his hands towards his throat, at which point Mia grabbed his wrist and put him in a submission hold again.

The big guy backed off, dazed, and beginning to get a bit upset that this little Chinese girl had stopped him twice. A small crowd was beginning to gather around the table and Mia could see from the look in his eye that he was thinking about taking a real swing at her. She looked him straight in the eyes without flinching.

"Thank you for your help. You can go now," she said.

Something about the look in her eyes made the man decide that twenty dollars wasn't worth the effort, and that his pride would be better off if he didn't try again.

"You're welcome," he said stiffly as he turned and walked away.

Mia heard clapping noises from behind her as the interviewer and a few other sorority members applauded her demonstration.

"I underestimated you, my dear," the interviewer responded. "You are hired."

The party was a typical sorority affair. Lots of girls, lots of guys, lots of booze. Mia's job was to hang around the main floor of the sorority house and serve as a bouncer if anyone tried to start a fight or make a big scene.

Mia had never been to such a party before. She had never even had a drink of alcohol. She wasn't quite sure what to expect, so she brought along a few tools of the trade. A telescoping police baton was clipped to her belt, and a knife was strapped to her calf, just under her jeans.

The night was proceeding without incident until an obviously drunken fraternity brother started making unwelcome advances towards his date.

"Stop it! Let me go!" the girl protested.

"Come on," the man slurred, "let's go upstairs where we can be alone," he said as he began dragging her towards the stairs by her wrist. The girl resisted futilely, outweighed by about a hundred pounds. Mia quickly positioned herself on the stairs in front of the advancing man and confronted him.

"Let her go," she said as she put up her hand towards the man in a stopping gesture.

The man looked up and laughed as he attempted to walk into and over Mia. Before he could touch her, Mia thrust her knee up into his solar plexus, grabbed his left hand while stepping behind him, placed her foot in the crook of his leg, and applied pressure to force him down onto the stairs. He was then left gagging for air, face-down on the stairs with his arm behind his back. Mia had her knee in his back so that he wasn't able to get up. During the brief melee, he had released the girl he had been dragging up the stairs.

Mia turned to the girl. "Are you o.k.?" she asked.

The girl looked stunned and was rubbing her wrist. "Yes," she replied, "thank you."

Mia turned her attention back to the man on the ground. "I'm going to let you go and you will leave the party now. Yes?"

"Yes," came the man's strained reply.

Mia released his wrist and took her knee off of his back while quickly moving up the steps and turning to face the man. The man stood up, rubbed his wrist for a moment, and then lunged at Mia without warning, throwing a punch at her face. Mia dropped down into a sitting position on the stairs and delivered a swift side-kick to the man's groin. As the man dropped to his knees cursing, she leaned forward while still in a sitting position and delivered a forearm strike to the side of the man's face, which was now level with hers due to his position on the stairs below. His head slammed into the side of the substantial bannister and he crumpled to the ground. Mia had already stood back up and was prepared to continue the assault, only to find that it was unnecessary, as her attacker wasn't moving.

"Bravo," came a voice from the main floor below. Mia looked down to see a well-dressed male student leaning against the archway leading into the next room.

"I don't think he will be bothering anyone else tonight, except perhaps for the ER doctor," the man continued.

Mia eyed him warily as she walked down the stairs. The man pulled a business card out of his pocket and extended it in her direction.

"How would like to come work for me?"

Mia took the card and read it:

Gaming Entertainment Enterprises
Nicky B.
555-724-9845

"What kind of job is it?" she asked.

"Oh, nothing you can't handle," he replied with a sly smile.

From that day forward, she became Nick Bartonovich's personal bodyguard and enforcer. It was good money and she liked the work. The job gave her frequent opportunities to take out her frustrations against her father on numerous unfortunate surrogates. Nick was amiable, and talkative – the exact opposite of Mia and Mia's father. It was easy to know what Nick wanted because he told her, and he always smiled when she delivered. It was a perfect match.

Now, as she entered her studio apartment, she stared into the mirror hanging on the wall, admiring the expensive necklace that Nick had just given her. She wondered for the first time in their relationship what it was, exactly, that Nick wanted. The possibility that he might be interested in her as a woman and not just a business associate caused her heart to beat faster. Many women her age had already married and had children, but Mia had such mistrust for men that she had never been comfortable progressing beyond a few dates with any potential suitor. Nick, however, was a man she trusted completely. She could envision a future with him. She noticed as she looked into the mirror that her cheeks were turning slightly red. She had never had this feeling before and it was confusing – but she liked it.

Chapter Thirty

J.T. got off the plane in Nassau and took a cab to the British Colonial Hilton, where he would be staying. He was nervous. He hadn't met any of his former victims face to face since the trial, and then only a select few had been brought into court to tell their stories for the jury. Back then, he'd felt no pity for them and no shame. Since that time, he had learned to stop objectifying his victims and begun to see them as real people, even to empathize with them. As that process had taken place, he'd begun to feel ashamed about what he had done. Over time, he'd worked through the shame and accepted responsibility for his own actions. Eventually, he developed a desire to make things right, or barring that possibility, to at least own up to what he had done and apologize to their faces.

He checked in to his room and deposited his suitcase on the bed, unpacking his clothes and hanging them in the closet. The sight of the suit brought back memories of the old days. Except for the ordeal at the Cayman Islands bank, he hadn't worn a suit in almost eight years. It felt as if he was staring at a relic from the distant past.

Once he finished unpacking, he grabbed the book he had been reading, *Compelled to Control: Recovering Intimacy in Broken Relationships* by J. Keith Miller, and headed down to the hotel restaurant for something to eat. The food in the restaurant was more than adequate. The wine he ordered was good, and he lingered at the table after his meal, drinking another glass of wine and reading more from his book. As he read, he came across a passage that hit home:

> *...the shift from being in charge of all outcomes to one*

of doing our best and turning the outcome over to God puts many of us into a spiritual life, a life controlled by the reality and power of God's Spirit instead of our own manipulations and controlling behaviors.

He thought about how his life had changed this past eight years. He had gone from being a corporate big-wig who thought he had it all under control – who felt the *need* to have it all under control – to an ex-con who was trying to make amends for the wrongs he had done, and to let go of the perception that he was by any means in control of anything other than his own actions. He was nervous about the meetings he had scheduled for tomorrow, but he knew in the final analysis, he wasn't responsible for what the other people did with his attempts to make amends. He was only responsible for what he did personally.

He pondered this thought as he went back up to his room and went to bed, saying the Serenity Prayer before he drifted off to a dreamless sleep.

The next morning, J.T. woke up and had breakfast on the beach at the hotel before heading back to make certain the conference room he had reserved was ready. Afterwards, he went back to his room and dressed in the business suit that he had brought for the occasion. He took out the disguise kit he had brought and began the practiced routine of pasting on the fake eyebrows and mustache, inserting the temporary dental implant, and putting the colored contacts in place. He had done this so many times in preparation for this trip, it was almost as routine as brushing his teeth. One last check in the mirror confirmed that everything was in place before he went back down to the conference room to await the arrival of his first appointment.

His first two guests arrived on time. Mr. and Mrs.

Thompson were a black couple in their sixties. The husband had worked for one of the companies that J.T. had sold off and which was subsequently liquidated. The man had suffered a heart attack the week after learning he was going to be let go and that his pension fund was insolvent. The wife was already retired at that point, but didn't have a pension. The husband went on disability, taking social security as soon as he could in order to make the house payments which they were already behind on. When J.T.'s lawyers had tracked him down, they had been about to lose their house. Through the foundation that J.T. had set up a few years before to help his former victims, the house had been saved and they were receiving a check each month, which was worth about twenty-five percent of what his pension would have been.

They exchanged greetings and J.T. introduced himself as Jack Smith – the alias he had chosen for the occasion. They exchanged small talk for a few minutes as J.T. asked them about the cruise and whether or not they were planning on shopping while they were on the island. They were a nice couple, easy to talk to, and J.T. felt horrible for what he had done to them. He let the feelings sink in, reminding himself that his worth wasn't defined by his past actions, but that he was still responsible for the damage those actions had caused. It helped him gain perspective before he spoke.

"Mr. and Mrs. Thompson, I arranged to come here today to talk to you for a very specific reason. You see, I am one of the primary people responsible for the demise of the company that you worked for and the failure of your pension fund. I'm here today to take responsibility for those deplorable actions and let you know that I am sincerely sorry for the pain those actions have caused you."

J.T. stopped and paused before he continued. He braced himself for their reaction. The old couple looked at each other in a bit of confusion and then back at J.T. There was silence that seemed to last for a thousand years before the old man finally spoke.

"I appreciate you saying that, son," the old man began. "You know, I was pretty devastated when all of it first happened. I had a heart attack and we almost lost the house – there were some pretty rough times. I was bitter and angry and it started to eat me up inside." The man turned to his wife and looked at her with eyes full of love. He placed his hand on top of hers and they smiled at each other before he continued. "But my wife came to me one day and challenged me about my attitude. She asked me why I was letting some company take away our happiness, when all they really had the power to do was take away some things that were going to turn to dust one day anyway." He looked back at J.T. and continued. "So I decided to let it go and move on. I decided to forgive whoever did it and move on with my life."

He reached across the table and patted J.T.'s hand. "So I thank you for your apology... and I forgive you." He smiled at J.T. and tears began to form in J.T.'s eyes.

"Thank you, thank you very much. You don't know how much that means to me," J.T. replied.

They talked for a few more minutes before the couple left, and they ended up hugging each other before the man and his wife walked out of the door. J.T. went back to his chair at the conference table and sat down, totally blown away by what had just happened. He sat there in a daze for several minutes before a knock came on the door.

He answered the door and introduced himself to an attractive woman in her mid-thirties. His briefing on her had indicated that her name was Theresa Borne of Toledo, Ohio. Ten years before, her husband had committed suicide after losing his job and his health benefits at one of the doomed companies that J.T. had helped to gut. Her husband had been on anti-depressants and could no longer afford the medication once his insurance was cancelled, being unable to afford the more expensive COBRA insurance. He'd committed suicide by slitting his wrists after getting drunk out of his mind. Theresa had found his body in the bathtub when she returned home from her job.

After the introductions and polite banter, J.T. began his confession.

"Mrs. Borne, I arranged to come here today to talk to you for a very specific reason. You see, I am one of the primary people responsible for the demise of the company that your husband worked for and..."

Before he could finish his sentence, Theresa Borne threw the glass of water at J.T. and began cursing at him. The base of the glass tumbler hit him in the forehead. Blood began trickling down his forehead from the gash that had been opened. Theresa had gotten up by this time, stepped over to where J.T. was seated, and begun hitting him in the face, all the while cursing at him. J.T. managed to grab her wrists and prevent her from continuing, only to have her spit in his face and begin kicking his shins.

The racket the woman was making had reached the front desk, and a security guard made it to the room just in time to see the enraged Mrs. Borne attempting to bite J.T.'s hands in order to get him to release her so she could continue to hit him. The security guard grabbed Mrs. Borne from behind, immobilizing her arms and pulling her back out into the hall.

J.T. decided that going out into the hall would not be a good idea and sat down to compose himself and catalog his injuries. He went to the men's room and cleaned up a bit before the next interview, re-applying a slightly sideways fake eyebrow that had been moved during the altercation. He made it back into the conference room just minutes before the next person arrived.

All told, J.T. had ten different interviews by the end of the day. There were a variety of reactions that he experienced, but the best and the worst had been the very first two interviews of the day. He caught the plane back to the Cayman Islands that night, texting Laura when he was able that he was on-schedule with no mishaps. He was exhausted. He had experienced just a small portion of both the venom and the forgiveness to be had from all the people he had wronged in his past, and he quietly began to weep as the mixed emotions of gratitude and sorrow overwhelmed him.

Chapter Thirty-One

Over the next several months after Nick had given Mia the ruby necklace, he began asking her to accompany him to an increasing number of lunches, dinners, and walks in the park that had nothing to do with business. It was quickly obvious that he was moving their relationship towards something more, but Mia was still unsure how to take all of the attention.

In the past, when Nick had been romantically involved, it usually ended up in sex with the woman in question on the second or third date. Gifts and parties, taking the private jet to various events and exotic locations for romantic weekend getaways, all followed by the inevitable breakup about six months later, when Nick became bored with the girl or she became too demanding. Yet, none of that was happening between Nick and Mia. Apart from the ruby necklace, no other gifts had been given. He had not attempted to make sexual advances, and everywhere they had gone together, outside of business trips, had been in town, within driving distance of Nick's house. It was unusual for Nick, but Mia was enjoying herself and decided to wait it out. She knew that Nick would tell her whatever he had to say when he was ready. Nick was nothing if not goal-oriented. She trusted him, and that was all that mattered.

One evening, Nick was scheduled to attend an art gallery exhibition. It was a black tie event. Mia always accompanied him to these events as his bodyguard and followed behind him as he moved through the crowd in his trademark style, saying his hellos to friends and making new acquaintances. Mia usually busied herself looking for signs that someone may intend bodily harm to Nick, making sure no one with a score to settle showed up close enough to pose a threat, and going over possible exit strategies in her mind to keep from getting bored.

In the past, events such as these would be where Nick would frequently find his next girlfriend. The interested female would usually wander over into his circle and at some point make it obvious that she was available and interested. One of two things would then happen. Nick might ask for her number and call her to arrange a date at a later time. If he was exceptionally taken with her and the woman was obviously willing, he would make his exit and take her back to his house, where they would usually end up having sex. Mia knew the latter because, on numerous occasions after dropping the two off at Nick's house, the women had still been there the following morning when Mia had come in to work.

The exhibition was following a predictable pattern. The champagne was flowing, Nick was working the crowd, and in between conversations, he was stopping to view the photography exhibits. This particular artist was focused on trees, specifically close-up shots of different parts of the trees, like the bark, a leaf with rain on it, and an exposed root system. Mia personally preferred performance art rather than photographs or paintings. She supposed this was most likely due to her background in martial arts.

A woman whose dress was showing entirely too much cleavage sauntered up to where Nick was standing and began talking to him about the photograph he was looking at. He responded politely and the woman stepped even closer to him, obviously flirting with him and attempting to get a response. Physically, the woman was Nick's type. Young, athletic build, blond, and busty. Mia felt her face getting hot. Her breathing rate increased and her jaw muscles started tensing up. She realized with some alarm that she was jealous.

All the dinners and walks and drives in the countryside with Nick over these past months had changed their relationship. She realized for the first time that, during this time, she had actually begun to develop romantic feelings towards him. She was falling in love and now this young woman was threatening that experience. Mia wanted to walk up and push her away from Nick, perhaps with a well-placed open-hand strike to the throat. But she kept completely still and watched, her gaze never leaving Nick and the woman.

Nick took a step back and attempted to extricate himself from the situation, telling the woman to have a nice evening and turning his back on her to move on to the next exhibit. The woman took several steps, going around Nick, positioning herself in front of him, pressing herself into him again, obviously not the type to give up easily. When it became clear that she was not going to take the hint, Nick turned to Mia and gave her the subtle but practiced sign that he wanted Mia to run interference. Mia smiled slyly as she gladly stepped forward to handle the situation.

Nick took a step back from the woman in practiced fashion just as Mia arrived at his side and slipped between him and the woman. Nick turned and walked away, leaving the two women alone.

"Mr. Bartonovich would like you to leave him alone now," Mia said to the woman, smiling as she did.

The woman, who had obviously had too much to drink, looked angrily at Mia. "Get out of the way, you slut!" she spat, and attempted to walk around Mia, in the direction Nick had walked.

As the woman attempted to walk past, Mia stepped into her, discreetly grabbed her wrist, and twisted it into a wrist lock so that the woman could not advance without causing herself considerable pain. The woman took in a gasp of air and was likely about to call out for help, but Mia had already begun to whisper in her ear.

"Find another man, honey, or I will break your pretty little hand."

No sooner had Mia finished her sentence than she had released the woman and stepped backwards, standing between her and the path that Nick had taken. The woman was obviously angry and was rubbing her wrist, but not drunk enough to miss the point. She turned away in a huff and walked in the opposite direction.

Mia caught up with Nick, who had just said hello to an old friend of his and was engaged in conversation. He caught Mia's eye as she took up her familiar position not too far from him, and he nodded his approval.

After the party was over, Mia escorted Nick home in the rented limo. Once she saw Nick had closed the door to his house, she had the driver drop her off at her own apartment. She thought back over the evening with some satisfaction, pleased that Nick had not taken anyone home with him. In fact, she'd noticed he hadn't even taken a phone number from any of the many available women he had talked with during the evening.

The next day, Mia arrived at work as usual and went to Nick's office, ready to work on the day's business. The morning progressed as it normally did, with Nick working on the laptop, talking on the phone, and frequently giving Mia items to put on her task list to be taken care of later in the day. It was a beautiful day, and when they stopped for lunch, Nick suggested that they take a walk down to the sandwich shop just down the street and eat in the park.

As they passed the park on the way to the sandwich shop, Nick stopped in front of the park's water fountain and began staring into the fountain, as if he was lost in thought. Mia stood beside him as she often did, waiting.

"Mia, have you enjoyed the changes in our relationship

these past several months?" he said without looking away from the fountain.

Mia felt her face getting warm. "Yes, I have," she replied.

"Me, too," Nick replied. He suddenly turned towards Mia and took her hand. "Mia, since I had cancer, I've changed. What I want has changed. I see things differently than I ever have before. I see *you* differently than I ever have before."

Mia's face was practically on fire. She could feel a burning sensation in her chest. She didn't move.

"Mia, I haven't loved anyone for a very long time; you know that. But I love someone now. And I want to be with that someone. Mia, I love you, and I want to be with you. Not like all those other girls, not a one night stand, not a six month fling. I want to be with you for the rest of my life."

Mia felt tears begin to well up in her eyes. She had never loved a man since her father had betrayed her all those years before. She had never trusted any man besides Nick. Now, as he spoke to her, she knew in her soul that she loved him, too.

Nick reached into his pocket and pulled out black box, holding it out to her. "Mia, will you marry me?"

Mia reached out her hands and cradled Nick's face, looking up into his eyes in a way she had never looked into them before. Then she answered with all of her heart, "Yes. Yes, I will."

They embraced in front of the fountain.

Nick and Mia were married a week later in a private ceremony with a few of their closest friends in attendance. A few days after that, they took a private jet to Charleston, South Carolina, where they stayed at the Wentworth Mansion for a week. Nick had booked the Grand Mansion Suite for their stay, a beautiful one-thousand square foot luxury suite complete with chandeliers and two floor-to-ceiling marble fireplaces. It was quintessential southern charm at its finest.

They toured Charleston and Fort Sumter, rode bicycles through the historic district, and ate at the finest restaurants. Mia had never been so happy in all her life. She got up each morning in the bed next to Nick and pinched herself to be sure she wasn't dreaming.

Nick was a changed man. It was as if he had been reborn. He was no longer solely focused on making money and achieving his business goals. He was actually enjoying life and was finding that Mia was so much more interesting and beautiful than he had ever imagined. He couldn't believe he had been so blind to the fact all these years.

On the jet back to New York, they viewed a slide-show of all the pictures they had taken and reminisced about the wonderful time they'd had in Charleston. Once they were back in town, Mia and Nick moved her things into the brownstone. That night, they sat on the couch and watched one of Mia's favorite movies – *Casa Blanca*. Mia was curled up next to Nick, who had his arm around her as she rested her head on his shoulder. For them, time had stopped. They had each other and they were in love. Nothing could have been better.

Chapter Thirty-Two

Silas stared at the dashboard of his police sedan in shock. All he had wanted since he was a kid was to be a cop. He had joined the Army at 18 and gone straight in to the NYPD Police Academy when he was honorably discharged at the age of 21. He eventually worked his way up to detective. He had been a good cop. Emphasis on the word *had*.

Somewhere along the way, Silas had discovered online gambling and gotten hooked. What started as an innocent pastime slowly grew to dominate more and more of his income. He started picking up extra shifts and side jobs as a security guard as his habit grew and his losses started getting larger. One night, he thought he was about to win big, enough to pay off the house. He was on a roll, working up a one thousand dollar stake into over 100K. One more good hand and he promised himself he was going to cash in and log off for the night. Then he started losing. Before it was over, he was 10K in debt to the house, and the house belonged to Nick Bartonovich.

That was when things had started going downhill fast. He had compromised his integrity to get rid of that debt, which eventually led him to where he was sitting right now. He had hoped that somewhere along the way he would find the path to redemption, to turn back the hands of time and somehow set things right, but it hadn't turned out that way.

After being tortured by Nick and Mia, they'd shot him up with some sort of drug and he had passed out. When he woke up, he was in a hospital in Nevada. After seeing he was conscious, a nurse had given him a sealed manila envelope with his name on it. She said that someone had delivered it the day after he had been admitted and asked her to give it to him when he regained consciousness.

As he looked through the contents of the envelope, his heart sank. In it was enough information to convict him as an accomplice to J.T. Thornbacker in the prison break. As part of the frame-up, his fingerprints were all over 'evidence' that was to be found by the FBI at a location near the Nevada prison where the break out occurred. Never mind that it was all fabricated evidence planted by Nick and company. His career would be ruined in the process of even trying to prove his innocence.

Of the two locations where evidence had been planted, the first had nothing tying Silas to the prison break. The second location, however, did. A note in the envelope said that the FBI had already received information about the first location, proving J.T. Thornbacker and company had planned the escape. It further stated that the information about the existence of the second location would only be turned in to the FBI if Silas decided to pursue Nick Bartonovich, J.T. Thornbacker, or anything related to the Cayman Island heist. The message was clear: leave us alone or we'll destroy what is left of your life.

After reviewing the information from a cop's perspective, he knew his chances of staying out of prison, should the FBI ever receive that second tip, were slim to none. There was enough money in the envelope for him to buy a bus ticket back home to New York. He went home with his tail between his legs, vowing to never gamble again.

His resolve to stop gambling lasted about three months. He kept the losses at a minimum for a while, but one night, he thought he had a chance to score big again, only to end up a thousand dollars underwater. He was tapped out. Maggie had told him that if he lost any more money gambling, that she would leave him, so he couldn't tell her. He needed cash fast. Then, later that week, Silas was cataloging some physical evidence from a small-time drug bust down at the station and he had an epiphany.

Silas and his partner Dave usually took turns taking the evidence down to the evidence locker. Today, his partner had a dentist appointment and had decided to leave before they were done cataloging the evidence. He'd told Silas to sign his name on all the necessary documents, because his tooth was killing him and he had to go to the dentist ASAP. After his partner left, Silas counted fifteen hundred dollars that they had retrieved from the perp when they'd busted him. Silas' partner had no clue how much money was there. Silas could log $500, pocket the rest, and no one would ever know. The perp would figure it out, but since it was drug money and he was a drug dealer, who was going to believe him over a cop?

Silas checked to make sure no one was paying close attention to him as he cataloged the evidence. He pretended to accidentally knock the money onto the floor. When he bent down to pick it up, he put a thousand dollars in his sock as discretely as possible before standing back up.

That was the first of many thefts that Silas began making to cover his gambling habit. He rationalized it in so many ways. It was drug money, so it was no big deal. He deserved it, after all – cops were underpaid and performing a public service. Why should the bad guys make all the money? He was putting these guys behind bars – shouldn't that be rewarded?

One day, Silas and his partner were going to stop at one of their favorite lunch hangouts. Silas parked the car, opened the door, and was about to get out when Dave put a hand on this arm.

"Hey Silas, hold on a minute. I need to talk to you about something."

"Yeah, o.k., what is it?" Silas said as he turned to his partner.

"Shut the door," Dave said, nodding at the open car door.

"Sure, Dave," Silas said, wondering what was up as he shut the door.

"Silas, how long have we been partners?"

"About ten years now, I think," Silas replied, wondering where Dave was headed with this.

"Yeah, that's right, about ten years," Dave echoed. "I don't know how to ask this, Silas, so I'll just come out with it. Are you stealing money from the evidence we turn in?"

Silas felt the blood drain from his face and hoped that it didn't show.

"No, Dave, why would you think that? I would never do that," Silas said, trying to sound indignant.

"Silas," Dave continued, "there was a little over two grand on the perp we arrested on 5th Street about two months ago. I counted it when you went to take the statement from the shop owner. I signed off on the evidence because it was your day to write the log and I didn't check on it too good, so I didn't see that you had only put down about a grand. Later that day, I found a cigarette lighter from the perp on the floor – you know the one with the skull and cross-bones case on it? I went down to check the log to see if we had recorded it and to add it into evidence, and that's when I saw that the money was short."

Silas tried to smile and laugh it off.

"So I maybe miscounted the money?"

"I counted it, Silas. The money's missing."

"Dave, I didn't take the money. There has to be some other explanation," Silas protested.

"Silas, I've been counting the money from the busts we've made ever since, when you weren't looking. Half of the busts we made whenever you were in charge of filling out the evidence logs were short."

Silas slumped back in his chair. He looked down to the floor. He was busted and he knew it.

"What are you going to do, Dave?" he said without

looking up.

"I don't want you to get busted, Silas, you've been a good partner and a good cop, but I can't trust you anymore. I'll keep my mouth shut if you resign."

Silas looked up at him in shock.

"Resign? Dave, I'm just a few years from retirement. That would ruin me."

Dave's face remained stern and un-moving.

"You should've thought of that before you went on the take. What you did was wrong, Silas. Once we go there, where's the line get moved to?"

Silas didn't answer; he just continued looking at Dave.

"You've got to the end of the day to turn in your resignation or I take what I know to IAD. I'll take a cab back to the precinct."

Dave got out of the car and shut the door.

Chapter Thirty-Three

It was 6:00 a.m. on a Saturday morning when Nick's cell phone rang next to his bed. He woke up immediately and reached over for the phone. Calls that came in this early on a weekend were usually important. Since he and Mia had married, he had begun instructing all of his business associates not to call until at least 8:00 a.m. on the weekend.

He looked at the caller ID and saw that it was Katrina Byers as he made his way into the bathroom and quietly closed the door so that Mia wouldn't be disturbed. In fact, he knew she was already awake. It was an occupational necessity for her that she was a light sleeper. But Nick liked to provide her with these small courtesies. It felt good to be looking out for someone besides himself these days. It was relatively new ground for Nick Bartonovich.

"Hello," Nick answered after he hit the 'answer call' button.

"Nick, I'm sorry to be calling you so early on the weekend, I know how you hate that," she replied. Katrina Byers was one of Nick's top CPAs, one who worked exclusively for him and was immensely valuable to his organization. If she was calling, it was important.

"What is it? What has happened?" he replied.

Nick listened as Katrina detailed the situation for the next fifteen minutes, asking few questions, just letting Katrina explain in her usual, very detailed way. When they were done talking, Nick said that he would call her back within the hour as he disconnected the call. This was not good news, it was not good news at all. He looked in the mirror, his mind racing, trying to decide what the best response to the situation would be.

He walked back into the bedroom and sat down on Mia's side of the bed, then began gently stroking her hair. She opened her eyes and smiled – something she had been doing an increasing amount of during the past year since they had gotten married.

"Mia, darling, we need to talk. Katrina Byers has just called with some bad news and we need to decide how to handle it. I'll make some coffee for us downstairs."

He leaned down and kissed her gently on the forehead before leaving to make the coffee.

Downstairs, Nick made the coffee mechanically as he thought about what he had just been told. When the buzzer on the coffee maker alerted him that the brewing cycle was completed, he poured two cups of coffee and took them to the den where Mia was already waiting. He thought about how many times in the past year he had enjoyed their morning coffee. How much he loved making Mia's coffee just the way she liked it – strong, black, freshly ground gourmet coffee that they purchased at the organic co-op. But today was different. Today they had bad news to discuss.

He went into the den area and found Mia sitting on the couch with her feet curled up underneath her, waiting. She took the coffee from him and cradled it in her hands, closing her eyes and inhaling the coffee's aroma. She waited for Nick to sit down in his usual chair before she spoke.

"So what is the matter?" she said at last.

Nick put his own coffee mug down on the side table, not really in the mood to drink it.

"Katrina has gotten considerably worse. The doctors don't think she will make it to the end of the week."

"Oh, my God," Mia exclaimed.

About six months prior, Katrina had been diagnosed with renal disease, a.k.a. kidney failure. She had told Nick about the dialysis treatments she would be taking and how the disease would affect her work hours. She had been put on the kidney transplant list and told she had a good chance of getting a transplant in time, based upon the current stage of the disease.

Once Katrina began going to dialysis, she needed someone to watch her daughter Sasha, who was nine, while Katrina was at the clinic for the lengthy dialysis process. She began making a short list of people that she trusted who could help with this task. She had noticed the radical change in Nick since he had married Mia. He actually smiled in a genuine way now, not in the sly way he had before, as if he was about to close a business deal. She'd noticed that Mia had changed, too. She'd seen them together several times at Nick's office when she would go by to cover the quarterly financial reports with Nick, and she had been impressed with the atmosphere change in the house. It was no longer a hard business atmosphere... there was love there now. She decided to ask Nick and Mia if they would be on the rotation to help watch Sasha a couple of times a month. After Nick and Mia talked it over, they'd agreed to do it on a trial basis.

Sasha and Mia hit it off almost immediately. Sasha was into the latest music, and fashions, like most kids – things Mia was never allowed to participate in when she was Sasha's age. Mia began asking questions and showing a genuine interest in what Sasha was doing. Soon, Mia was downloading the latest music and taking Sasha shopping. Sasha even helped Mia open up a Facebook page and they friended each other. It was as if Mia was re-living her own childhood in a way she had never been allowed to experience before.

Nick's affection for Sasha had grown, as well. He began to accompany Mia and Sasha on some of their shopping trips and they would all eat lunch together. Once, on the spur of the moment, Nick suggested they all go out to the horse farm where Nick and Mia kept their horses, and go for a ride.

Sasha's eyes lit up like it was Christmas morning. They had a blast and Sasha was continually asking if they could go back. Nick and Mia enjoyed these outings so much that, after three months, they had asked Katrina if they could up the ante and watch Sasha once a week. Katrina had obliged, glad to be able to rely on them for more help without feeling like she was imposing.

They had all known the possibility existed that Katrina wouldn't get a transplant in time, but no one had seriously considered it. Mia put her coffee cup down on the table in front of her.

"Is there anything we can do to help?" Mia asked.

"Actually, there is something Katrina asked us to do. She asked us to adopt Sasha," Nick replied.

Mia inhaled slowly, looking away from Nick at a painting of a lone ship in the ocean that was hanging on the wall. She held the breath in as she allowed the words Nick had just spoken to roll around in her head. Then she looked back at Nick.

"What do you want?" she asked.

"I want one of my best accountants and a good friend not to die," Nick replied seriously. Then he added, "I'm almost fifty years old, Mia. I've never brought up having kids with you because I thought I was too old. These past few months spending time with Sasha have been good. She was like the daughter I never thought I would have. And the three of us together have such a good time...." He looked Mia in the eyes. "Look, I don't want to pressure you into anything, but if you want to do this, I'm willing to jump off the ledge with you. You know I like a good rush."

He smiled as he waited for Mia to respond to what he had just said.

Mia looked back at the painting on the wall. The painting reminded her of her own life's journey in many ways. In it, a single ship was out in the ocean with no land in sight. The seas were rough and the crew was struggling to keep the ship afloat. They were struggling for their very lives with somber determination. She continued looking at the painting as she spoke.

"I know what it is like to be on your own, without your parents for support, without anyone you can count on except yourself. It is a hard life with no guarantees that you will make it. We could give Sasha a good life. We could love her and give her all of the things that I never had when I was growing up. I want to protect her. I want to help. Yes," she said, turning back to look at Nick, "I want to do this."

Nick reached over and placed his hand on Mia's, squeezing it gently.

Chapter Thirty-Four

Nick and Mia called Katrina immediately and let her know that they would be happy to adopt Sasha. They visited Katrina later that same day in the hospital. Sasha was at her mother's side when they arrived and was very upset. When Nick and Mia entered the room, she walked over to Mia and hugged her, tears streaming down her face. Nick could tell by the look on Katrina's face that she was in a bad way.

Katrina spoke to Sasha and explained that she would be staying with Nick and Mia while Mommy was in the hospital. After they had visited for a little while, Nick asked Mia if she would take Sasha down to the car, saying that he would be there in a few minutes. Sasha didn't want to go, but Katrina told her that she could come back and see her tomorrow, but that her mother needed the rest right now. Reluctantly, Sasha kissed and hugged her mother goodbye before she left with Mia.

"Have you told her yet that you don't have long?" Nick said when they were alone.

"Not in so many words, but she's a smart kid. She knows," Katrina replied.

"You should tell her yourself. It would be best if she hears it from you, to help her let go and all," Nick continued.

Katrina looked up at Nick with tired eyes. "Thank you."

Nick nodded his head.

Later that day, Katrina's lawyer came by and she changed her will to indicate that she wanted Nick and Mia to be Sasha's legal guardians. She decided not to discuss the matter with Sasha. It would be enough for her to deal with Katrina's impending death. Katrina reasoned that Mia and Nick could tell her when the time was right, after she had some time to grieve. They had decided that Nick and Mia would adopt Sasha as soon as possible after Katrina passed. Katrina dictated a letter to her lawyer to be given to Sasha upon her death, explaining that this was her wish so that Sasha would hear it straight from her.

    Once the whole legal process was completed, Katrina felt relieved. Over the next few days, Sasha came by every morning and they spent many hours together. They talked, played cards when Katrina felt able, and Sasha would read the latest novel she had been reading out loud to her mother. Nick and/or Mia would drop Sasha off, then pick her up for lunch and bring her back by in the evening. These precious days went by so fast for Katrina. She was relishing the time with her daughter, but she was grieving for herself at having to leave Sasha when she was so young.

    On the fourth day, Mia had dropped Sasha off and was saying goodbye to Katrina as she prepared to leave, but Katrina asked her to stay. Katrina looked much weaker than she had the day before. She could barely talk and Sasha had to bend her ear down close to her mother's mouth to hear what she had to say. Katrina whispered in her daughter's ear, "I love you, Sasha. I will always love you...."

    "I love you, Mommy," Sasha said with tears beginning to flow down her face.

    The alarm on Katrina's heart monitor went off and soon the medical staff was rushing in with the crash cart to try and revive Katrina. Mia pulled Sasha back as the doctors and nurses worked, but it was soon clear that Katrina was not coming back. Sasha turned to Mia, who pulled her close while Sasha cried.

    The funeral was brief and attended only by a small circle of Katrina's friends, and her younger sister. Her own mother was dead, and her father was in a nursing home and unable to attend. After the service, Nick and Mia took Sasha by her house to pick up some of her things before returning to their house. They simply said that Sasha would be staying with them for a while and Sasha didn't ask why, too overcome by grief to ask any questions of them at the moment.

The hours turned in to days and weeks, and eventually years. Sasha began to move on with her life and acclimate to life in her new family. Nick and Mia officially adopted her on her eleventh birthday.

There were many changes that took place in the Bartonovich household over the next several years. Nick moved his office to the second floor so that Sasha could have a bedroom upstairs next to Nick and Mia's bedroom. They bought Sasha her own horse, which she named Katrina's Pride in honor of her mother. She became quite an accomplished rider and even won some riding competitions. Nick and Mia had to develop new work schedules. Mia began farming out some of her more dangerous activities to other members of their company. Nick even began shifting some of his business activities towards more legitimate enterprises, not wanting Sasha to associate with some of his former colleagues who had frequented the house prior to her arrival. Overall, the addition of Sasha to the Bartonovich household was resulting in a kinder, gentler family atmosphere.

Nick was amazed at how much better his life had become since getting married and adopting Sasha. He now had a purpose beyond himself and he was finding genuine fulfillment in his role as a family man like he had never had before when business was his primary focus. Mia, too, was blossoming into her role as mother and wife. While both Nick and Mia still pursued the business side of their lives, they made the adjustments necessary to make home life a big priority. Life for the Bartonovich family was good.

Chapter Thirty-Five

Laura sat beside Valerie in the crisis center and held her hand as she cried. She had a busted lip and her left eye was almost completely swollen shut. She listened to the story patiently, a variation on a similar theme she had heard a hundred times.

"He saw me in the supermarket and followed me outside. He grabbed me and drug me down an alleyway. He tried to get me to tell him where I'm staying. When I refused, he did this to me."

Valerie paused in telling her story and sobbed before continuing.

"He wants our daughter. He said that he will find out where she goes to school and take her from me." She turned and looked at Laura with a look of desperation in her eyes. "Ms. Laura, I can't let him take my daughter! He was abusing her sexually, and that is why I left him! I can't let him take my daughter!"

"It's going to be o.k., Valerie. We're going to help you, just calm down," Laura replied.

But even as the words came out of her mouth, she wasn't sure how much she believed the words herself. If Valerie's ex had found her in the supermarket, then he was too close to finding out that Valerie was staying here at the crisis center, which was only a few blocks away. Assuming Valerie hadn't been followed back to the center today, it was likely only a matter of time until she was. Laura could feel her blood begin to boil as she thought about her own past experience with sexual abuse, how powerless she had felt, and now to hear that this woman's young daughter had been sexually abused by her ex. It was too much.

She tried to remain calm as she continued. "Valerie, do you have a picture of your ex?"

"Yes, yes I do."

"Good, I want you to go and get it. Then I want you to write down his address where he lives and works. I'm going to call the police and we'll report him."

"O.k., Ms. Laura," Valerie replied, getting up and walking off to her room to get the picture.

Laura called the police and asked them to send someone down so they could report the attack; then she went out back behind the crisis center, and once the door was shut, she let out a scream. "Ahhh!" She turned around and saw a metal trash can and kicked it with the side of her foot. She paced up and down the alleyway for several minutes before finally feeling calm enough to step back inside.

She found Valerie sitting down at a table in the common area, writing down the information Laura had requested on a piece of paper. Laura took it from her and went into the office, making a photocopy of the information and the photograph. She folded the copies and put them in her back pocket before she went back out to where Valerie was sitting. She handed the originals back to Valerie.

"Valerie, hold on to these for when the police get here. You just tell them exactly what you told me. I have to go right now, but I'll be back to check on you later. Just grab one of the other volunteers when the police get here and they will help you with everything. O.k.?"

Valerie nodded her head up and down.

Laura took out her cell phone and punched in the home address of Valerie's ex. It was about five miles from here. If she went on her bicycle, it would take her about twenty minutes. She unlocked the bicycle lock, removed her bike from the bike rack, and began pedaling.

The address was for a second floor apartment. It was a small duplex unit, with one apartment on the bottom floor and the other on the second floor. A stairway led up the exterior of the unit to the second floor apartment door. Laura positioned herself across the street where she would be hidden from view by some shrubbery. She parked her bike out of view and stood behind the plants, watching.

It took about an hour before the police finally came by. They walked up the stairs and knocked on the door. A medium-sized man answered the door. After he had talked with the police for a few minutes, they escorted him down the stairs and put him in the police cruiser.

Laura waited until they were gone before crossing the street and going up the steps to the apartment. She knocked on the door and waited for someone to answer, but no one did. She tried the door and found it locked, so she went back down to her bicycle and rode home.

It was a few days before she found out from Valerie that her ex had been released on bail. Valerie was scared out of her mind that he was going to take her daughter away and hurt her again. Laura tried to comfort her, but she was beside herself. She was still crying when Laura left for the day.

Laura wasn't scheduled to volunteer at the crisis center for a few more days. She went to her apartment, packed a few things in a backpack, and rode her bike back to the apartment where Valerie's ex lived. It was around 6:00 p.m. when she arrived. She hid her bike in the foliage and positioned herself in the same location as before so that she wouldn't be seen.

At about 7:00 p.m., the ex left the apartment. It was a Friday night, and from the way he was dressed, he was going out to party. She waited until he was out of sight before crossing the street and going up the stairs. She knocked on the door just to be sure no one else was home. No one came to the door. She looked around to be certain she wasn't being watched by some nosy neighbor. When she was certain she wasn't being watched, she slipped on some latex gloves and tried the door. It was locked, as expected. She retrieved some lock picking tools from her bag and picked the lock – a handy skill she had picked up in her drug dealing days.

Once inside, she shut the door behind her and locked it. A quick look around the house revealed that this door was the only entrance to the apartment and that no one else was around. She retrieved a black ski mask from the bag and a junior sized baseball bat. She positioned the mask on top of her head so that she could pull it down in a moment's notice, and then she looked for a place to sit where she would not be seen from the outside. Once she was positioned, she waited.

There were some down sides to this plan. If someone else came back with the ex, Laura could be in trouble. In that case, she might need the gun she had brought along that was tucked in the back of her pants. From the looks of this place, though, he wasn't going to bring a girl back here. She supposed he was the type of guy who would convince the girl to go back to her place. That way, if it got rough, he could leave after he smacked her around a bit and she wouldn't know where to find him. Scum. She could hardly wait until he got back.

There were a few false alarms from neighbors coming home or leaving, but Laura's mark finally returned at 1:00 a.m. He was whistling as his foot hit the bottom stair. She pulled down the mask over her face so that he wouldn't be able to identify her later. The door was solid wood and he hadn't left a light on inside when he left, so he wouldn't see Laura until it was too late to do anything about it.

He had just opened the door and reached over to turn on the light when Laura sprang into action. She slammed the big end of the bat hard into his solar plexus, and then she kicked him between the legs. He dropped to his knees and she easily tipped him back out the door and onto the landing with her foot. He lay there in a fetal position on his back, gasping for breath. She stepped across the threshold and took a small can of pepper spray out of her pocket. She aimed it at his face and sprayed it in his eyes. While he was screaming and trying to wipe the pepper spray out of his eyes, she reached down with both hands and rolled him down the stairs as hard as she could. She was pleased to see that he made it all the way to the bottom before he stopped. She quickly gathered her things and walked down the stairs. Laura bent down beside him as he lay there moaning, pointed her phone at him, and hit he 'play' button on the pre-recorded message she had created using an internet app that disguised her voice.

"If you touch Valerie or her daughter again, it will be the last thing you ever do," said the creepy-sounding automated voice.

She quickly crossed the street into the alleyway where her bicycle was hidden, and turned around to make certain she wasn't followed. The whole episode had taken about thirty seconds. As she turned around, she just saw the door begin to open on the bottom apartment as someone came out to see what all the noise was about.

A few days later, she read about the attack in the local paper. The man had apparently sustained a concussion, broken a leg, dislocated his shoulder, and required ten stitches to close a gash in his cheek caused by an exposed nail on the wooden staircase.

"Those darned nails," Laura thought to herself as she smiled.

Chapter Thirty-Six

Silas looked down at the document that had just arrived in the mail. He knew what it was, but forced himself to open it anyway. He had to read it for himself. There was something about reading it in print that seemed to hit him like a ton of bricks. Maggie and Silas were now officially divorced.

Resigning from the force had been a hard blow to Silas. He started drinking heavily. He told Maggie why he had quit – the truth, and she was mad as hell. He swore to get help. He even attended Gambler's Anonymous for a while, but the itch just wouldn't go away. He kept thinking that all he needed was one big score to set things right.

He was making ends meet with private detective and security work, but kept skimming money off of his paycheck to gamble with on the side so that Maggie wouldn't know. They began to have more and more fights over money. There were many times that Maggie would borrow money from her sister to cover the mortgage payment when they couldn't come up with the funds because of his gambling losses. Their marriage continued to disintegrate. Finally, Maggie gave him an ultimatum. Either stop gambling for good, or their marriage was over.

One weekend, Maggie and their son Tommy had gone to visit her sister. An old friend invited Silas over to watch the football game. Once the game was over, the guys wanted to play some cards. Silas knew he should say no, but he stayed. He told himself he would just spend twenty dollars on the game and then bow out for the night if he lost it. He ended up losing one hundred and fifty dollars before the night was over. It was money they had needed for groceries.

Maggie and Tommy returned from their trip and Maggie eventually asked Silas for some money to go to the store and buy the groceries. When he confessed that he had lost the money, she went ballistic. It had been the last straw for Maggie. She took Tommy with her and moved in with her sister that same day.

Silas put the divorce papers down on the kitchen table and poured himself a tall glass of scotch. All of this could have been fixed with money, he told himself. He thought back to when it had all really started to go downhill several years ago, and fixated on the Bartonovich affair as the starting point. The online gambling site must have been rigged, he told himself. How else could the site have won so much money back from him in so little time? That led to the debt that caused him to decide to take the job from Bartonovich in the first place. Since it was Bartonovich's site, Silas reasoned in his inebriated stupor, it was his fault that Silas' marriage had fallen apart. That was the last coherent thought he had before he passed out on the couch.

While he was asleep, he had a dream about the bank in the Caymans where Nick Bartonovich had taken J.T. Thornbacker. In the dream, he saw large bundles of cash fall out of the duffle bag that Nick was carrying out of the bank. He simply walked away without picking the bundles up. Silas ran up and began picking up the cash, stuffing it into his pockets and into his shirt until he couldn't carry anymore.

He had the hangover from hell when he woke up the next morning. He drank two glasses of water, showered, and made himself some strong coffee with two slices of toast on the side. He sat at the breakfast table eating the toast, drinking coffee, and staring at the divorce papers. By the time he had finished his toast and coffee, he had convinced himself of two things. Firstly, if he had enough money, Maggie would take him back and he would have his family again. Secondly, if his money problems had gotten drastically worse because of

Nick Bartonovich, then Nick Bartonovich could make those same financial difficulties go away for good.

Silas started spending every spare moment he could researching Nick's businesses and watching his house. He determined he would learn everything he could about the man, find his weakness, and exploit that weakness to score a big pile of cash for himself.

One afternoon as he was watching Nick's house, he saw the girl leave with Mia in a car. He had determined her name was Sasha some weeks before by going through the Bartonovich's discarded trash. He followed the car as inconspicuously as he was able. They left the city and made their way over to Newark, New Jersey. Their first stop was at a florist, where they came out with a bouquet of flowers. From here, they proceeded to Fairmount Cemetery.

Silas pulled into the cemetery behind them, far enough back so as not to be noticed. He followed them until he was forced to turn down one of the side roads to prevent being discovered tailing them. He quickly exited his vehicle, grabbing his binoculars and finding a spot where he could see their car fairly well.

The car stopped. Mia and the girl got out of the car with the flowers and went over to a grave stone. He couldn't make out the name on the grave stone, but the girl appeared to be crying. They stayed a few minutes, the girl put flowers on the grave, and then they got back in the car. Silas pretended to be visiting a nearby grave when they drove by the road where he was positioned. Once they had left the cemetery, Silas got back in his car and drove down to where the girl had put flowers on the grave. It didn't take him long to locate the grave with the particular bouquet he had seen them place. He took out his phone and took a picture of the grave stone before getting back in his car and heading home.

This was something significant. Sasha was the key to Nick Bartonovich's money – he was sure of that. This graveside visit just might be the leverage he needed to turn the key. He didn't know who Katrina Byers was or how she was related to Sasha, but he would find out soon enough. And once he knew, he would be able to exploit that information to achieve his goal. He slept well that night and had the same recurring dream. In the dream, Nick Bartonovich was dropping bundles of cash for him to collect.

Chapter Thirty-Seven

It was a beautiful day for sailing. J.T., Laura, and James had taken the sailboat out in the morning. They had been out for around two hours and were about to stop and drop anchor for lunch.

Since starting their new lives in the Cayman Islands, J.T. had developed a passion for sailing. About a year before, he had purchased this thirty-two foot Hunter 326 sailboat. It had one mast with two sails in the classic Bermuda rig style. There were two couches in the main cabin, with a table in the middle, two sleeping areas which were each behind their own bulkhead, a lavatory, and an open galley.

James went below and was beginning to get the meal ready. He had developed into quite an amateur chef and had prepared one of his latest dishes for them to try. Today it was going to be jalapeño Tilapia served over angel-hair pasta with grated Parmesan cheese, accompanied by a white wine.

J.T. was at the wheel and was about to lower the sails and come to a stop. Laura had just come up from the hold after retrieving some sunscreen. She put her sunglasses down on a small seat located at the stern of the boat just behind the wheelhouse. The seat was built into the railing, with the second rail curved out and around the seat to provide back support.

She was just about to put sunscreen on her face when the movement of the boat caused her glasses to slide off of the seat and onto the ledge below, just past the railing at the back of the boat. She put the sunscreen in the cup holder next to the seat and grabbed the railing, stepping over the side of the boat and onto the ledge. As she was reaching for her glasses the boat hit a wave and lurched to the side, causing Laura to lose her balance. She fell forward, hitting her head on the side of the boat before falling into the water.

"Wow, did you see that wave we just hit?" J.T. said as he turned around to where he thought Laura was sitting. He saw her orange PFD in the water about twenty yards behind the boat, where she was floating face down. He immediately began turning the boat around, heading back in her direction.

"James! Get up here! Laura fell off the boat!" J.T. yelled.

James came rushing up from the galley. "Where is she?!"

By this time, J.T. had succeeded in turning the boat around and was headed straight towards where Laura was floating, still face down in the water.

"Right there!" J.T. exclaimed as he pointed to where she was. "I think she hit her head and got knocked out. I'll pull up alongside and you jump in to get her."

When the boat was close enough, James jumped in and swam over to Laura, immediately flipping her over so that her head was no longer face-down in the water. He began swimming with Laura in tow back to the boat.

"Hang on, Laura! Hang on!" he exclaimed.

J.T. turned the boat back around once more after passing by Laura, dropped the sails, and engaged the motor so that he could come up slowly on his friends. When he got close enough, he tossed out a life preserver. James grabbed on with one arm and held Laura with the other as J.T. hauled them in.

Once they had Laura on the deck, J.T. could see that Laura's lips were blue, indicating she wasn't breathing. He immediately removed her life vest and began performing CPR. After about thirty seconds of CPR, Laura vomited. J.T. rolled her onto her side so that the vomit wouldn't go down her windpipe. Laura began coughing and spitting, gasping for air.

"James, go get a blanket," J.T. ordered.

James came back with a blanket and wrapped it around Laura. After a few minutes, Laura's lips started turning pink again.

"Are you o.k.?" James asked.

"Give her a minute, James," J.T. said. "Don't you worry about talking right now, Laura, just focus on breathing." Turning to James, he continued, "It takes some time to get your breath back after something like that. I know, I almost drowned as a kid. Took me about an hour before I could speak."

After they took Laura below, J.T. told James to watch her and make sure she didn't go to sleep. He was concerned that she might have a concussion, and felt that they needed to have her checked out at the hospital to make certain it wasn't too serious.

J.T. turned the boat around and set sail back to the marina. He called ahead so that an ambulance was there waiting on them by the time they returned. The doctor in the ER gave Laura some oxygen and checked her over. Eventually, he diagnosed her with a concussion and sent her home with James and J.T., giving them a print-out on what symptoms to look for at home. He told Laura that she needed to gets lots of rest and take it easy over the next few days. She was to let him know if any of the symptoms listed on the sheet he gave her persisted or got worse.

J.T. suggested that they all stay at his house for the next day or so. That way, he said, he and James could take turns keeping an eye on Laura's condition. Laura protested a bit, but in the end, she was too exhausted to give them much resistance and she capitulated.

A few weeks after the boating incident, they were all eating over at J.T.'s house, and Laura brought in two presents from the car. She gave one to J.T. and one to James. They looked at her with questioning looks until she said, "Well, go on. Open them up."

J.T. unwrapped his first. It was a beautiful stained glass piece of a sailboat on the water. Laura had included a note inside the box. J.T. opened the note and read it to himself. "Thanks for saving my life," it read. James opened his and found a similar note. His stained glass scene depicted a boy riding a bike down the beach.

J.T. went over to Laura and gave her a big hug.

"I'm just glad you are o.k. Thanks for the gift."

"Yeah," James added, "thanks. That was pretty scary. Next time, you stay inside the railing, young lady," he said in mock sternness, wagging his finger at Laura as he spoke.

"Yes, sir!" Laura said with a mock salute.

Laura's near-drowning had been concerning on more than one level. The x-ray that had been performed on Laura in the ER had revealed the implant which had been installed for monitoring the prisoners while they were at Utopia. The doctor started asking questions about it. Laura had told him that it was a private medical issue, and that she didn't want to discuss it. After a few more prodding questions, the doctor finally let it drop.

They were all concerned that if they didn't get the devices removed, it might lead to their true identities being revealed and land them back in prison. They began discreetly searching for a good hospital somewhere other than the Cayman Islands where they could have the devices removed. The Caymans were too close to home and too many questions would be asked. It had to be somewhere else.

They finally located a good hospital in Costa Rica. Research had revealed that Costa Rica had some of the finest medical care in all of South America. The whole procedure would cost them each ten thousand dollars, plus the cost of the charter plane split three ways. They flew into San Jose on a Friday afternoon, spent the night in a hotel, and then had all three of their devices removed on the following day at a local clinic – no questions asked. One more day in town to monitor for any signs of infection, and it was back to George Town on Sunday.

All in all, life had been good for the three of them during these past eleven years since they had been kidnapped from Utopia. Not only had they escaped re-capture, but they had been able to build new and fulfilling lives in Grand Cayman and become good friends all around. They had no idea that their world was about to be turned upside down once more.

Chapter Thirty-Eight

Sasha's eighteenth birthday party had been a huge success. The party started out with a trip to the Trapeze School of New York, where Sasha and a group of her friends tried out swinging from the trapeze. Next, it was back to the Bartonovich's brownstone for a catered birthday lunch, complete with three-tiered birthday cake, presents, music, dancing – the whole nine yards. Lastly, they finished it off with a movie.

The following morning before breakfast, Nick and Mia asked Sasha to come into the library so that they could give her one last birthday present. They sat down around the coffee table and Nick placed a manila envelope on the table that had Sasha's name on it. Sasha was still on a party-high from the events of the day before and she was grinning from ear to ear.

"Thank you again for the party yesterday, Nick and Mia. It was the best birthday party ever."

Although it had been years since they had officially adopted her, she still preferred to call them by their first names. Mia could understand completely. No one could replace Sasha's mother, nor did she want to. She was just glad to be a part of Sasha's life.

"Sasha," Nick began, "I'm very glad you had a good day. We have one more present to give you, but it's not what you might expect. I have some very good news for you, but it also might be very difficult news."

Sasha looked from Mia to Nick and back, a quizzical expression on her face. "O.k., what is it?" she asked.

"When we adopted you, there were certain facts about your life that we didn't feel you needed to know at the time,"

Nick continued. "Mia and I talked about it and decided that you needed time to grieve and adjust to your new life before we told you. Due to other circumstances that will hopefully be clear in a few minutes, we decided it would be best to wait until you turned eighteen to tell you those details."

Sasha had moved to the edge of her seat with curiosity, wondering what was about to be revealed.

"Sasha, your biological father is still alive." Nick paused to let Sasha process what he had just said, knowing that her entire world would shift with the words he had just spoken.

"That can't be possible," a confused Sasha replied, "my father died in a car crash in Canada when I was a baby."

"Sasha," Nick continued, "I know this is hard to accept, but your mother didn't tell you the truth about your father."

"So you're saying Mom lied to me about my father's death? Why would she do that?" Sasha said, visibly upset.

"Look, I know this is a lot to process, but your mother had a very good reason for not telling you the truth about your father. Your father is a man named J.T. Thornbacker. When you were born, he had just been sent to prison for twenty-five years. He didn't even know your mother was pregnant with you. In fact, he doesn't even know you exist at this moment."

"I'm sure your mother just did it to protect you," Mia added, touching Sasha's hand gently as she spoke.

"Why did you guys wait so long to tell me?" Sasha asked, looking hurt.

Nick and Mia looked at each other.

"Your father is currently on the FBI's wanted list. He escaped from prison nine years ago," Mia answered.

Sasha's eyes widened and her mouth came open with a look of surprise.

"What?"

"I know it's a lot to take in. Everything you need to

know is in this envelope," Nick said, tapping the envelope on the coffee table with his finger. "Once you have had a chance to look over it, ask me anything you like."

"So no one knows where he is?" Sasha asked, picking up the folder and placing it in her lap.

"*We* know where he is, Sasha," Mia said.

Sasha looked at Mia with a mixture of surprise and bewilderment.

"He is living under an assumed name in another country," Nick went on. "We can arrange for you to meet him, but there are some complications. Because he is a wanted man, if the FBI finds out about him, he will go back to jail for the rest of his life."

Sasha stood up, clutching the manila envelope in both hands. She began backing away from Nick and Mia. She was upset, her brain not sure which question to ask first. Should she be mad at Nick and Mia, or her mom, or at anyone? She didn't know. Her thoughts were a jumble of emotion-filled firecrackers.

"I need some time to think," she said as she turned and practically ran out of the library and up the flight of stairs to her room. Nick and Mia heard the door slam.

Sasha sat down on her bed. She opened up the manila envelope and poured out the contents onto her bed. Her eye was caught by an 8 ½ by 11 inch photograph of J.T. Thornbacker. He was smiling as he faced the camera, and dressed in a three-piece suit. She went over to her mirror and held the picture beside her face as she peered into the mirror so she could see her image side by side with her father's. The resemblance was undeniable. She wondered when the picture had been taken.

There were various articles in the pile on her bed. One was about J.T. being appointed CEO of some company. Most of the others were about his arrest and trial for embezzling funds and various other illegal business practices. She read them all, devouring them for information about who her father was and what he was like. The last article was about J.T. Thornbacker's amazing escape from prison, along with two other prisoners. It detailed how the hideout that they had fled to after leaving prison had been discovered, and that all indications pointed to their plan to flee to Europe and live under false identities. She wondered how Nick and Mia had found him after all these years.

Before today, she had believed her father's name was Steven Byers, and that he'd been a school teacher who had died in a car crash in Canada. Today, she had learned that she had been lied to by both her mother and her adoptive parents about one of the biggest facts in her life. It was unsettling. The more she thought about it, the madder she became.

She needed someone she could talk to, someone she could trust. She called her best friend Marty to see if she could come over and talk.

"Hi Sasha," Marty answered.

"Hi Marty. Can I come over? I need to talk to you."

"Sure. What's up?"

"I can't talk about it on the phone and there's something I need to show you first."

"O.k. When do you want to come over?"

"I have to wait until the coast is clear. Maybe in about an hour?"

"No problem. Just text me when you leave to come over, o.k.?"

"O.k. See you soon."

She was taking a risk in talking to Marty about her real father. But she needed someone she could trust to listen to her. Right now, she was having some definite trust issues with Nick and Mia. Marty had been her best friend since grade school. She had been Sasha's confidant when her mom had died. If she couldn't trust Marty, then she couldn't trust anyone.

Sasha grabbed her backpack and tossed in a windbreaker, a flashlight, and her phone. She collected all of the papers spread out on her bed and put them back in the envelope, tossing that into the backpack too. Now all she had to do was wait until Nick and Mia went to bed. She didn't want them knowing where she was going and she certainly didn't want them asking a lot of questions or trying to stop her. She was eighteen, after all – old enough to do what she wanted.

Mia came and knocked on her door around 10:30 p.m.
"Yes?" Sasha responded.
"Are you o.k.?" Mia said without opening the door.
"Yeah, I'm o.k. I just want to be alone right now."
"O.k. If you need anything, just come and get me."
"Alright. Thanks."

Sasha heard Nick and Mia's bedroom door close down the hall. She waited another thirty minutes until she no longer heard any sounds coming from the direction of their bedroom. She slipped on her backpack and quietly opened the door, looking down the hall to make certain the light was off in her parents' room. She had practiced going downstairs without making a sound, marking each place she would need to step without making the floors creak. She paused before each floor to carefully peer around the wall separating the stairs from the rest of the floor before coming down to the landing, making sure Nick wasn't still up. She went all the way down to the basement, punched in the security code to turn off the alarm, and exited the door that led out to the sidewalk. She closed the door as quietly as she could, locking it with her key.

She started walking in the direction of Marty's house. She turned the corner and was about to walk past an alleyway when she was grabbed roughly from behind. She tried to scream, but there was a cloth over her mouth. As she inhaled, she felt weak and couldn't keep her eyes open. In seconds, she lost consciousness.

Silas McGruder dragged her into the alleyway, out of sight of anyone who might be passing by.

Chapter Thirty-Nine

Sasha's phone didn't have a password on it, which was good for Silas. That way, he didn't need to use the burn phone he had purchased to send a message to Nick Bartonovich. It was 6:00 a.m., time to get the ball rolling. Silas took a deep breath and exhaled it slowly. This text was about to start the events moving that he had planned for so long. He had checked and double-checked all of the details. Everything was in place. Now all he had to do was send this text.

He scrolled through Sasha's contacts and selected both Nick and Mia's numbers, and then he typed out the message:

> I have sasha. 10 million in cash, one hundred dollar notes, or you never see her again. Put the money in a big cooler with wheels on it. J t thornbacker must deliver the money. Will contact you in 24 hours to tell you where to meet me with the money. No cops or else.

He checked the message twice to make sure he had all the details right, then hit the send button. He then took a picture of Sasha, duct-taped to the captain's chair in the RV, and sent it through, as well. Once the message and picture were sent, he removed the phone's cover and popped out the battery. It was just a precaution so that they wouldn't be able to track the phone. He checked Sasha's restraints one more time before climbing in to the driver's seat of the RV and driving away.

As Silas drove along, he thought about the events that had led up to this moment, and a smile came across his face. All of the planning, all of the time spent surveilling and researching, the investment he had made in the miniature microphones that he had placed around the Bartonovich's house – it had all paid off. Now the brass ring was in sight.

Many months before, when Silas began to focus on Nick Bartonovich as the key to his future success, he had started looking for a way to spend more time staking out their house. He'd found a basement efficiency apartment on the opposite side of the street from the Bartonovich's home, down on the corner. It was the perfect place from which to surveil all of the comings and goings at their residence. Besides, he had needed a place to stay since he'd lost the house in the divorce.

He had purchased a set of high quality remotely accessible microphones that he was going to use to bug their house, but he needed a way to get inside undetected in order to plant them. One day, the HVAC company that the Bartonoviches used was out doing routine maintenance on their system. Silas was home and was watching the Bartonovich house that day. He noticed that Nick and Mia left together shortly after Sasha headed off to school, leaving the HVAC technician alone in the house. Silas had simply walked over with a box containing the bugs, tipped the HVAC tech a hundred dollars to let him in the house, and planted the bugs.

He had been settled on the kidnapping scheme for some time. He decided that nothing else would provide the leverage he needed to get what he wanted. He had everything planned out except how he was going to get Sasha alone so that he could grab her. Breaking into the house would set off the alarm, and doing something in broad daylight near their house was too risky. Then, when he had heard from the bug in Sasha's room about her plan to leave the house after dark without her parents' knowledge, that problem was solved. Finding out that J.T. Thornbacker was her father from the bug in the library was just icing on the cake. He couldn't resist using J.T. as the courier. The last thing Nick wanted was for J.T. to get caught by the cops – then he would be connected to the prison breakout he had orchestrated and go to jail. Every bit of insurance Silas could get to make certain the authorities stayed out of his way was welcome. Yes, this was going to be sweet revenge indeed.

Nick Bartonovich reached over to the night stand and picked up his phone. He looked down at the sender and wondered why Sasha was texting him this early in the morning from the next room. He opened the text and read the message. Then he saw the picture that came through next and he immediately jumped up out of bed, ran down the hall to Sasha's room, and threw open the door.

"Sasha!" Nick exclaimed. "Sasha, if this is a joke, it isn't funny. Where are you, sweetheart?" There was no answer.

By this time, Mia had put on her robe and was walking down the hall to Sasha's room.

"What is going on? Where is Sasha?"

Nick handed Mia his phone.

"Oh, my God!" Mia exclaimed.

Mia and Nick began a hurried search of the house, each of them calling her name as they checked each floor, hoping and praying this was all a joke. When they had gone through every room, they met back up in the kitchen. Nick placed his hands on Mia's shoulders and looked straight into her eyes to make certain he had her full attention.

"Mia, I need you to call the airport and have them get the plane fueled and ready to go to Grand Cayman. You stay here and get the money. I'll call you once I'm in the air and we can work out the details."

Nick dressed quickly and left the house for the airport. He pulled out his phone and dialed a number. It was 5:00 a.m. in the Cayman Islands, so it was a long shot that his office administrator would be awake, but he dialed anyway. It rang several times before finally going to voicemail.

"This is Nick Bartonovich. Drop everything you are doing and call me as soon as you get this message. This is an emergency."

He hit the disconnect icon on his phone. His mind was racing. How had Sasha been kidnapped? Why was J.T. being pulled into this? He could only speculate at this point as he drove as fast as he could to reach the airport.

When Sasha came to, she was sitting in a captain's chair in the back of an RV. Her hands and feet were duct-taped to the chair, and her mouth was gagged. She could tell by the road noise that the RV was on the move. The drapes on the windows were all drawn, and a curtain which separated the cab of the RV from the rest of the vehicle was also drawn. She could hear country music playing on the radio.

She began breathing faster as the fear hit her. She tried desperately to break free of her restraints and to scream. After a few minutes of struggling, she realized that she was getting nowhere, and stopped pulling against the restraints. She started looking around to see what information she could gather from her environment that might help her escape or notify someone that she was a captive.

It was an hour or more before the RV slowed to a stop. Sasha could hear the driver getting up from the driver's seat. She heard the curtain rustle as the driver stepped back into the main cabin. Sasha's chair was turned to face the rear of the vehicle, so she couldn't yet see her kidnapper. A mixture of fear and curiosity gripped her as she waited to see who it was and what they would do next. Silas stepped in front of Sasha and sat down on the couch across from her.

"I'm glad to see you are awake," Silas began. "I'm not planning on hurting you, Sasha. You are simply a means to an end. You see, your daddy has a lot of money. And he owes me. But what you need to know right now is that, as long as you do what I tell you to do, I won't hurt you. On the other hand, if you try to escape or start screaming, then I will hurt you. Do we understand each other?"

Sasha nodded her head up and down to indicate that she understood.

"Good. Right now, we are off of the interstate and pulled over on a side road. There's nobody here to hear you if you scream, so don't even try it. I'm going to let you go now so that you can go to the restroom here in the RV and get something to eat and drink. If you cooperate with me, this doesn't have to be a horrible experience."

Silas produced a knife and began cutting away the restraints from one foot, then the other. He did the wrists last, letting Sasha remove the gag herself. Sasha eyed him warily the entire time, wondering if he was going to assault her or if he was telling the truth. She massaged her wrists where the duct tape had been constricting the blood flow as she walked over to the lavatory.

The bathroom ventilation window was too small for her to fit through and the privacy glass obstructed her view, but she was able to get a look at the surrounding area. All she saw was the woods. After she had relieved herself, she began looking around for anything she might use as a weapon or to cut the duct tape with, but she didn't find anything. She finally decided that she couldn't stay in the bathroom forever and came back out.

True to his word, there was a bottle of water and a pre-packaged sandwich sitting on the table for her when she came out. Silas motioned for her to sit down opposite him, where the food was placed, and she complied. She ate the sandwich, which tasted just shy of edible, and drank half of the water before Silas looked at his watch.

"O.k., time's up, back in the chair; we have a long way

to go yet."

"Where are you taking me?" Sasha asked.

"Don't you worry your pretty little head about that," Silas replied.

Sasha thought about making a break for the door on the way back to the chair, but Silas had positioned himself strategically in front of the door as he motioned for her to sit back down in the captain's chair. She reluctantly complied and sat back down. He picked up the duct tape and began securing her to the chair once more. When he was done with the duct tape and gag, he went back to the front of the RV and soon they were back on their way to wherever it was that they were going. As they drove down the road once more, Sasha prayed to God that Nick and Mia would give this man whatever he wanted so that he would let her go back to her family.

Chapter Forty

Nick Bartonovich exited the plane practically jogging down the steps to the awaiting car. Tammy, his local office administrator, was sitting in the back seat. The driver opened the back door for Nick and then sprinted around the front of the car to the driver's side. Nick had prepped Tammy on the phone about what he needed done while he was in the air. He turned to her as soon as the door was shut, hoping everything was taken care of.

"Give me a status report," Nick said.

"He is in the house out on Rum Point. I have a local resource out there right now watching him. Sam was seen this morning watering his garden and hasn't left the house since," she reported.

"Good work, Tammy. Jared," Nick said, addressing the driver, "I want you to come with me to the door just in case the greeting is less than amicable."

Jared nodded as he glanced at Nick's face in the rearview mirror. Jared was one of a few local heavies that worked for Nick from time to time as drivers and/or security personnel. He was a first-rate martial artist, not to mention that he was also a body builder who could probably bench-press a small car.

It took less than fifteen minutes to arrive at the house. Nick didn't wait for Jared to come around and open his door. He exited the car and briskly walked up the ramp to the side door of the house. Jared had to jog the first few steps to catch up. Nick rang the doorbell and looked down at his watch impatiently as he waited for someone to answer the door.

J.T. had just finished his morning coffee and was about to log in to his online brokerage account to check on his investments when he heard the door ring. He glanced over at the security camera monitor that he had installed on the side of his desk before getting up. When he saw who it was, he couldn't believe his eyes. He switched the view on the monitor to single out that lone camera for magnification, just to make certain. His heart started beating faster. He grabbed his cell phone and quickly sent out a text, and then he opened a side drawer and pulled out a Smith and Wesson .45 caliber revolver before he went to answer the door.

    Nick was reaching his finger down to depress the doorbell once more when the door finally opened. J.T. was standing there with the gun in one hand, pointed down at the floor. He said nothing, but stared at Nick warily, waiting.

    "Hello J.T.," Nick said without smiling, "I need your help."

    J.T. was shocked a bit at Nick's introduction. This wasn't the Nick he knew from years before, who demanded cooperation at the point of a gun.

    "What are you doing here, Nick?"

    Nick reached his hand into his coat jacket pocket. J.T. started to raise the pistol and Jared started to grab Nick to pull him to the side of the door, out of range of the gun. Nick put out his free hand and said, "Hold on, I'm just going to retrieve my phone."

    Once J.T. lowered the gun, Nick slowly retrieved his cell phone and pulled up a picture of Sasha. The resemblance to J.T. was unmistakable. He turned the phone around and handed it to J.T.

    "J.T., this is your daughter, Sasha. She is also my adopted daughter. She has been kidnapped, and I need your help to get her back safely."

    J.T. slowly reached forth his hand and took the cell phone from Nick. He looked down at the face smiling back at him on the phone and felt like he had been hit with a sucker-punch in the stomach.

"Come in," he said as he turned around, still clutching the phone in one hand and the gun in the other.

He walked slowly over to the couch. Once they were seated on the couch, J.T. took his eyes off of the phone and looked up at Nick.

"This is impossible. This is a young woman. She would've been born sometime when I was in prison," J.T. said.

"True," Nick replied.

"Assuming this is true," J.T. continued, regaining some of his composure, "who is the mother?"

"Katrina Byers."

J.T.'s mind recalled back almost nineteen years before, to when he had met a young woman who'd worked for Nick. She was an accountant who would give J.T. information from Nick that was deemed too sensitive for email or other forms of communication. They had hit it off instantly. She was funny and vivacious, full of life. J.T. asked her out to dinner after their second meeting. It was a risk that they might be seen together and his connection with Nick might be discovered, but she was worth it.

Then the investigation began. Nick and J.T. terminated communication with each other. They wanted to avoid being discovered working together, bilking the company that J.T. was currently working for as a CEO. He and Katrina continued to meet on the weekends at a hideaway in the countryside so they wouldn't be discovered together. During one of their rendezvous, Katrina had asked J.T. what he thought about starting a family one day and what he thought about children. J.T., always the self-confident, self-centered business man, told her that he didn't think that would fit in with his plans. He didn't want children, he said.

He remembered the fight they had after he made that statement. She accused him of not loving her. He said that he wanted to be with her, but that love, marriage, children –

those weren't things he was interested in. She stormed out of the house and drove back home that night. J.T. tried to contact her, but she didn't return his calls. Shortly after, he was arrested, and he never heard from her again.

"How do I know you are telling the truth and that this isn't just another one of your scams?" J.T. said warily. "And if this girl whom you claim is my daughter is in so much trouble, why isn't Katrina here to help convince me all of this is true?" he demanded.

"Katrina is dead, J.T." Nick replied somberly.

J.T. could tell Nick was telling the truth. Nick was many things, but in all the years he had known Nick, J.T. could never remember one time that Nick had lied to him.

"How?" he asked.

"Kidney failure. She died eight years ago. It's a long story that I don't have time to get into, but Mia and I got married. We helped watch Sasha when Katrina was sick. Katrina asked us to adopt her when she knew she wasn't going to make it. We did. It's all here." Nick put his briefcase on the table and opened it up, dumping out a set of papers that included Sasha's birth certificate, the adoption papers, pictures of Sasha with Katrina, Katrina's death certificate, and pictures of Mia, Nick, and Sasha together. He waited as J.T. looked through the information. Finally, J.T. looked up at Nick.

"This isn't the Nick Bartonovich that I knew," he said finally.

Nick paused, trying to decide how to best answer that charge. Honesty, he decided, was the best approach. "Look," he began, "I got cancer. I had an operation followed by a long recovery...it changed me."

J.T. was looking straight into Nick's eyes, looking for some sign of deception.

"If I could go back and do things differently... there are a lot of things I would change," Nick continued, "but right now, I don't have time to go through all of that. Sasha needs our help and I'm asking you to please help me."

J.T. picked up a portrait-sized picture of Sasha. He could see the eyebrows and mouth were his, no doubt. The nose was thankfully Katrina's. He remembered Katrina's perky nose. He smiled. If there was any way this girl was his, and she certainly looked like she was, then there was no way in hell he was going to pass up the chance to help her. He wanted to get to know her, to make sure she was o.k., and to have some kind of relationship with her.

"O.k.," he said, still looking at the picture. "Tell me what I need to do."

"The kidnapper wants a ransom and says that you must be the one to deliver it. He will call in about eighteen hours to give more details. No police or else. I need you to come back to the States with me. I have a plane waiting at the airport for us now."

J.T., still looking at the picture, began to nod. "O.k., but I have a request, too," he said.

"Name it," Nick replied.

"James and Laura will be coming with us."

"I hardly see how they can help," Nick replied.

J.T. looked up at Nick with determination in his eyes.

"Eight years ago, you used me to take almost eighty million dollars out of a bank, leaving me a fugitive from my own country and living under a false identity. Now you waltz in here and tell me I have a daughter that you have known about for years but haven't bothered to tell me about until now. In addition to that, you want me to risk going back to prison for the rest of my life to help get her back from a kidnapper."

"Back Stateside, you have money, power, resources, everything. You have your own network of contacts and hired hands. James and Laura *are* my network. They are the people I have had to rely on for years. We trust each other with our lives because we can't fully trust anyone else. I'm willing to take it on faith that this girl is who you say she is. I'm willing to go out on a limb and believe you don't have some scheme up your sleeve to lure me back to the States and turn me over to the feds. Now I'm asking you to trust me a little bit and bring Laura and James along to help out. I trust them, and if everything is what you say it is, we need people we can trust to help us out on this."

"O.k., I hear what you are saying," Nick replied. "If you think they can help, then bring them along, but we need to leave soon. She may be your biological daughter, but she is my adopted daughter and I love her very much. The clock is ticking and we need to get moving. Where are they and when can they get here?"

J.T. went to his office to retrieve his cell phone. He called James and Laura on a three-way call. Once he had them both on the line, he briefly explained the situation and asked them if they would consider coming back to the States with him to help get his daughter back.

"Wow," Laura exclaimed. "That is a huge bombshell, J.T. I don't want to be the black cloud here, but are you *sure* she's your daughter?"

"Well, the paperwork looks authentic enough, and then there's the pictures. She's not my spitting image, but the resemblance is pretty strong. I think there is a good chance Nick is telling the truth. Besides, he could have turned me in at any time in the last eight years if he wanted to, or sent his goons to kidnap me again, for that matter. Nick's changed too, he's different somehow. Strange as it is for me to say this, I think I trust him on this one."

"Well, if you feel that confident about it, I'm in," Laura replied.

"What about you, James?" J.T. asked.

"With all we've been through, I'm not about to let you two go back to the States alone. I'd be glad to help you out,

J.T. Just tell me when and where."

"Be at the airport in twenty minutes. I'll text you the gate info on the way."

J.T. threw some items in a backpack and headed out the door with Nick. Thirty minutes later, James, Laura, J.T., and Nick were on an airplane and headed back to New York.

Chapter Forty-One

Silas pulled in to Toakama, West Virginia at about 10 a.m. in the morning. He pulled the RV behind one of the abandoned buildings and shut off the engine. It had been a long day. He cut Sasha loose so she could go to the facilities and eat something, then secured her back to the captain's chair with a generous amount of duct tape. She would be uncomfortable and probably wouldn't sleep much through the night, but she was young and would be fine after a day's rest back home in her comfy bed in New York City.

Toakama was an abandoned mining town in the middle of nowhere. It had been a thriving little town until the mine shut down after an explosion that had killed twenty workers back in the 1950s. The mining company had shut down the mine and moved the workers to a more profitable location about a hundred miles away. A few residents stayed around, but without anyone to support the local businesses, eventually everyone had either died or moved away.

There was only one road leading into the little town, making it perfect for this ransom exchange. The road was about three quarters of a mile long and terminated in a cul-de-sac that served to allow people to turn their vehicles around and head back out of town. The road into town crossed over a fifty-foot gorge just before the city limits. The gorge had a bucolic stream flowing at the bottom of it and the whole town was surrounded by forest. The mountains rose behind the town, leading further up into the Blue Ridge Mountains. A post office, a barber shop, a grocery store, a hardware store, a diner, and even a small town hall at the end of the street were among the various brick buildings that lined the main street that was Toakama.

Silas had liked hiking since he was a kid. He had discovered this place on a hiking trip that he had taken years before. Being in the great outdoors helped him clear his head. When he had begun to plan the kidnapping, this was the first place that came to his mind as a potential exchange location. It was perfect. It was surrounded by rugged terrain, he could see anyone trying to enter the town on the one road in or out, and you could hear a pin drop in the deserted streets. The buildings offered perfect cover so he could watch the whole drop-off without being seen. And best of all, it was in the middle of nowhere, with the next populated town being twenty-five miles away.

He reached into the refrigerator and pulled out a six-pack of beer, then headed up the hill about a hundred yards. From this spot, he could see the RV and the whole town below. He popped the top on the first beer and enjoyed the view. Not too long from now, he was going to be a very rich man. He smiled at the thought and took a drink from the can.

After he had finished three beers, he went back into the RV and took a nap in the back. Later in the day, he would have to double check on all the preparations he'd already made, and there was no sense being tired when he did so. He slept like a stone and dreamt of buying a nice house somewhere in a tropical island, and being reunited with Maggie and Tommy when this was all over.

He woke up about two hours later, feeling an intense need to relieve himself. He went outside and up the hill a few yards behind a tree and took care of business. He thought to himself that he felt like a million dollars. Then he laughed and said out loud, "I feel like *ten* million dollars!"

Before he made his rounds to check on all of the items he had prepared for the ransom exchange, he went back into the RV and took Sasha's gag off to give her a drink of water. After all, he told himself, he was no monster. When that task was done, he went to work.

He walked behind the row of buildings on the upperside of the town's main street. He could see the tarpaulin-covered Jeep from where the RV was parked. It looked just the way he had left it a few months before, except for the generous dusting of pine needles and small twigs on top of the tarpaulin.

After he removed the cover, he reached far under the seat and retrieved the keys, checking first to make certain there were no black widows or other creatures lurking underneath. He popped the hood, connected the battery, and jumped in the driver's seat. He had brought an extra battery just in case, but he hoped he wouldn't need it. He turned the key and the engine tried to turn over twice, then roared to life. He smiled. Everything was going according to plan.

He un-holstered his .38 revolver, which he carried in a shoulder sling, and checked the ammunition. It was good to be prepared when you were in the woods by yourself. You never knew who, or *what*, you might run into. He left the jeep running to warm up the engine and went back inside to get Sasha. He walked her out and put her in the passenger's seat, leaving her hands bound and putting on the seatbelt for her. He couldn't afford to leave her here alone – she was his ten million dollar ticket.

He climbed up in the driver's seat and put the Jeep in gear, driving up a mountainside road that looked like little more than a trail. He needed to make sure this old logging road hadn't been blocked by any fallen trees during his absence. It would be a shame to get stuck trying to remove a tree from across the road with ten million dollars in the back of his vehicle. He was under no illusions about what he was about to do. He knew Nick Bartonovich would come after him as soon as he knew his daughter was safe. Having a quick escape route available was essential.

He drove for about thirty minutes up the winding road before he had to stop and remove a small tree that had fallen across the pathway. Luckily for him, it had cracked in two when it hit the road, making it easy to roll out of the way and down the hill into the woods to the left of the road. He had a small chain saw in the back of the jeep in case he needed it, but rolling the broken parts of the tree downhill was even easier. He got back in the Jeep and drove for a few more minutes without encountering any obstacles, and decided he had come far enough. He turned the Jeep around and headed back to town.

Back at the RV, he let Sasha sit at the table inside while he cooked some hamburgers for them on the stove. He waited to remove the duct tape from her hands until they were ready to eat, just in case. She ate like a horse. Silas thought to himself that it must be the mountain air. He was hungrier than usual himself and cooked them both another hamburger.

"You eat pretty good for a girl," Silas said, putting down the second hamburger in front of Sasha.

"Thanks for the second hamburger," she said as she began eating. "Why are you doing this?" she said at last.

Silas looked up at her from his hamburger and smiled, "You mean, besides the money?"

"Yeah, I guess," she replied hesitantly.

"It's complicated. I gambled, I lost a lot of money on a crooked gambling site that your dad ran, I lost a good job, my wife left me, yada, yada, yada." He took another bite from his hamburger and washed it down with a swig of beer. Sasha didn't say anything, just waited.

"I guess at some point I decided that I deserved a better hand than the one I had been dealt. I was a cop, at one time, and I saw a lot of crooked guys get away with a lot of money while I was keeping the law and struggling to pay the mortgage." He shrugged his shoulders. "So I decided it was my turn to walk away with some of that money."

He looked at Sasha. "It's nothing against you, but whether you know it or not, Nick and J.T. Thornbacker didn't get rich because they were nice guys. This money they are paying me with was stolen from some other people."

Sasha's anger got the better of her and she said without thinking, "Nick is not a crook!"

Silas looked at her for a minute before he spoke. "Listen, Sasha, I don't expect you to agree with me. But enough about me, it's time for dessert."

Silas went to the refrigerator and took two ice cream bars out of the freezer, handing one to Sasha before sitting back down at the table. She took it from him and opened it up, thinking how strange it was for this man who had just kidnapped her to be giving her ice cream. They ate dessert together in silence.

After they were finished, Silas said, "O.k., time for you to go back in the chair. I can't have you running off now, can I? Go to the bathroom first, though; it may be a while before you get a chance to go again."

Sasha reluctantly got up to go to the tiny RV bathroom. Silas remained in his seat while she did. When she came out, Silas was still seated, finishing up his beer. She walked over in the direction of the captain's chair, resigned to being restrained with duct tape again. When she got close to the door and noticed Silas wasn't out of his seat yet, she suddenly saw an opportunity to escape. She lunged for the door, opened it up, and dashed outside before Silas could stop her.

Silas realized his mistake too late, jumping up and heading out the door, running after her. Sasha had a good head-start on him of about fifteen feet. Silas had never been much of a runner, and he knew he couldn't outrun her if all things were equal. Just as Sasha began opening up a bigger lead, she tripped on the exposed root system of a large oak tree and fell down. Silas didn't miss his opportunity, closing the distance between them before Sasha regained her traction.

He reached down and grabbed her arm. Sasha turned and bit him as hard as she could. Silas released her and let out a yell, but he shot out his leg and kicked her in the stomach before she could stand up. She buckled to the ground with a groan as Silas briefly looked at his bleeding hand to assess the damage. Silas' days as a cop subduing suspects on the streets of New York had been fine-tuned over the years. No uptown socialite teenager was going to get the better of him in a street brawl.

Sasha sat up on the ground, trying to breathe and stand up at the same time. Silas' anger got the better of him and he stepped forward and back-handed her hard across the face with the same hand she had just bitten. Sasha went down like a sack of potatoes, letting out a whimper as she hit the ground. Silas didn't wait for her to regain her footing or even sit up. He grabbed her by the forearm and began dragging her back to the RV.

"I told you that you would get hurt if you tried to get away, didn't I? Why did you have to go and do that?! Huh?!"

By the time they had reached the door of the RV, Sasha had still not regained her footing. Silas grabbed the top of her pants from behind with one hand and the back of her shirt with the other, lifting her up onto her feet and pushing her into the RV. Sasha collapsed onto her hands and knees on the floor.

Silas stepped into the RV and shouted at her, pointing to the captain's chair, "Get in the chair!"

Sasha practically crawled up in the chair. She was bleeding from her lip and her left eye had already started to swell up. Tears were coming down her face as Silas busied himself taping her hands and feet into position. When he was done taping her to the chair, Silas grabbed another beer from the refrigerator and stormed out of the RV.

Chapter Forty-Two

The airplane ride back to New York was filled with activity. After an awkward first greeting between Nick, James, and Laura, Nick began a briefing that covered everything he had told J.T. Once James and Laura were up to speed, Nick began making phone calls.

He first called Mia to make certain she had obtained the required ten million in one hundred dollar notes, as the kidnapper had specified. She confirmed that all was ready. The next call he placed was to someone that J.T. knew from personal experience – bad personal experience.

"Victor, I need your assistance on an important job.... Yes, we leave tomorrow morning at 6:00 a.m. This is not the usual job. It is a rescue of sorts. It seems some lunatic has decided to kidnap my daughter.... Yes, the usual fee, plus a bonus when she is returned unharmed. A six man team would be fine.... We don't know yet where it will be. I suggest you have your plane fueled up and ready to go anywhere. Oh, and Victor, you remember that job a few years back in the Cayman Islands? Well, those three will be joining us.... Yes, life is strange sometimes. It's a long story and I don't have time to tell you now, but suffice it to say that this time we are all working together.... O.k., I'll call you at this number as soon as I have more details."

Nick disconnected the phone.

"You're still hiring that mercenary to do work for you?" J.T. asked.

"Yes, he's the best. As you know from personal experience, he gets the job done," Nick replied without his usual sly smile.

"I thought you said the kidnapper said no cops? How

do you think he is going to react to a bunch of commandos armed to the teeth showing up on the scene?" J.T. queried.

"Probably not very well if he ever sees they are around, but I'm not prepared to depend solely on the promises of an unscrupulous kidnapper for Sasha's safe return. I'm planning on being prepared."

"I can't argue with that. Just make sure these guys stay out of sight unless we need them. We don't need the kidnapper or kidnappers to be spooked and do something crazy. By the way. Do we know anything more about him/her/them?"

"Nothing," Nick replied. "I received the message on Sasha's phone and the battery was taken out shortly thereafter, preventing us from tracing the call."

J.T. turned to James and Laura. "Thanks for coming, you two. I needed to have some familiar faces backing me up on this," he said.

"Don't mention it," James replied. "Business down at the shop was getting a bit slow anyway," he continued with a smile.

"Yeah, besides, it will be good to see if these fake IDs are as good as Nick said they were," Laura quipped.

The plane landed at the airport and everyone filed into an awaiting SUV once they had de-planed. James, Laura, and J.T. were relieved that they were able to avoid any scrutiny of their documents for the time being. They sped along the highway and into the city, arriving at the Bartonovich residence in early afternoon.

When they entered the house. Nick greeted Mia, who was busy packing the ten million dollars into an oversized cooler. with Marcus' help. Nick skipped the awkward introductions and instead offered everyone some lunch. Mia had ordered some gourmet sandwiches, which were already laid out on the dining room table.

J.T. noticed that both Nick and Mia checked their phones frequently. He assumed they were checking to see if the kidnapper had provided any additional instructions. Once the money was packed, the cooler full of cash was rolled in to a closet until it was needed.

After lunch, Nick showed J.T., Laura, and James to the downstairs guest bedrooms where they would be spending the night, and then everyone migrated up to the library. Drinks were served to everyone as they prepared to pass the anxious hours until the kidnapper sent further instructions.

"Nick," J.T. said, "I'd like to see Sasha's room, if that's o.k."

Nick looked up, as if he was caught off-guard by the request. He turned to look at Mia in order to ascertain what she felt about it.

"I'll take you up," Mia said in response.

J.T. walked slowly into the room, taking his time, looking around at everything and soaking it all in. There were traces left of the girl Sasha had been when she'd first moved in to the room. A plastic pony, some softball trophies, a few books that an eight-year-old girl might read intermixed with more recent teenage selections. He walked over to the desk that now held a laptop. He looked down at pictures of Sasha and her friends from school. There were freshly opened presents piled high in one corner of the room, remnants of the birthday party the day before she'd been kidnapped. He picked up a picture of Sasha from the table. He held it in both hands as he sat down on the bed and began to cry.

Mia was watching the whole scene from the doorway. When J.T. started to cry, she turned to walk away, intending to give him some privacy.

"No, wait," J.T. said as Mia turned to go. "I'd like you to stay. I want to know more about her...about Sasha."

Mia turned back around, taking a look around the

room herself as if to conjure up in her mind memories from the day before, when Sasha had been in the room.

"Sasha is a very strong person. A free spirit. She loves to ride horses and take risks. She reminds me of you, in many ways."

J.T. looked up at Mia. "I wish you would have told me about her sooner," he said.

"We did what we thought was best," Mia replied.

"I guess my sins are catching up to me," J.T. continued. "All those years when I took from others things that were important to them. Now the most important person in the world to me has been temporarily taken away from me before I even got a chance to meet her, and I'll do anything to get her back."

Mia crossed the room and put a hand on J.T.'s shoulder. She looked him straight in the eyes with that determined, steely look that only Mia could deliver as she said, "We *will* get her back."

The remainder of the evening was uneventful as everyone stayed in the house in case the kidnapper contacted them. No one was very hungry after the late lunch they had consumed, so they ate a light dinner consisting of soup and crackers. After they had finished eating, Nick turned on the sports channel as he, Mia, and J.T. reclined in the game room. He and Mia continued to check their phones alternately every few minutes. Finally, Mia went to walk on the treadmill to burn off the nervous energy that was building up as they waited for the next communication, leaving J.T. and Nick to pretend to watch sports.

James and Laura wandered up to the library where James retrieved a copy of *The Adventures of Huckleberry Finn* and picked up reading where he had left off a few days before. Laura retrieved her Kindle from her backpack and pulled up a new book she had just downloaded about stained glass. They curled up next to each other on the couch in the library as they read, just like they liked to do back home.

By 10 p.m., everyone was ready for bed. Nick promised he would wake J.T. as soon as further instructions were delivered, and everyone went off to their rooms for the night. J.T. lay awake for about an hour, thinking of the amazing fact that he had a daughter who was eighteen who he had never met. He prayed to God that she would be returned unharmed tomorrow before he finally drifted off to a fitful sleep.

Chapter Forty-Three

J.T., Nick, and Mia were all dressed for the day and assembled in the kitchen by 5:00 a.m. Both Nick and Mia's phones lay on the kitchen table. Marcus hung back in the corner, trying not to intrude. Nick made a pot of coffee for everyone while they waited anxiously for the message they were all expecting. James and Laura wandered groggily into the kitchen at 5:30 a.m., still in their p.j.s. Laura began nursing a cup of coffee like it was a spiritual experience. It was like a séance as they all took up places around the kitchen table and stared at the phones, willing the phones to communicate with them. No one was willing to speak out loud and break the silence.

At 5:50 a.m., James whispered into Laura's ear, "I'm going to go get dressed; things are probably going to hit the fan in a few minutes when the kidnappers call, and we should be ready to go." With that, he headed back downstairs as quietly as possible. Laura took the remainder of her coffee and chugged it, then made her exit as well.

A few minutes later, both phones buzzed almost simultaneously, indicating a message had been delivered. Nick and Mia both grabbed their respective phones and opened the text message that had just been delivered. J.T. quickly came around behind Nick as they all read the message simultaneously in silence.

> Toakama, WV. 12 pm noon EST. Bring the cash in the cooler with wheels with the lid duct taped shut. Only j.t. crosses the bridge into town alone with the cash. He will walk down the main street to the end. Further instructions will be given to him then. Give him one of these

phones. No tricks or else.

The message was followed by another picture of Sasha, with a copy of a Roanoke, West Virginia newspaper from the day before featured prominently so that the date could be seen.

"Mia, find the nearest airport to Toakama and get the plane ready," Nick said urgently.

"I'm on it," Mia replied. She went over to the kitchen computer desk and sat down to search for the airport.

Nick speed-dialed Victor.

"Victor, the exchange is at 12 p.m. noon, Eastern Standard Time, in Toakama, West Virginia. We'll be flying in to the nearest airport at..." He looked over at Mia.

"Roanoke, West Virginia," Mia said.

"Roanoke, West Virginia. I'll call you once we are in the air to coordinate where to meet. I'll get us three SUVs to use. I'm forwarding you the message we received from the kidnapper right now. Don't be late, Victor, I'm counting on you."

Nick hit the disconnect icon on his phone.

"Meet at the car out front in five minutes," Nick said as he rose quickly from the table and left the room.

J.T. went down the stairs to the recreation room and repeated Nick's announcement to James and Laura in a loud voice, "Meet at the car out front in five minutes."

The trip to the airport seemed to take an eternity. Once they arrived, they quickly boarded the plane. Soon after, they were up in the air on their way to Roanoke, West Virginia.

Silas had reviewed the message carefully before hitting the send key. He waited to make certain the message was delivered before he shut the phone off and removed the battery. Cell coverage had come a long way since the early days. Still, he'd had to climb to the roof of one of the abandoned buildings to get even one bar in order to send the message.

He went back down to the RV and began to cut Sasha loose so that she could go to the bathroom and eat some breakfast. The swelling from where he had hit her on her face had mostly gone down. There was a bump on her lip and the cut had scabbed over during the night. Her eye had a bruise under it, too.

Silas stepped back from the chair and stood with his back to the door, facing Sasha, and cutting off any hope of escape.

"Now, go to the bathroom and then sit down over there for some breakfast," he said.

Sasha dutifully complied, not seeing any opening to try for another escape. When she came out of the bathroom, Silas motioned to the seat at the table farthest away from the door, where a bottle of water and a breakfast bar were placed on the table top. Sasha sat down and began eating.

"You know, you don't have that much longer to be here. Your dad will be bringing the money at noon, and you'll be going home. So don't try anything else, o.k.?"

Sasha continued to eat without saying anything. When she was done, Silas stood, blocking the door again, and motioned with his head to the captain's chair. Sasha went over and sat down for their now practiced routine as Silas secured her to the chair with yet more duct tape. Once that was done, he exited the RV to complete the preparations for the arrival of J.T. and the money.

Victor was waiting at the airport when Nick and company de-planed. Once they had rented the SUVs and exited the airport grounds, Victor told them to pull over next to a mini-van taxi that was waiting on the side of the road. The five other men from his team exited the taxi and loaded several large black duffel bags into the back of the SUVs. Victor got in the vehicle with Nick, Mia, and J.T.

The caravan took off, following a route that Nick had already laid out to their destination. He had printed off a map on the printer while they were flying, just in case the GPS on the SUV malfunctioned for some reason. He was leaving nothing to chance.

Victor turned to J.T. and held out a small black box with some wires extending out of it.

"This is a two-way radio transmitter. I'm going to put it on you so we can communicate while you make the drop. This piece goes in your ear so we can talk to you, and this piece will be positioned near your collar so that we can pick up anything you say."

"O.k.," J.T. replied as he watched Victor hold up the various parts of the device.

"Now take off your shirt so I can tape everything in place."

J.T. removed his shirt and Victor began securing the various wires and the box with a special type of tape. He placed the earbud in J.T.'s ear and worked the wire into place so that it was less visible. After he was done, he flipped a switch on the black box, and then he put on his headset and told J.T. to say something.

"Check, check," J.T. said into the microphone.

"That's good," Victor said. "I'm going to tap on this microphone; tell me if you hear it in your earpiece."

Victor tapped on the microphone and J.T. heard the soft tap-tap sound in his earpiece.

"I hear it," he replied.

"O.k., when you walk down the street into town, speak out anything that might seem out of the ordinary, anything that seems out of place. We may not be able to get eyes on you, depending on where we are positioned. If things go bad and you need us to come in after you, just let us know over the mic," Victor concluded.

It was one hundred and thirty miles from Roanoke to Toakama. The winding mountain roads slowed down their average speed to around forty-five miles an hour. It was almost twelve when they approached the bridge that crossed in to Toakama. Victor instructed Nick to pull off the road right before the bridge. He had studied the aerial photographs available on the internet and seen that, after crossing the bridge, the road took a sharp turn left. They would then be inside the town limits.

"We go on foot from here," Victor said. "Be quiet when we get out of the car, we don't want them to think we came in with this many people. Let's hope they don't have eyes on us already."

Once they exited the vehicles, Victor turned to his team and gave them hand signals indicating they should switch on their two-way radios and stay silent. The men quietly complied. Two men opened up the duffle bags and began handing out the weapons they had brought along, including two sniper rifles. They all put on camouflage hats and face paint. The team assembled next to Victor near the lead SUV at 11:57 a.m. Two of the commandos unloaded the cooler with the ten million dollars and put it beside J.T.

Victor handed Nick, Mia, James, and Laura two-way radios so that they could all communicate. He told them to leave the radios on so that they could hear if he needed them to bring the SUVs up to their position quickly. Nick walked over and handed J.T. his phone.

"Take this. The kidnapper said you should have it for the drop. Be careful out there, J.T.; Sasha is counting on you."

J.T. nodded his head, then picked up the handle and began pulling the two-wheeled cooler behind him as he approached the bridge. Three commandos followed on one side of the road, three on the other. Nick, Mia, Laura, and James all stayed behind in the SUVs so they could quickly drive into town should they be needed.

The bridge was barely a hundred feet long. The frame was made of steel, with wooden cross-planks that served as the road surface. The steel was rusted with patches of the original red paint still visible here and there. The wood looked sturdy enough in most places, but J.T. noticed several spots where it had begun to rot. The cool mountain air and the sound of the stream running under the bridge provided a peaceful setting, but J.T. was sweating nervously as he stepped off of the bridge and began walking slowly around the corner.

Victor and his men had quietly slipped off of the road and into the woods as J.T. rounded the corner and the first buildings came in to view. The sign on the side of the road read, *Welcome to Toakama, population 312.*

"Just keep walking down the center of the road slowly. We'll keep eyes on you from here," J.T. heard Victor say through the earpiece in his ear.

J.T.'s heart was beating faster as he continued walking down the road into Toakama, and he wondered what was going to happen next.

Chapter Forty-Four

Silas saw J.T. Thornbacker through his binoculars as he rounded the corner from the bridge to Toakama at 12:03 p.m. He appeared to be alone and pulling the cooler filled with cash, but Silas knew better than to think that Nick didn't have some hired guns nearby. Fortunately for Silas, he was prepared for such an eventuality.

It took J.T. the better part of five minutes to walk the entire length of the street and arrive at the cul-de-sac at the end. When he arrived there, he saw a chair with a note taped to it and a cable with a hook on the end which led off to the right-hand side, through an alleyway and behind a building. The note read: *Hook the cable to the handle of the cooler, then back away from the chair ten paces and wait for further instructions.*

J.T. read the note out loud for the benefit of the listeners on the other end of the two-way radio, and then he took the rope and tied it to the cooler as indicated, backing off ten paces as instructed when he was done. Once he began backing away from the cooler, he heard a distant whining sound and the cable grew taught as the cooler began moving along the ground and down the alleyway, out of sight from where J.T. was now standing. About a minute later, the whining stopped.

Silas un-hooked the cooler from the winch and cut the tape so that he could open the lid. He smiled as he saw bundles of one hundred dollar bills. He took one out and examined it more closely to make certain that it was a genuine one hundred dollar bill. He was no treasury agent, but he had gotten pretty good as a cop in telling the genuine article from a counterfeit. Satisfied it was the real thing, he re-taped the cooler top closed and pushed it up into the back of the Jeep via the ply-wood ramp he had constructed, securing it with several elastic tie-downs for safety. He glanced down the alleyway to ensure that no one was there before he got into the Jeep and started the engine. He reached over to where Sasha was seated in the passenger's seat and cut loose the duct-tape from her feet. Then he cut her hands loose from the tape that held them to a bar that ran along the side of the doorframe of the jeep.

"Get out and go down the alleyway; your father is waiting for you," Silas ordered.

Sasha got out of the car and began running down the alleyway, tearing the tape away from her mouth as she ran, and yelling, "I'm here! I'm down here!"

Silas gunned the engine of the Jeep and headed up the old mining road, out of town and in the opposite direction from where Sasha was running.

When J.T. heard Sasha calling out, he ran towards the alleyway and towards Sasha. He immediately recognized her from the pictures he had seen. "Sasha!" he cried as he reached her and hugged her in his arms. She had recognized him from the pictures Nick had shown her and didn't resist as J.T. embraced her.

"She's safe!" he said into the two-way radio microphone.

As soon as he had uttered the words, he heard Victor respond. "Bring the SUVs up now!" Nick hit the accelerator on the lead SUV and the wheels spun wildly as the vehicle sped forward, closely followed by James and Laura in the other two SUVs. They rounded the corner into town to see Victor and the rest of the commandos quickly working their way along opposite sides of the street, clearing each alleyway and moving towards Sasha and J.T. Nick roared past the commandos and came to a quick stop, pulling up alongside Sasha. Mia and Nick jumped out of the vehicle and embraced Sasha.

Victor ran over to where they were standing. "Are you o.k.?" he said to Sasha.

"Yes, I'm fine," she responded.

"I heard a vehicle drive off; which way did it go?" Victor asked.

Sasha turned and pointed down the alleyway. "Down there is an old road leading up into the mountains."

"How many people were there in all?" Victor continued.

"It was just one man," she responded.

Victor turned and pointed to two of his men, "You two stay here with them. The rest of you come with me."

He motioned to James with his thumb, indicating he should exit the SUV he was driving. As soon as James was out of the seat, Victor jumped in. Once his men were in, he hit the gas and tore down the alleyway and up the old mountain road, following the path Silas' Jeep had taken. Victor took a tracking device out of one of the utility pouches on his uniform and turned it on. A blinking dot appeared towards the edge of the screen. He knew he had to keep that dot within a two-mile radius or the transmitter that he had put in the bottom of the cooler would be out of range.

Silas stopped the Jeep and got out. He probably only had a few minutes head start before some of Nick Bartonovich's hired guns would be storming up the mountain to hunt him down. He walked to the uphill side of the road, to a large pile of logs that were being held in place by three upright posts supported by a rope tied between two large trees. Silas took out his knife and quickly sawed through the rope, making sure to stand behind the tree and out of the way of the soon-to-be rolling logs as he did.

Once the rope was severed, the mass of logs quickly rolled down onto the road below Silas' Jeep, hopelessly blocking the road for any following vehicles. Silas jumped back in the Jeep and drove away. He wanted to be long gone when his pursuers arrived. While they couldn't pass this point with a vehicle, they could still shoot him if he didn't make it around the next bend in the winding road first.

The SUV Victor was driving lurched up the mountainous road at a speed almost too high for safety, tearing around the corners and on up the next incline in an effort to gain on the man they were pursuing. As Victor rounded the next bend, he saw the mass of logs up ahead and brought the vehicle to a stop about twenty yards away. He peered through the window, looking around to see if there was someone positioned nearby to ambush them.

"You two take the upper side; Miles and I will take the lower side," he ordered.

The men exited the vehicle with their weapons drawn, immediately taking cover behind the available trees as they worked their way forward and beyond the pile of logs that blockaded the roadway. Once they had ascertained there was no one waiting in ambush, they re-grouped on the far-side of the log jam from where they had parked their vehicle.

Victor looked down at the mass of logs, estimating several of the logs weighed in at four or five hundred pounds each. There was no way they were going to move them quickly, especially since their SUVs didn't come equipped with winches. The forest above and below the road was too steep and forested to drive around the log jam. He spoke into his two-way radio.

"Tommy, is everything stable back down there?" he asked.

"Yes. We've searched practically the whole town. No one else is here but us," he replied.

"Good. You and Vlad get up here ASAP. We need to move some logs that our man blocked the road with."

"O.k., we're on our way."

Forty-five minutes later, Victor's team was finished clearing the road so that the SUVs could pass. The exhausted team re-entered their vehicles and continued the search for the kidnapper. Victor periodically checked the tracking device on the off chance that the kidnapper's location would re-appear on the screen. After about thirty minutes of driving, a blip suddenly appeared.

"We've got our target on the tracking screen, a little over two klicks out," he said to the rest of the team.

As they approached the target, Victor began to slow down. He and his men were scanning the surrounding areas, trying to get a visual on the target. They were practically on top of the signal, but still they could see nothing. Victor stopped the car and said into his microphone, "Fan out and find this scum bag. We're practically on top of the transmitter."

The team exited the vehicles and fanned out in practiced fashion, with three men sweeping uphill and three down. They located the cooler in a few minutes, discarded and empty on the downhill side of the road. They quickly re-entered their vehicles and resumed the drive along the mountain road, which had leveled off and begun to descend slightly. Around the next bend, the road intersected a paved road. Victor slammed his fist down on the dashboard of the SUV, realizing that their chances of finding the kidnapper had just plummeted.

The team split up, taking opposite directions on the paved road. They drove for another hour before Victor called off the search and headed back to Toakama.

Chapter Forty-Five

"Are you o.k.?" Mia said to Sasha, looking at her bruised eye and cut lip. All she felt for the kidnapper at that moment was hatred. She prayed he hadn't sexually assaulted her daughter. God help him if he had. On second thought, she hoped God *wouldn't* help him in that case.

"I'm o.k.," Sasha said, giving Mia another hug. "I'm just so glad to be free now."

"Sasha, I need you to be honest with me," Nick said. "Did that man touch you inappropriately? Did he rape you?"

"No. No. he didn't," she replied.

"Guys, you should come see this," James yelled from down the alleyway that Victor had driven down earlier.

Everyone walked *en masse* down the alleyway to where James and Laura were standing. There, behind the building, was the RV where Sasha had been held captive.

"That's where he kept me hostage," Sasha informed them.

Mia left Sasha's side and walked determinedly towards the RV. She went to the driver's door, opening it up, and began to look around the cab.

"What is she doing?" J.T. asked Nick.

"She's looking for clues to who this man is or where he went. She's quite good at it, actually. It's a skill she developed years ago when she used to track down some of our more recalcitrant debtors," Nick replied. "I'd wager, if there is anything he left behind that indicates who or where he might be, she'll find it."

"I think I can help you with that," Sasha replied.

Nick and J.T. both turned to look at Sasha.

"Do you know who he is?" asked J.T.

"Not exactly, only that he said that he had been ripped off by a gambling website that you owned, Nick. He also mentioned that he used to be a cop," Sasha continued.

Nick's face showed a glimmer of recognition, which he quickly hid. "Describe him to me," he said.

A quick description of the kidnapper from Sasha confirmed Nick's suspicions.

"We'll get a sketch artist to help draw a picture of him so that we can identify him and stop him from doing things like this to anyone else," Nick said with finality. He was going to find him alright, and when he did, there would be hell to pay.

Back in the RV, Mia had conducted a thorough search and collected all the receipts and paperwork that she could find. A quick review of the material indicated that the kidnapper had paid cash for everything except the RV rental, which had required a credit card. The RV rental paperwork she found in the glove box listed the name of Silas McGruder.

Leaving his real name on the rental agreement was either stupid, sloppy, or a planned deception. Mia had encountered a few of the people she had tracked for Nick in the past who had used this tactic. They had deliberately used their real names to lead her off of their trail just enough to buy an airline ticket using an alias and temporarily escape to some far-off destination, supposedly out of her reach. If that was what Silas had planned, she knew just what to do. Whatever the reason for using his real name, she was anxious to find him as soon as possible.

Mia exited the RV and walked back to where Nick, J.T., and Sasha were standing.

"We need to get back to New York, *now*."

Nick nodded in agreement. He turned on his two-way radio, but got nothing but static when he tried to reach Victor. He tried Victor's phone, but it only went to voice mail. He left a message telling Victor to call him with a report as soon as possible, and let him know they were returning to New York. If Victor had apprehended Silas, they would know soon enough. If not, they needed to get back to New York and start tracking Silas down from there.

They collected James and Laura, who had finished a cursory search of the remaining town. They had found nothing else that might be of help in tracking down the kidnapper. Everyone piled in to the remaining SUV and headed back to Roanoke. Three hours later, they were in Nick's plane and headed back to New York.

The next day, James, Laura, and J.T. boarded Nick's plane and went back to the Cayman Islands. Even with their new identities, they reasoned it wasn't safe to stay too long in the States. Before they left, J.T. arranged for Sasha to fly down and visit him in Grand Cayman on her spring break. J.T. and Sasha shared a tearful goodbye as he boarded the plane.

Within a week, Sasha's face had healed and life was beginning to return to the new normal. Mia and Nick had insisted that Sasha have a bodyguard for the time being, and she'd had to answer a million questions from her friends due to the fact that he followed her everywhere except to the ladies' room. Over time, though, it became second nature to have the bodyguard around, and it only irritated her when she went on a date with her new boyfriend.

Over the next few months, before Sasha visited him on spring break, J.T. kept in touch with her via facebook, twitter, and phone calls, trying to catch up for lost time. He was thankful that she wanted to have a relationship with him and was looking forward to seeing her when she came down to visit. He was determined not to let her slip away the same way he had let her mother exit his life. He had learned many things since going to prison and beginning recovery. He had learned that although relationships could be messy, it was worth it to work through your problems and continue to reach out and invest in relationships with those you loved.

James had been in contact with a youth center in the United States for several months before the kidnapping episode. Once they were back home, he continued working out the final details to arrange for a yearly retreat in the Cayman Islands for at-risk teens. The youths would fly down and spend a week biking around the island, camping out, and fishing. He wanted to help other kids avoid taking the wrong path like he had. In addition to working on starting the youth camp, he finally convinced Laura to marry him. They had a quiet marriage ceremony in the garden at J.T.'s house. Laura continued to work at the women's shelter, occasionally providing some extra unlisted services to certain women whose abusive former husbands or boyfriends just couldn't take the hint.

Nick and Mia continued to search for Silas. Mia recognized that one of the receipts she'd found in the RV was from a sub-shop in a part of town that she recognized. It was located near where they had obtained the identification documents for J.T., James, and Laura. A visit to the document forger, along with a memory-enhancing bribe, soon revealed the name of Silas' new alias – Bob Conner. They put Silas' new name and picture out through their usual channels in hopes of tracking him down, but it had been two months and they still hadn't heard anything. It appeared that Silas McGruder had fallen off the face of the earth.

Chapter Forty-Six

Nick and Sasha were sitting on a bench in Central Park. It was a beautiful day. Everything was beginning to bloom as spring made its reappearance, and all seemed right with the world. Walking in the park was something Sasha had done regularly with her mother when she was alive. It calmed her and helped her remember the good times she'd had with her mother. Nick had walked with her through this section of the park many times when Sasha's mother was sick, and they had continued the practice in the years since.

"Nick," Sasha began, "I want to ask you something and I want you to tell me the truth."

Nick raised an eyebrow and looked over at Sasha with interest. Whenever she asked him a question like that, he knew what came next was going to be serious. He remembered the first time she had used that phrase with him, "I want you to tell me the truth." It was after her mother had died. She had asked him then if he believed in Heaven. Nick had never been one to prevaricate. He had always told the truth boldly and without reservation. He was always direct in asking for what he wanted. He admired that same quality in Sasha. And so, when she had asked him that question, he'd told her what he really thought. He simply said, "I don't know if Heaven exists or not. I can't say I believe in something that I'm not certain exists." That seemed to satisfy her and she had never asked him that question again.

"Go on," Nick prodded.

"When that man kidnapped me, he told me that you were a crook and that the money you were paying him for my ransom was stolen from someone else. Is that true?"

Nick smiled in spite of himself. He regretted what Silas

had said to her, but he admired the fact that she was bold enough to confront him about it directly. He looked her in the eyes as he answered.

"Many years ago, I made a lot of money by conducting illegal business deals. I was convinced that nothing mattered but making money. A lot has changed since then. Now, I'm not going to tell you that everything I do to make money today is completely legal, but I don't do things the same way anymore. I'm more selective about my business dealings today."

"Were my mom and J.T. involved in what you did before?"

"Yes," Nick responded flatly, wishing she hadn't gone in that direction.

"What did my mom do?"

"She was an accountant. She helped us launder the money and disguise the transactions so that we didn't get caught."

"But J.T. did get caught. He went to prison for what you all did, right?"

"Yes, he did." Nick looked at Sasha, watching the wheels turn in her mind, both regretting the end of her innocence and feeling proud that she was ready to tackle the muddy truth of it all on her own.

Sasha didn't ask any more questions. She just turned and watched a man playing frisbee with his dog in the field across from where they were sitting.

About a week later, Sasha knocked on the door to Nick's office.

"Come in," he said.

She came in and sat down in one of the big wing-back chairs facing Nick's desk.

"What can I do for you today, m'lady?" Nick asked playfully.

"Be careful what you ask for," she said in reply.

"Ah, methinks the lady doth have something weighty on her mind. What is it, my dear?"

"I've been thinking about that conversation we had in the park the other day."

"And?"

"And I want to ask you a few things."

"The usual part about telling the truth applies, I suppose," Nick responded.

"Yep."

Nick prepared himself. "O.k., fire when ready."

"Are you and J.T. still working together?"

"No, my dear. We stopped working together a long time ago. Now we are simply friends who share a relationship with you."

"O.k. Next question, sort of. I've been thinking a lot about what you all did to make money back then, and I've been having a hard time reconciling the fact that I love all three of you, and Mia, too, whom I assume was involved in it with you, as well. I need to be able to process it all somehow, to make sense of it." Sasha fidgeted with the corner of her shirt with her fingers as she paused before blurting out, "Well, I'm having a hard time with the fact that you were all doing illegal things to make all of this money. There, I said it. I want to undo it but I can't. So instead, I want you to help me set up a foundation to do good things with that money. I want to do something good with the money you made doing something bad. I want to know that our family is doing something to make the world a better place, not a worse one."

Sasha slumped back into the chair, obviously relieved at having spit it out, but unsure about what Nick was going to do with the request she had just made. Nick sat behind his desk with the inscrutable poker face which she could never read. It was the same way he'd looked at her the first time she had asked if she could go out on a date with Teddy Fromeyer. That look betrayed nothing. It was stone. She waited.

Nick looked off to a painting that hung on the wall behind Sasha. It was a painting of ancient Rome being re-built after the fire that had burned it down in 64 A.D. He'd always liked that painting. It symbolized something good coming out of a tragedy. Like his marriage to Mia coming out of his battle with cancer, like Sasha coming into their lives out of the tragedy of Katrina's death. And now he was being given another opportunity to bring something good out of a past that had produced wealth, but no happiness. A past that had produced riches with emptiness that was devoid of more than temporary fulfillment. It provided power and influence, which was nice, but ultimately, it lacked the power to fill one's soul with real contentment.

He was not the same man as he once was. True, he was no saint and probably never would be. He still ran an illegal gambling business along with many legitimate gaming enterprises. But as he grew older, he began to see the point that J.T. had made to him years ago on the yacht while they'd been moored outside of Grand Cayman. He wasn't sure exactly where it came from or if he even believed in God, but he did feel a sense of guilt about some of the things he had done to gain the wealth he had acquired – especially in the early days with J.T.

His greed to get that money back from J.T. had ultimately paved the way for Sasha's abduction. Silas wouldn't have even known she existed if Nick hadn't hired him to track down the money in the first place. Now, Sasha of all people was beckoning him to come over from the dark side, to turn over a new leaf, to rectify some of the past wrongs. It was as if some cosmic force in the universe, call it God if you like, was luring him to change his ways and become a force for good.

He stared at the picture for a good few minutes. Sasha could tell he was deep in thought, so she didn't interrupt him or demand an answer. That's one thing she had learned from

Mia. When dealing with Nick, it was best to wait it out and not push him. He would answer when he was ready.

Ever since he'd had that bout with cancer, Nick had been pondering what his legacy would be after he was gone. He knew that Mia loved him. Since Sasha had entered his life, he had come to know that Sasha loved him. But beyond those two relationships, what would there be in the world when he was gone that was a result of his having lived his life? Money? Many people had money. In and of itself, it meant little. A business? His businesses consisted largely of gambling, both legal and illegal, as well as a healthy real-estate portfolio – hardly what he considered a worthy legacy.

He supposed that Sasha's challenge was fortuitous. He realized in that moment that she had just helped provide the answer he had been looking for. He decided it was time to take the plunge and take action instead of simply pondering the possibilities. He looked back at Sasha.

"What, exactly, did you have in mind?"

"Well, I have a few ideas. One was a scholarship fund for medical students, a possible grant program for research on renal disease and cancer treatments. There are a lot of things we could do. Are you interested?"

"Yes. As a matter of fact, I am," Nick replied, almost as astonished as Sasha to hear the words coming out of his own mouth. "But we should discuss it with Mia first. If we are going to do this, we need to make the decision as a team."

Sasha was beaming. She ran around behind the desk and gave Nick a big hug.

"Thanks, Nick, you've just made my day!"

"And you've just made mine," he said as he returned the hug.

Nick and Sasha talked it over with Mia when she returned to the house for the day. She liked the idea of doing something to help eradicate the diseases that had taken Sasha's mother and almost taken the love of her life away from her. It was a way to fight back, and Mia had always been a fighter. She had never been one to just sit around and do nothing when faced with a challenge.

She and Nick had a private and more serious discussion later that day. They decided to begin phasing out their illegal enterprises in favor of legitimate businesses in gambling and real-estate. Nick came up with a plan that would accomplish the task in a little over a year. They decided that there was no reason to continue to run the risk of getting sent to jail for mere money's sake. They would remain millionaires by virtue of the income from their legitimate businesses alone.

They established the Katrina Beyer's Foundation for Public Good with an initial endowment of seventy-five million dollars. The money was invested, and the grants and scholarships would come out of the earnings, not the principle, so that the foundation could continue to operate indefinitely. Sasha decided that she was going to major in business with an emphasis on non-profit management when she went to college in the fall, so that she could take an active role in managing the foundation.

On spring break, as promised, Sasha traveled to the Grand Cayman Islands to spend the week with J.T. Nick insisted that her bodyguard accompany her. J.T. and Sasha had a great time and Sasha discovered that she shared a passion for sailing with her dad. They worked out a plan where Sasha would come and visit a few times a year. J.T. hated to see her leave at the end of the week, but he was pleased to know that she would be pursuing her plans for the foundation. He was as proud as a father could be.

Chapter Forty-Seven

Silas McGruder, alias Bob Conner, came in the door of his Nassau, Bahamas home whistling one of his favorite songs. He was riding high after a good night at the blackjack tables at the Crystal Palace Casino. He'd gone in with ten thousand dollars and was coming home with fifty thousand. It didn't matter right now that, over the last few months, he had racked up a net loss of one hundred thousand dollars. Right now, he was on top of the world.

He went into his office and opened up the closet door, revealing a large safe. He placed the briefcase containing his winnings on the ground and kept whistling while he worked the dial of the combination lock. He turned the handle and opened the safe to reveal stacks of one hundred dollar bills. He smiled even more as he removed the money from his briefcase and began putting it in the safe.

Suddenly, he heard a door creak somewhere in the house. He quickly reached into the safe and grabbed a .45 caliber revolver before spinning around and bringing the gun up to firing position. He slowly got up and began working his way over to the office door. Besides the light in the office, there was a single lamp on in the living room, as well as the light in the kitchen range hood. It was too dark for comfort, but he couldn't exactly run around flipping light switches now.

He cleared the doorway as quietly as he could, looking first one way, then the other. The back part of the house was completely dark. He was taking a chance either way, but he guessed whoever or whatever had made the sound was probably in the front part of the house. He went left out of the office, moving as quietly as he could, his gun at the ready.

He heard a sound in the kitchen, just ahead and to his right. He quickly stepped forward and brought the revolver around, using the door frame for cover. When he did, he saw the neighbor's cat jump down from the counter. He let out a sigh of relief and lowered the gun.

"You almost scared the crap out of me, Melvin," he said as he tucked the gun behind his back and into his waistband.

He picked up the cat and walked over to the door, opening it and tossing the cat outside. He locked the door and began walking back towards the office to finish what he had begun a few minutes before. He had taken one step into the office when something hit him hard in the side of the thigh, causing his knee to buckle. He cried out in pain as he dropped to one knee.

He reached behind him to grab the gun in his waistband, only to have someone grab his wrist and twist it behind his back. He felt the gun being removed as he was shoved forward onto the floor.

"The money is in the safe; you can take it all, just let me live," he said to his yet unseen attacker.

"Turn around," a voice behind him said.

He pushed himself up into a sitting position and turned around slowly. As he saw Mia Bartonovich standing before him with his own revolver trained on him, his eyes widened in fear.

"How did you find me?" he said, shocked that he had been tracked down. He had been so careful.

"It's very hard to completely disappear. First, I found out the name of your alias, and then I waited for you to contact your ex-wife. I traced one of the calls you made to her and found it came from Nassau; then, all I had to do was show your picture around the casinos to find out where you were. You should have stopped gambling."

"Son of a gun," Silas said in disbelief.

"You should not have kidnapped my daughter! You should not have hit her!" Mia said, her voice growing louder with increasing emotion.

"I...I'm sorry about that, o.k., I wasn't planning to hit her. I'm very sorry about that. Please, just take the money and go."

Silas began bringing his knee up slowly as he talked, trying to get the backup pistol he had strapped to his ankle within reach without being noticed.

"You are just like my father. He used to hit me when I did not do what he wanted."

"Look, I regret what I did, really. I lost my head and I'm very sorry. Will you please forgive me?"

He was close now, very close. If only he could get her distracted for a moment. Then, as if on cue, Mia tossed the gun into the far corner of the room. As soon as she let go of the gun, Silas went for his backup. He almost had it out of the holster when the telescopic baton that Mia carried slammed into the back of his hand, causing him to involuntarily release his grip on the handle of the gun.

He brought his other hand around and attempted to punch Mia in the stomach as she was standing in front of him. His punch never found its mark. Mia stepped inside of his swing and brought up her knee, catching him in his face and breaking his nose. Silas' head snapped back as blood spurted out of his nose.

He quickly regained his balance and lunged forward with everything he had. It was a last-ditch effort to grab Mia and wrestle her to the ground, where he could use his size and physical strength to his advantage, but he was too slow. Mia stepped to the side and connected a side-kick to Silas' head, sending him off of his trajectory and causing his head to slam into the door jamb. He crumpled to the floor and didn't move.

Mia had already re-positioned herself for another

offensive, but Silas remained motionless.

A few days later, Sasha came running into the kitchen, where Nick and Mia were just finishing up their morning coffee. She was ecstatic.

"You'll never believe what just happened!" she exclaimed.

"Tell us, my dear," Nick replied.

"An anonymous donor has just given 9.5 million dollars to our foundation!" she replied, barely able to contain herself.

"That's wonderful, Sasha!" Mia responded.

"The weird thing is, we haven't even been running a donation drive. I can't figure it out," Sasha continued.

"Well, I'm sure the word has gotten around the philanthropic community about the work we'll be doing. I'm just happy there is someone who believes in the mission enough to write a check for the cause," Nick said.

"Yes, I'm sure that's it," Mia agreed, taking a sip from her coffee.

Later that week, Nick Bartonovich was seated in his office perusing his email. He noticed an email from Mr. Watanabe – the man they frequently used to track down delinquent debtors. Inside the email were two sentences, followed by a link. The message read simply, *"This will interest you. Not our doing though."* Nick clicked on the link and it brought up a story from the *New York Times*.

> A man was found dead in his home in Nassau, Bahamas yesterday, the apparent victim of a robbery gone wrong. An undisclosed amount of money was missing from an open safe found near the body. The man has been identified as

Silas McGruder, a former New York City policeman who was living in the Bahamas under the alias of Bob Conner. Police have no leads on who may have committed the crime at this time.

Nick raised an eyebrow in interest. *Well, that's one potential problem we don't need to worry about any more,* he thought to himself. He forwarded the article to Mia before moving on to other emails.

Note from the Author

Utopian Day is filled with interesting characters, most of whom are deeply flawed by way of being thoroughly human. One of the main themes I attempted to weave throughout the story was the theme of redemption and positive change in the lives of people whose past and present is marred with moral and personal failure, greed, and tragedy. There are a number of questions that are touched on throughout the story that are related to these themes. How does positive change happen? What is the process a person goes through to decide that they want to change? What does that process look like? How can a person who starts out life with a series of moral failures and bad circumstances actually turn their lives around?

One set of characters in this story decide they want to turn their lives around and pursue that process of recovery and positive change through a unique prison program that intertwines psychology, religion, and a twelve step program. Another set of characters evolve over time from criminals who appear to enjoy their lives of crime and the fortune it brings them to a place where they have developed a different set of values that is no longer compatible with the old criminal lifestyle. The transformation for both groups of people is gradual and incomplete when our story ends, but the change is undeniable and the process is ongoing.

We live in an imperfect world where there is good mixed with bad. We see people commit crimes and atrocities on the one hand, while others do good deeds – sometimes there is a progression from one to the other for the same person over the course of time. My hope and desire is that you found this book entertaining on the one hand, and encouraging on the other. Wherever you are in life, know that positive change is possible. You can be different, and you can stop the unproductive habits of your past or present and begin the process of positive change. I hope this book has given you some ideas about how you might begin to do that if you so desire, or perhaps encouraged you to continue on the journey of change that you are already on.

I encourage you not to allow yourself to be defined by your mistakes. Instead, I challenge you to allow yourself to be defined by Whose you are. We are all God's beloved children and are intrinsically valuable by virtue of that fact. When we live life in that reality and combined with God's assistance, positive change is always possible.

Thanks for reading,

C. L. Wells

Thank You

If you enjoyed this book, I would appreciate a short review on the site where you purchased the book. If you know of others who would enjoy reading this book, please pass the word along. Your participation is greatly appreciated. Thank you!

To join my email list and be informed about new books as they become available, or simply to ask a question or make a comment, you can email me at creativefiction@outlook.com.

Acknowledgements

Thanks to my wife for her support and encouragement during the writing of this book. Thanks to Alcoholics Anonymous for the twelve-step program that organization initiated that is referred to in the book, along with references to some of the principles taught by that organization. Thanks to Reinhold Niebuhr, the author of the Serenity Prayer, portions of which are used at various points in the book. Thanks to Jennifer Collins, my editor, whose work and comments helped to make this a better book. Thanks to Monique Nelson, who designed the cover of the book. Both Jennifer and Monique can be reached at Elance.com should anyone desire to enlist their valuable services.

About the Author

Christopher Wells holds a Bachelor of Arts in History from West Georgia State University and a Master's Degree in Computer Information Security from Capella University. He lives in South Carolina with his beautiful wife and three wonderful children. His hobbies include kayaking, paddle boarding, hiking, and bicycling.

Made in the USA
Charleston, SC
18 May 2016